LUST, LOVE & PIXIE DUST
LAVENDER FALLS
BOOK TWO

ISABEL BARREIRO

Published by Isabel Barreiro

Copyright © 2024 Isabel Barreiro

All Right Reserved

Paperback ISBN: 979-8-9902878-9-1

Lust, Love & Pixie Dust

Genre: Small town paranormal romance

Cover Design: Jennette Perdomo

❀ Created with Vellum

To those who need to remember to let go
And to the ones whose love language is acts of service
Caleb loves to be of service

THINGS TO KNOW

This an **open door romance** book so there are **adult scenes.**

Spicy chapters:

    2, 9, 15, 16, 18, 20, 30

Playlists:

Eleanor's Playlist

Caleb's Playlist

PROLOGUE

Eleanor

There were three women dressed like Tinker Bell flirting with Caleb and I wanted to turn them into pixie dust. The fates, the universe, whoever and whatever must really fucking hate me.

I had been sipping on the same caipirinha for the past hour. And by sipping I mean my glass was empty and I was waiting for a refill. But the tavern was bustling with tourists and therefore I needed to wait.

Which was a good thing. It was the Full Moon Fall Festival. People were drinking, smiling and having a great time. Ticket sales had gone up and it was slowly turning into a success, all thanks to the amazing volunteers and town staff.

My best friend Lily had managed to become a marketing queen that helped create this success despite all her anxiety. On top of that she pioneered the Cursed Bar Crawl with our mutual best friend, Celestino, who recently moved back. And I bet right now they were confessing their love for each other in the attic of the haunted house.

How romantic.

I glanced at my phone. My other best friend Lola was still at the petting zoo, taming baby dragons in disguise. It would be a while before she could join. I eyed the stoic elf who was manning the bar.

His blue eyes that matched the same shade as my favorite flower were focused on the beer he was pouring. His silver hair that reminded me of starlight, was braided back. His pale skin shimmered beneath his black henley. I chewed the useless straw attached to my empty drink.

One of the Tinker Bells leaned over the bar, pushing her breasts up to her neck and attempted to flirt with him. I snorted. She was bold but there was no way he would give her the time of day. However, I did applaud her attempt and her outfit was super cute. At least she was going for what she wanted.

Our eyes connected and I mentally cursed at the way my stomach dipped. My body always betrayed me when it came to Caleb Kiernan. I hated his eyes; so pale and perceptive they unnerved me. He handed the Tinker Bell her beer without letting go of my gaze. His eyes followed the slope of my neck, over my scale cladded bra and down to my mishap fishnet skirt. With our fall festival being close to Halloween, many people came in costume. I decided to dress as a sexy zombie siren.

He took a deep breath, his hand reaching for the bottle of *cachaça* and the air fizzled.

I could imagine his hands on me, his fingers scraping the netting against my thigh until my flesh turned pink. I could almost feel his other hand slip up to wrap around my throat as his lips nipped at the weak spot right below my ear.

His hand tightened around the bottle as his eyes darkened in the haze of the tavern. My cheeks felt flushed. I could feel the body glitter slipping down my back. This is what always happened. A stare down filled with desire, sly glances, flushed cheeks and the occasional breathless banter. But nothing ever happened. *Ever.* There was never a climax of any kind. We've known each other for four years and something or someone always got in the way.

Another Tinker Bell waved her hand for his attention, breaking our tug of war. I was five seconds away from blasting her but that wouldn't be pixie-like for someone who was deputy mayor of Lavender Falls.

Instead, I did what I always did where Caleb was concerned. I looked around for someone else to occupy my time. After the year I had, I was tired of waiting for him. I was drained from our constant tango of sexual tension and I was exhausted from giving effort towards people who wouldn't or couldn't reciprocate.

What I needed was to let go, a break. What I needed was a good fuck. A nice, no strings attached, getting twisted in the sheets, sweaty and steamy lay. Sex was a great way to destress and with the end of the year being the craziest time in Lavender Falls, I needed to relax.

A flash of blonde caught my eye. I smirked. The vampire at the end of the bar could do.

I did like when someone could sink their teeth into me.

CALEB

There were about 85 people inside my bar which meant there were roughly 60 pairs of eyes I needed to stab. Why the fuck did she think she could come to my bar dressed like that?

My hand gripped the bottle of *cachaça* as our eyes undressed each other. It was the same dance we've been dancing for four years. I noticed Eleanor's drink was empty and was in the middle of making her a new one when some Tinker Bells showed up.

It must have been a cruel twist of fate to have three drunken women dressed as pixies badger me for drinks when the only pixie I wanted was across the room.

In my tavern's lighting, her honey eyes looked the same color but I knew better. One of them was the same shade as an olive. Her cheeks were flushed and by the rise and fall of her chest that was barely being covered by her bra she was feeling the same way.

My eyes traveled down to her skirt. Fishnet was wrapped around her hips and I wanted to dig my fingers into her flesh and feel her muscles tightened against me. Before my thoughts could spiral, another Tinker Bell waved her hand in my face. I glared at her.

"Yes?" My voice sounded bored.

"I was wondering," she pushed her breasts further up, "if you were busy later."

I looked back towards Eleanor but she had already disappeared. My eyes wandered around the bar, trying to find my pixie.

"I'll be busy," I said, keeping my voice short. She pouted. If she thought that was going to work she had another thing coming. My younger brother Flynn patted my shoulder. He was around my height with dirty blonde hair and brown eyes, a replica of our father.

"Excuse my brother. He's a stick in the mud but I'd be more than gracious to provide whatever your heart desires."

I snorted. Flynn was always flirty with the customers. I didn't understand why. They ordered, we served. There was no need for small talk. The Tinker Bells smiled. My brother waved his hand towards the end of the bar.

My eyes narrowed at the sight. The bottle of *cachaça* in my hand shook slightly. Eleanor grazed her fingers delicately on the vampire's hand, her eyes hooded. She was on the prowl tonight.

I recognized that look. It was the same look she gave me.

She threw her pink hair back in laughter and I watched the asshole's eyes wander down her bronzed neck. There was no fucking way she was going home with him.

She's not going home with you either, a tiny voice whispered in my head. It's not that I didn't want to take her home, to my bed and then stay under the sheets until her body was sweaty and flushed. I did. But I couldn't. Not yet anyhow.

Not until I got rid of my stupid curse.

CHAPTER 1
SPREADSHEETS NOT BED SHEETS

ELEANOR

T*wo months later*
        TAB. =AVERAGE(C2, C3, C4).
=J1+J2+J3.
DEL.
DEL.
DEL.

My computer screen consisted of letters, numbers and symbols blurring and bubbling together like one of Priscilla's potions. I groaned into my perfectly manicured hands. Leaning back I spied my clock on the desk. 8:30 PM. *Fuck.* I was supposed to leave the office three hours ago. I glanced around. Everyone had gone home like normal supernatural beings.

Kraken's crap, even Lily was out of the office. Although knowing her she was probably curled on the couch with Celestino and her laptop still working.

I entered a few more numbers before hitting save. I was helping with a few finance reports since Chelsea's assistant Alex just had a baby with his high school sweetheart, Thalia. Why did I agree when I already had so many responsibilities? No fucking clue. My heart must be made of pure gold.

Stepping into the frigid air of Lavender Falls I tightened my coat. We were officially at the very end of November and the chill of winter was in full swing. My brain was swamped with so many things. After the success of our Full Moon Fall Festival thanks to my best friend, tickets sales for our Whimsical Winter Wonderland Festival were going up.

The fall festival was *so* successful that we needed to make sure the winter festival was a big hit. On top of that I had to maintain the mayor's whole entire life. There were meetings she needed to attend, hearings to be heard and problems to be solved.

With every step towards my favorite pub I felt the weight of everything settle on my shoulders. Sure the mayor ran the town but I ran the mayor *and* the town. Which I didn't mind. I liked the responsibility. But I couldn't lie that spending most of the fall season helping with the festival ignited a spark. I hadn't felt that feeling in a long time. It reminded me of the parties I would put together in high school and the events in college.

This winter season was going to kick my ass. I wouldn't be acting as deputy mayor in my full capacity this time. Nope. I was fully in charge of the festival. Well I would oversee Ben Chaves who was in charge of Culture Affairs and Special Events. I cringed at my conversation with Mayor Kiana. I wish she had told me sooner.

"Ms. GLADD's granddaughter will be interning under you this winter season," Mayor Kiana said. Her curls were pulled to the top of head and today she wore an aqua blouse that set off the warm undertones of her brown skin. Her eyes narrowed at me and I felt like I was back in her chemistry class with Lily, Lola and Celestino.

"How come?" I asked. I felt my heart thump against my chest. Another responsibility.

"She wants to get into politics. Figured it would be a good experience plus I need you to focus on one thing," she said. One thing? This wasn't good.

"What do you need me to do?"

"Emily will be taking on your usual responsibilities since I want you to focus solely on the festival," she said, sitting back in her leather chair. I bit the inside of my cheek to keep from screaming why? Did I not handle her and the fall festival well enough for her to trust me?

"I know you've already been working on it and I don't want to split your workload between working for me and helping with the event. I want this to be just as successful as the fall festival." Mayor Kiana shuffled some papers on her desk. My eyes twitched. She was hiding something.

"And?" I said with an eyebrow raised.

"Well as you know Ben and Celestino handle the events and you'll be overseeing things so they run smoothly just like you usually do," she said as her fingers flipped through more papers. My heart rattled against my chest.

"And?" I stressed the word. I wish she would just come out and say it.

"You'll be working…" she trailed off.

"Yes?" I said impatiently.

"With your sister," she said, finally looking at me. I froze. Three words. Three words was all it took for my body to turn into ice. No. There was no way.

"Why?" I croaked out. I wanted to throw up.

"Your family's company is one of our sponsors this year. They decided to opt in at the last minute. They want to make sure the festival is a success and I trust you to take this task on while I continue making sure the town is running with Emily." Mayor Kiana knew about my strained relationship with my family. But she wouldn't do this if she didn't need my help.

"Your family relationship is why I'm entrusting this to you. Ben has

agreed. Hale's Lumber Industry is helping with quite a bit of funding,"
she continued. That translated into we need this sponsorship. I nodded
wordlessly.

"I know this is a big ask-"

"No problem," I said, cutting her off.

THOSE TWO WORDS rolled off my tongue with ease. Since working for
the town I've become accustomed to it.

"Eleanor the copy machine has no ink." "No problem, I'll fix it."
"Eleanor, I need a meeting with the mayor next Tuesday." "No prob-
lem, I'll schedule it." "Eleanor the numbers aren't adding up." "No
problem, let me see."

And so on and so on. It's not that I hated my job. I was just tired of
doing everything for everyone. I felt cramped in a box. I, Eleanor
Silva, was not meant to be trapped in a box. I grimaced. I had to work
with my sister? A shiver ran up my spine and it wasn't because of the
cold.

Staring up at the moon my heart sank. The chill of winter no longer
cut my skin but settled against it. Memories of the past resurfaced.

I broke us into pieces, packed my bags and left for college with
Lily. They moved to a nearby town when I left. I hadn't seen my sister
in a few years.

We tried reconnecting after I graduated college and moved back to
town but my father wouldn't have it. And now we needed to work
together? Now their company was a sponsor? Fuck. This meant I had to
work with my father and whatever the hellhound he wanted for the festival.

I pushed the wooden door of The Drunken Fairy Tale Tavern open
and warmth spread through me like it always did. The booths were
filled with people that I grew up with. People who knew me, well the
fashionable bubbly version of me.

Irish music played softly in the background. Their lights were dimly lit giving a more serene feel. Tatiana was behind the bar with Caleb today. She recently discovered, thanks to Lily's help, that her family used to own the pub.

Her great uncle decided to leave town, wipe everyone's memories that he existed and leave the pub in Caleb's family's hands. And now that the truth was out both Caleb and Tatiana co-owned the joint. While Caleb might not admit it I think it gave him some relief. He's always enjoyed pouring the drinks and he looked damn sexy doing it. Tatiana leaned towards Caleb to say something. His lips quivered slightly up and he nodded.

I turned immediately away. I didn't need my feelings about Caleb bubbling up tonight. My brain was overloaded enough as it is. And while he did occasionally preoccupy my mind with his sexy brooding scowl tonight was not the night. I snuck around back to my favorite booth, hoping to not catch his eyes. I glided into the worn leather seat and placed my cheek on the table ignoring the fact that it could be covered in germs. I closed my eyes.

Maybe the germs could give me a mystical illness that would render me motionless and speechless. Then I wouldn't have to work with my father. I snorted. The town might erupt into chaos if that were to happen. Things might be set on fire while the town is chased by baby dragons and griffins. I shuddered.

I just needed a few minutes to breathe in the smell of hops and fried goodness. But my body refused to relax. I was already thinking in overdrive. I had a list of things to get through to prepare. Training Emily was at the top of my list. I needed to talk to Ben to see how preparations were.

The smell of mint smacked my nose. I knew who was next to me without opening my eyes.

"Eleanor," his deep voice rumbled. I straightened up and shot him a flirty smile.

"Hey there hottie. I would like a glass of water and a basket of monster-ella sticks pretty please," I said as sweetly as I could. His piercing pale blue eyes made my skin prickle. His hands flexed on his hips. He wore a pensive look on his face.

"What's wrong?" he asked. I kept the smile on my face. The one thing I disliked about Caleb was how easily he read into me. Okay, I also couldn't stand how my body became like a live wire every time he was around.

"Nothing to worry your pretty white blonde hair about, Elfie," I said. He leaned forward onto the table and the smell of mint soothed me. I forced my body to stay still, for my breathing to be as even as possible as his presence deliciously washed over me.

Staring into his eyes I felt compelled to tell him everything, like always. No matter how hard I tried to fight the pull that he had over me there was something about Caleb's presence that tempered my restlessness. He dipped his head down and I couldn't help but glance at his pretty pink lips; lips that begged to take me.

"Eleanor," he said. His voice felt like sandpaper and I leaned in begging to feel it scratch against my skin. I'm surprised he didn't comment on the nickname. He usually got annoyed with the amount of times I called him random shit. Elfie. Honeysuckle. Beer Master. Pumpkin. Starlight. The list had been growing for almost four years.

"What's wrong?" he asked again. My eyes widened at his concerned tone. It almost felt real. Caleb and I have always heavily flirted and sure we argued but discussing my worries? Expressing interest in me other than what could happen behind closed doors? Never. The man was like a sealed vault, never letting anyone in.

Well Sailor and Celestino were exceptions. Now that I think about it, I don't think I ever saw Caleb date anyone since he moved back. While Caleb's family grew up in Lavender Falls he moved away with his dad when he was young.

"Do you date?" I blurted out. His eyes widened a fraction. He coughed, awkwardly.

"Date? No. Hook up? Sometimes," he said honestly. Mhm. Interesting. And yet we haven't done anything.

"Really?" I asked. He rolled his eyes.

"Yes," he said curtly. Then why the fuck won't he give me the time of day? Was I not appealing to him? Most people found me appealing. I'm sexy, smart, funny. I do have relationship issues-

"What's wrong?" he asked again, breaking through my egotistical thoughts.

"I'm fine," I responded. Another phrase I've grown accustomed to saying over the past few years. It was a lie. I was anything but fine. I was tired. I was miserable. I was worried. The vibrator in my night stand recently broke. I was hungry. Instead of responding Caleb did what he always did. He walked away. I sighed into my seat, breathing slightly easier.

What was I going to do? I hadn't seen my sister in years. We used to be so close. She was only four years younger than me. We would have makeover Mondays where after all of our homework was done we would sit on my bed and do each other's makeup. We practiced magic and glitter. We told each other about our crushes, our dreams.

But as I got closer to graduation my father and I began arguing more and more. He wanted me to take over the family business. *Hale's Lumber Industry.* One of the top companies in the northeast that provided high-quality and affordable lumber materials. The company borders the Hollow Tree of Lavender Falls.

The Hollow Tree is a sacred tree for pixies. It was planted around the same time the town was founded and imbued with magic. The magic helped us pixies give our talents an extra boost. What made Hale's Lumber Industry one of the best was the particular way my father used pixie dust to lengthen and strengthen the wood that gets chopped.

It helped that my father specialized in nature. He's always been environmentally careful with his work and magic. Probably one of the only decent things about him. He wanted *me* to take over. I had the same specialization as him but I didn't want to be stuck working for him my entire life. I enjoyed nature but it wasn't what I excelled at. I was better at tinkering, creating, and problem solving. At least humans got one thing right about pixies.

I sighed. He said I needed to stop partying and slutting around town and get serious. Okay, he didn't use the word slut but it was heavily implied. He couldn't see that I always maintained top scores while enjoying life. That life wasn't just sitting behind a desk. Life was meant to be *lived.*

By the stars I had the second highest GPA in my grade level in high school. But everything to him was a competition. I couldn't take it anymore. I said I was going to be studying what I wanted in college and go after *my* dreams, not his.

So I packed up and left. The last thing he said was to never come home because there wouldn't be anyone waiting for me. I remember seeing the pained look in my sister's hazel eyes. I realized what I had done.

By ignoring my responsibilities as the eldest I had forced my little sister to take on the role. She had no idea what she wanted and I pushed her into the same fucking box I was desperately trying to escape from. I tried to reconcile with her. I called and texted her but the messages went unanswered. I tried reaching out on socials but I could never find her. And at some point I stopped looking. Time moved on and I became comfortable in the bubble I created for myself.

After graduation I did come back though. I went to the office when I knew my father wouldn't be around. He had kept the same routine since I was child. Wednesday between 12-4 he was out. I had walked in and my sister stared at me in shock.

"Crystal," I had said, my voice breaking. But before she could say anything my father surprisingly walked in, took one look at me and called security. And since then I'd been too griffin shit to reach out to her. That was four years ago.

What the fuck changed that my father was sponsoring the festival? Before I could continue to spiral downwards, my phone began ringing. I sighed. Without glancing at the screen I picked up.

"The financial reports have already been sent," I said automatically. But it wasn't Alex who was on the phone. Not Alex, who called me every day at around nine every night this week to talk about the reports and his ever growing bundle of joy.

"So now you're willing to handle numbers." A deep accusing voice made my stomach drop.

"Father," I said, keeping my voice monotone.

"Mr. Hale," he corrected me, reminding me that I had no right to call him that title. I glanced over at Caleb who was walking over with my order. Fuck, I didn't want him to hear this conversation. But the man on the other side of my phone kept me glued to my seat.

"This is just me warning you that while you'll be working with Crystal I hope you can keep your silly wishy washy antics to a minimum." His voice was steel. I felt my anger spike. Of course the man still thought that even though I was 28, with a master's degree in business, a minor in hospitality and deputy mayor of Lavender Falls I was still the same wild teenager that would go out partying every night. Granted I still partied just more responsibly.

"If by silly wishy washy antics you mean living a full life you don't have to worry. My only concern is making sure the winter festival is a success," I said and my father grunted. Caleb slid into the booth across from me. Why the fury fuck was he sitting down?

"Are you talking back to me?" he questioned. I rolled my eyes at his accusation. He always had a way with words.

"I'm not talking back but simply responding to you. It's not my fault that you don't like what I'm saying," I said. Caleb raised an eyebrow and I looked away from his assessing eyes.

"And it's my fault I have such a disrespectful daughter?" he said. My heart pounded against my chest. Tears welled up in my eyes and I hated myself for my body's reaction. My father always managed to make me feel small and this time he did it within five minutes of speaking. A new record. He always did like winning.

"Last time I checked I wasn't your daughter," I said, venom dripping, reminding him of my place. I could feel Caleb's eyes burning into me. There was a quiet pause. My father let out a tired sigh.

"Crystal will be meeting with you next week Ms. Hale." His voice was curt. He was over this conversation but I would be damned if after these past few years I would let him have the last word.

"Mr. Hale, please let her know if she wants to set up a meeting to do so during working hours. My email is on the town's website. After hours are only reserved for friends and family. And one more thing. It isn't Ms. Hale. It's Ms. Silva." I hung up before he could get another word in. He may have disowned me as being a Hale but I was still my mom's daughter.

My mom passed away in a car accident when my sister was still very small. I know for a fact she would be disappointed in the man my father had become. I bit the inside of my cheek. He wasn't always like this. He used to care about family dinners and Sunday picnics by the Hollow Tree. But after she passed he became a different person. He definitely needed therapy.

It felt good putting him in his place. I sighed, my muscles dropping with mental weight. I felt utterly exhausted. My father was up to something. I just had no idea what it was.

"Who was that?" Caleb cut through my thoughts again. I looked at him. His brows were furrowed and his lips were set in their usual frown.

"Why are you sitting down?" I asked. He pushed the monster-ella sticks toward me.

"Great thing about having a co-owner is I can get off my shift early," he said. He crossed his arms over his chest.

"Okay and why are you here?" I asked, annoyance slipping in. I could still feel the emotional damage of my father's words on my skin. It was poking through my tone.

"You are going to eat the food and then tell me who was on the phone," he said plainly. A laugh bubbled out of me.

"And why would I tell you?" I said, leaning my hands on the wooden table.

"Because we're friends," he said. I blinked at him for a second.

"Friends? Caleb be serious," I said. His eyes narrowed.

"Are we not?" he asked. He couldn't be serious. There was no way we knew enough about each other to be friends.

"You realize the majority of our conversations these past few years have consisted of alcohol and making jabs at each other, right?" I said. His nostrils flared slightly.

"We know each other enough to be friends," he stated. I raised an eyebrow.

"What's my favorite color?" I asked. He snorted.

"Pink," he said. I rolled my eyes.

"That's obvious because I wear it all the time," I pointed out. He shrugged his shoulders.

"You specifically prefer a pale pink, like your hair," he said. I blushed against my will.

"Favorite drink?" I asked. He smirked.

"Caipirinha for an alcoholic drink. If you're feeling extra you'll add strawberry to it. For nonalcoholic drinks you like strawberry lemonade or honey lavender tea. You prefer your coffee light and sweet," he said, sitting back triumphantly. I glared at him.

"Okay, maybe I should ask something that doesn't involve what I eat or drink. How about-"

"You're fiercely loyal to your friends and this town. You like making people smile and laugh. Your best friends are Celestino, Lilianna and Lola. You're also incredibly smart and have a wicked memory," he said. I bit back a smile. I always knew he was too perceptive.

"Okay. Maybe we are sorta of friends. But if we're friends we should know a bit more about each other," I said, taking a sip of my water.

"Like what, Starburst?" he asked in a teasing tone. He crossed his arms, tilting his head in amusement as he watched me. I mimicked his head tilt as I stared into his eyes in thought.

"Favorite food, movie and activity." I listed off the top of my head. Caleb pushed the basket closer to me, urging me to eat.

"Irish beef stew for food. For my favorite movie it would have to be The Princess Bride," he said. That was surprising. My cheeks pinked at the thought of Caleb in a black mask and cape.

"I can see the similarities between you and Westley," I said, glancing away. "Activity?" I asked, refocusing. He leaned towards me, capturing me in his gaze. My heart skipped.

"Besides soccer I think you and I both know what it is. How about you answer the same questions," he said. I cleared my throat, fidgeting in my seat.

"*Caldo verde*. It's a Portuguese soup. For my favorite movie it would have to be The Princess Bride as well or The Swan Princess," I said.

"And activity?" he asked, raising an eyebrow.

"Shopping, getting my nails done, reading," I paused in thought before smirking, "I think we both know what else, don't we?" I said. He chuckled and fuck it was delicious. The sound scratched out of him as if he wasn't used to laughing. It was beautiful to watch his face shift into something like happiness. For a grump he really was handsome.

"Now that we've established we're friends and we have a few things in common, how about telling me who was on the phone," he demanded. I grimaced as the playful mood vanished.

"Can we just forget about it? I'm tired," I said. He stared at me for a second, watching. "Caleb," I warned. I knew that look. It was the, *I'm not letting go of this look*. His jaw was set, arms crossed and his lips were set in what was supposed to be a frown but looked more like a pout. He wasn't going to let this go.

"Eleanor," he said with an authoritative tone that I didn't want to fight against, not now anyway. I was too overloaded. "You need to relax," he said simply. My shoulders sagged as a helpless chuckle escaped.

"And how do you know that?" I questioned. He leaned forward again, trapping me with his gaze.

"Because despite you thinking we don't know each other well enough, for the past four years I've been watching you from behind my bar. You walked in here with tight shoulders and avoided eye contact with everyone. That smile you gave me? Fake as a stork dropping off babies. You're stressed," he said confidently. My stomach dipped.

I knew this fucking grumpy elf was too attentive. I *was* stressed. There was so much pressure over this winter festival and its success. Now with my family on top of everything I felt anxiety bleeding into my system.

"You sound like you have a solution." My voice trembled slightly. His next six words had my jaw dropping and my thighs clenching.

"It involves you in my bed."

CHAPTER 2
BED SHEETS NOT SPREADSHEETS

CALEB

I knew something was wrong the second she stepped into the pub. Her shoulders were drawn in, the skin under her eyes were dark with shadows and she avoided meeting anyones gaze. Another give-away was the fact that her eyes matched in color. That only happened when her mood was down. And that fucking smile? Fake as shit.

The second I heard her on the phone my blood boiled. From her sentences it had it be her father; a man I knew nothing about. Eleanor never talked about her family in the four years that I've known her.

Instead she would always skirt around the conversation. Dodging and weaving away, not wanting to reveal her past to me or to too many people which I understood. I had my own secret. He made her tear up and I wanted to pull the phone away, reach in and punch the asshat.

I told myself during the festival last month that this tango we've been dancing was over. I was tired of circling around each other. I had never planned on wanting to break the curse but ever since Eleanor twirled into my life I began singing a different tune.

Every time she walked in, her perfume imprinted on my skin. Every light graze of fingers as I handed her order to her was like electricity sparking. Her presence, her laughter, her smile, her fucking sharp tongue begged me to come alive. I don't know what compelled me to say what I said but there was no going back. She was tired, stressed and if I could relieve some of it I would.

However, giving in to our sexual desires had conditions. My curse for example. There were a lot of things I could do to make Eleanor forget her own name but the only thing I couldn't do was kiss her lips. My eyes flickered to them. They've haunted me for four years; a beautiful temptation. Her eyes widened at my words.

"You're lying," she said. I smirked. Of course she would be hesitant.

"I would never lie to you," I said honestly. I would rather cut out my own tongue than have her lose trust in me. She stared at me in disbelief.

"Why?" she asked. I couldn't help but scoff at her. After four years of us edging each other on I finally gave in and she was questioning it. I leaned forward and watched her breathing falter. Her cheeks turned the prettiest shade of pink and she pulled at her bottom lip with her teeth. I forced my eyes to focus on hers.

"This thing between us ends here. So you tell me what's wrong and as your *friend* I'll help you unwind," I stated plainly. She still hesitated.

"Why?" she asked again. The word was beginning to irritate me.

"Because we want each other Eleanor and I'm tired of pretending I don't," I confessed. "Also you're not the only one stressed. The fall festival was the busiest the tavern had ever been. I can't imagine what the winter will bring," I finished. Lilianna had already called me to set up a meeting for the winter pub crawl.

Eleanor finally broke away from my gaze to stare at her food. I sat in silence waiting. I pushed the food towards her again and she began eating. When she was ready for her decision I would be here. She picked up a cheese stick, eyeing it.

"So we're both stressed," she said. I nodded. She hummed, taking a bite. After she ate her third monster-ella stick she finally looked at me.

"It was my father," she said, eyes devoid of emotion but her fingers twitched slightly. I could tell she had practiced talking about him without flinching.

"I gather that much," I said, nodding at her to keep going. She sighed.

"We basically had a falling out right before I started college. We haven't spoken in almost ten years. Now the company, Hale's Lumber Industry, is going to be a major sponsor of the festival. Mayor Kiana wants me to oversee and apparently work with my younger sister, Crystal. We used to be close but then I left and she had to take over as next in line."

She paused to take a sip of water and I fought the urge to say what was on my mind. To tell her that I could hear every word her father said on the phone and how I wanted to punch him in the face. But this wasn't about how I felt about the situation, it was about Eleanor venting to me.

"So I'm just a bit stressed out about it. I know the festival will be a success because hello I'll be running it with Ben and Tino's help but I just feel like my father has something up his sleeve because why now? And then there's my sister. I've tried reaching out before but nothing. She probably hates me." Her eyes filled with tears of worry. My heart cracked slightly. I had never seen that look on her face. Eleanor was always happy and flirty. A swirl of emotions I kept at bay waved up to the surface; emotions I hadn't felt in a long time.

"No one could ever hate you," I said. She snorted. They couldn't. Eleanor was sweet, bubbly, confident. She walked in and faced every problem head on without batting an eye. But the Eleanor sitting before me was someone I didn't recognize. I had never seen her so…sad, unsure, lonely.

"My father does…I think but I could care less how he feels about me. My sister though?" Her voice cracked slightly. There was another crack in my heart. As someone with three other siblings I understood her. I would do anything for them.

I grew up away from them but we always called and spent summers together. My thoughts briefly drifted to my younger sister.

The only one I kept a distance from for a good reason. I felt my throat tighten. I couldn't be thinking about that right now.

"Is there anything you need from me? Maybe I could help out somehow? I have more time off now that Tatiana helps," I offered. Her eyes scrutinized me again. I didn't blame her. We never really hung out outside of festivals and if we did it was with Lilianna and Sailor.

"I'm trying to not ask why because I've said the word twice already," she stated.

"I want to spend time with you and I'll take it however you'll give," I said. Her cheeks flushed again and I began wondering what other places I could make her skin turn pink.

"So you're going to help me with my family problems just because?" she said warily.

"Yes," I stated. Could she not fathom that I wanted to do something decent for her besides making a drink?

"Friends-ish with benefits?" she asked. I nodded. "I haven't had one in awhile. Might be nice," she said absentmindedly. She stuck out her hand. "Friends-ish with benefits," she said with a real smile. I took her soft hand in mine, liking the way it felt. Her left eye began to slowly shift to a more olive tone.

"Friends-ish with benefits." I repeated the words back to her.

"So do we go to bed now?" she asked, raising an eyebrow. I bit the inside of my cheek to keep from grinning. "Wait, don't you live upstairs?" I glanced around the bar. People were beginning to head home for the night.

"Yes," I said.

"Should we wait for everyone to clear out?" she asked, finally taking another bite of her food.

"Don't want people to hear you, Starburst?" I asked with a smirk. I had been calling her Starburst ever since we met. She was an explosion of brightness and sparkle, bringing light to my world. A sly smile pulled on her delicate full lips and she leaned forward.

"It depends if you're good, Elfie," she said. Her voice wrapped around my body and set my blood pumping. She was going to be the death of me.

"Finish your food and we will head upstairs," I grumbled. I watched her lips wrap around the fried cheese stick. Her eyes remained locked on mine. What the fuck was she doing? My hands dug into my knees. She took a bite and slid her tongue out to lick her lips. I stifled a groan. Only she could make a cheese stick erotic.

"Eleanor," I growled, growing impatient. The pixie simply shrugged her shoulders.

By the time she had her last bite I was already up and reaching for her hand. She barely had her bag on her shoulder when I began tugging her towards the back of the pub to the stairs that led up to my apartment. I ignored the eyes of the few patrons that were left. They've been whispering about us for years. Tonight they'll actually have something to discuss.

"Caleb," she said, her voice slightly out of breath. With my magic I unlocked the door, dragged her inside and pressed her against the wall. Her eyes widened as her face slowly flushed. It was like watching a rose unfurl its petals.

I pressed myself against her, groaning at how she felt. She dropped her bag on the floor, hands roaming my body with anticipation and excitement. She gripped my hips urgently and pressed into my growing erection. My fingers dug into her. She felt like pure sunshine against me.

"Fuck," I whispered into her neck. She hummed in agreement as she scraped her fingernails up my back, lifting my shirt. I placed a chaste kiss on the side of her throat and felt her shiver. This time I took a gentle nip and she bucked against me.

"Yes," she hissed. My hands slipped down to grab the ass that I've been dreaming about for years. It was soft in my hands. Her whole body softened against mine, letting me mold her into how I wanted her to be. I kept tracing kisses along her neck, gently sucking and biting, making her grab onto me tighter.

"Harder," she whispered as her hands frantically pulled at me. I leaned back to get a look at her. Her cheeks were pink, mouth open gasping for air and her pupils dilated. She was better than any fantasy I spent years conjuring. She leaned forward to kiss me and I gripped her throat.

If she kissed me I was done for and my only focus was making her come. Her eyes widened and before I could think I took it too far she smiled. She fucking smiled, eyes filling with lust.

"You like that?" I grunted, grinding my cock against her core. She attempted to nod and I squeezed her throat. She gasped, eyes closing shut in bliss, a moan escaping her mouth. It was fucking music to my ears and I wanted it to play like a soundtrack on repeat.

"C-Caleb," she stuttered. Her voice was breathy, filled with need. Need *for me*. I slid one hand up to tug her blouse from her pants. I needed to feel her skin. She moved her leg up to hook around my waist. She held herself in place as my fingers traced lines across her waistband. I slipped a finger beneath her pants and she sucked in a breath.

"Yes," she moaned. She had no idea what was coming for her. I lifted her up and she wrapped both of her legs around my waist. The heat between them was making me mad. I carried her towards my bedroom and threw her onto the bed. She looked at me in shock.

"Stand," I demanded. Instead of worrying about being too aggressive she listened. I knew she would after seeing how much she enjoyed having my hand wrapped around her delicate neck. She stood on my bed with shaky legs. Her chest was rapidly rising and falling, her hair was already coming out of her ponytail. She looked disheveled compared to her always tailored look.

I wanted to ruin her perfectly manicured persona and by the stars I would. I moved to stand at the edge of the bed. I motioned for her to come closer and she obeyed. She obeyed *so* fucking easily.

"Strip," I growled. Her hands trembled as she began unbuttoning her blouse showing off her breasts cladded in thin purple lace. Her nipples were already puckered and begging to be sucked. She tossed the blouse to the side. With one hand she slowly cupped one of her breasts, pulling at the lace.

"I said undress," I said, smacking her hands away from doing my job. Her jaw was set. I could tell by the look in her eyes she wanted to defy me. But I was in charge. She unbuttoned her pants to reveal black satin underwear and thick tanned thighs. I couldn't wait to bury my head between them.

She pushed them down her legs and kicked them off. I dragged my hands up her thighs, digging into her flesh, following the pale streaks marked on her skin. She threw her head back with a moan.

"Lay down," I murmured against her skin. She shivered and scrambled quickly with a smile. She was a vision to behold against my gray sheets. My blood was pounding in my ears as I watched her open her legs for me. She was fucking eager. We both were. After four years we were finally in this position. She arched her brow.

"Well?" she asked, her lips pulling into a smirk. I chuckled. I always knew she would be bossy in bed.

I responded by taking a bite of the inside of her thigh. I wanted to devour her. She pushed her cheek into the pillow, one leg stretching out. I had been dreaming of this moment for years.

I wondered how she would taste, how she would sound moaning beneath my hands and tongue. I could feel my cock straining against my pants as I kissed my way up her thigh, hands massaging her legs. She slowly began rocking, urging me to her most sensitive area.

But I promised myself I would take my time with her. I licked the apex of her thigh, pulling out another moan from her.

With my thumb I brushed the lace roughly against her nipples. She squirmed beneath me. My fingers traced the outline of her delicate bra. Her eyes snapped at me. Impatience painted her beautiful face.

"If you don't take my fucking bra off and lick me I will scream and not in a good way."

I let out a chuckle, my hands squeezing her. So impatient. I bit the top of her bra and pulled back. She gasped as the bedroom air hit her exposed skin. Goosebumps rose against her skin.

"Let me remind you who is in control." My voice was rough against her body. She cursed but refused to move her hands and forcibly dragged me to where she wanted. My hands continued their tortuous pattern of squeezing, grazing her nipple and lifting her bra up just enough for the air to caress it. Her legs kept moving, trying to find to create the friction she needed against me as her hands twisted my sheets.

Instead of unhooking her bra I kissed my way back down, my tongue once again teasing the hem of her underwear. She needed to know who was in charge and it sure as fuck was me. Giving in for half a second I moved to run my tongue over the expanse of her covered pussy lips eliciting a whimper from her.

"Do you want more?" I asked teasingly. Her eyes sharpened with a mixture of lust and annoyance. She must have truly ran out of patience because she sat up and practically ripped her bra off. Her breasts hung low, fuller at the bottom and her nipples were a beige color and begging for me.

"Well?" she taunted. I shook my head in disbelief. Of course she would be this demanding in bed. But after years of bickering with her I knew how to handle her. Pushing her to lay back down, her hands slipped into my hair, pulling apart my braid as I sucked her nipple. Her whole body shivered. I felt her hand inch down between us and I snatched it holding it over her head. I pulled back enough to glare into her eyes.

"Keep them up here or I'll stop right now." She rolled her eyes and complied. I smirked as I continued to give her languid licks across her breasts, squeezing them under my hands until she was gasping in pleasurable pain. She hissed as my teeth grazed her overly sensitive nipple.

I groaned deeply as I slipped one hand beneath her underwear and between her folds. She was fucking drenched.

She moaned as I found the bundle of nerves that demanded my tongue. Soon I was going to taste her. Eleanor rocked her hips faster but I refused to give into her pace. I let my finger slide further down until it slipped inside. She clenched and I wished it was my cock. I pulled at her nipple with my hand and she arched her back. She was fucking magnificent. After a few pumps I slipped my hand out earning a delectable whimper.

"These are in the way, lovely," I whispered, kissing the center of her chest. I fisted her underwear and ripped them off. She gasped.

"Those are some of my nice ones!" she said, sitting up. I held them to my nose. I could get drunk on her scent. My cock continued to push against my jeans, begging for freedom.

"I'll buy a new one now the lay the fuck down. I've been starving to eat your pussy." My voice was husky, urgent. Her eyes lit up again. She liked being told what to do. I smirked. I wondered what else she liked.

"Yes sir," she said out of breath. I groaned at the term. How was I going to survive this night?

"Knees up and open wide for me," I demanded. She listened. One thing I've always admired about Eleanor was her confidence. Not just in who she is but with her body.

My eyes traced her figure. From her full tits to the slight dip in her waist down to the way her hips curved. Her body was made to be savored and adored. My eyes snagged on the landing strip of dark curls that led me to paradise. She was dripping for me. I bet it wouldn't take much longer to have her screaming my name.

I couldn't believe this was finally happening. After years of pining Eleanor was naked beneath me. My heart rattled against my chest. I've been in this position before with other women and while I always wanted this with Eleanor a small bit of trepidation began settling. I felt a small tap on my head. I looked up to stare into her enchanting two tone eyes. Her eyes reflected my thoughts.

This was happening and there was no turning back.

"Make me come, Caleb," she said urgently.

I dug my hands into her thighs and gave a slow, rough lick from her needy hole to her clit. Her thighs immediately tightened against my head. While I would gladly welcome dying from being strangled between her legs I needed her to keep them open for me.

I pushed her legs back apart as I flicked my tongue against her clit. She kept her feet planted and tilted her hips up. Her hand found its way back into my hair tugging me harder against her. I groaned low in my throat at her taste. *So fucking addicting.* She thrashed in my sheets, sweat making her skin glisten in the dim lighting.

Mine. Mine. Mine. The possessive word repeated over and over again. I wanted to remind myself of our friends-ish with benefits agreement but some primal part of me was taking the reins. I covered her sensitive bud with my lips and sucked while slipping two fingers into her. She bucked harder. I watched her, calculating what pressure to use to have her lose control. I wasn't even done with her yet and I needed more.

"Yes! Fuck. Caleb. Yes," she panted. I curled my fingers inside, making sure to hit her sweet spot and she rocked faster against me. She arched her back, eyes squeezed shut as she cried out my name in release. Her sound was never going to leave my head.

I drove my hips into the bed, pressing my cock against the mattress. I continued with gentle licks against her clit until her body stopped trembling and she was shoving me off by my shoulder. I sat back up and watched her body sag into the mattress. This was my eden, her naked and satisfied in my bed.

"Kiss me," she said, eyes heavy now that I made her scream my name. I crawled back up her body, kissing my way back up. She squirmed under me. I nipped the underside of her breast and she yelped, bucking up. "Caleb," she begged.

I groaned. Fuck, she could make me do anything by saying my name that way. I would give up every spirit in the realm, including my own, to be with her. I would even punch Rudolph in the nose for her. He was a little too merry and bright anyway. Either way there was one thing she could never make me do…at least not yet.

"I am kissing you," I murmured into her neck. She already had bruises where I spent extra time sucking and biting. I smirked. I was happy that I marked her. Fuck did it make me nearly come to think she'd be walking around town with me all over her body. She narrowed her eyes on me, the dreamy spell of her orgasm easing away.

"Why won't you kiss me on the mouth?" she asked. I could see the wheels turning in her head. My heart rattled against my chest, the truth sitting on the tip of my tongue. She pushed me away and sat up on her knees, naked, glistening like a goddess and grabbed my shirt, pulling me towards her. *Fuck.*

"Tell me," she demanded. Do I tell her? Would she run away? Would she be mad? She was probably going to be mad.

"Tell me or I'm going to kiss you," she said, pulling me closer. My eyes drifted down to her full breasts, nipples raw from my tongue. My throat tightened. How was I supposed to lie to her when she looked like this? I sighed and pulled from her grip. Staring at my hands I finally told someone the secret I've been hiding for over 15 years.

"I got cursed by accident when I was younger and if I kiss someone I get turned into stone."

CHAPTER 3
THE SLOW BURN BEGINS

I blinked. And then blinked again before my body got its shit together. I reached for a pillow and threw it at his stupid Elf King of Eating Pussy face. However, he caught it. *Jerk.*

"Eleanor," he said in his stupid grumpy sexy voice.

"You. Fucking. Idiot," I yelled, reaching for another pillow.

"Is that how you thank me for giving you the best orgasm of your life?" he said in a cocky tone that twisted my insides as much as I twisted in his sheets.

"First, it wasn't the best. Second, you fucking almost kissed me. I *almost* kissed you," I said, launching off the bed to grab the pillow he tossed on the floor to suffocate his tantalizing mouth.

"First, it was. Second, we didn't. I'm always careful," he said nonchalantly. I shook my head as I began pacing around his room. He'll turn to stone if we kiss? What kind of twisted curse of Medusa was this? What kind of fucking asshole curses someone to never be able to kiss? Fall in love? Sure. But kiss?! That's too cruel. Kissing was nice. Kissing was good exercise, fun exercise.

"Eleanor, say what's on your mind," he demanded. My nose

28

twitched. I hated how he read me so easily. I even hated how he understood my body and how I melted under him so damn easily. *Too easily.*

"Who cursed you? Why are you cursed and what are the exact details of the curse because clearly my other lips won't turn you into stone." I felt anger bubbling through me. I was upset at him. I was upset at how careless he was being. We could have kissed. We almost did! Why the fuck would he risk something like that just to give me orgasm? Granted it was a mind blowing, toe curling one but still.

"Do you want me to tell you while you're still naked," he asked, eyes devouring my body. I felt wetness between my legs as his eyes consumed every inch of me. I placed my hands on my hips ignoring the sensation rippling up and down my body.

"Will you be distracted?" I asked.

"Yes," he said. I rolled my eyes.

"Now he's honest," I mumbled. With my bra back on and I stared at my shredded underwear on the floor. I pointed to it. He had the audacity to smirk. He got up and tossed me a pair of boxers. I pulled them on, ignoring that they were stretchy and soft. I was absolutely keeping these as payment.

"You can keep them as payment for ripping yours," he said, sitting back on the bed. I sent him another glare. Was he a mind reader too? I continued to give him the silent treatment.

"Is the wall pillow seriously necessary?" he asked, arching a brow as I piled the pillows.

"Yes. We could accidentally kiss and you could turn into stone and never eat me out again. It would be a horrible day for me if that were to happen," I said. His cheeks flushed slightly and a part of me felt giddy for breaking him out of his icy armor.

"So I am the best." He snickered and I wanted to throw another pillow at his gorgeous face but that meant ruining the pillow wall I carefully crafted. Caleb eventually sighed and laid down next to it.

"My younger sister Bridget. She was about five when my parents divorced. I was 12. She didn't take the news very well. She slipped into my dad's study and grabbed one of his spell books. She found what supposedly looked like a love spell in hopes to get my parents

29

back together." Caleb's voice carried around the room and I found myself laying down, listening to the tragic tale.

"Her reading skills weren't the best yet. I walked in on her just as she was attempting it. She had just finished watching the Medusa episode in Hercules. Remember the show? She got frazzled and mixed up the words. I ended up cursed. If I ever kiss someone on the lips that I love I turn to stone," he said, taking a shaky breath.

"Bridget was distraught. She couldn't stop crying over what she did and my parents did everything they could to break it. But she couldn't remember how she said the incantation. Afterwards she had trouble sleeping. She felt horrible. Our parents were separating, I was cursed..." Caleb stopped. "They took her memories." I stifled a gasp. Love spells, curses, taking memories away?

That was serious magic.

"And so I've never kissed anyone. I've kept everyone at a distance in terms of relationships just in case," he said. I stared up at his white ceiling. I can't imagine the weight he had been carrying all these years. And he's been doing it alone.

"But how did you know about the curse working in that way?" I asked. Something must have happened for them to realize the curse's intention.

"The words my sister said. Half of it was in Gaeilge, the other half was in English. The problem was figuring out what Gaeilge words were spoken. Because she was five it wasn't perfectly said. We couldn't get a solid understanding and she couldn't remember. But the second half of the curse? Kiss of love will make you stone. I think she meant to say: kiss of love will make you one," he finished. My eyes widened as the realization sunk in. That's why we never hooked up all these years. But that one night...

His hand, which was surprisingly warm, slipped to cup my cheek. I was on edge the whole night. It was finally happening. Us. After years of tension we finally reached our breaking point. Caleb's blue eyes were drinking me in and I couldn't help but lean into his touch. He leaned in closely. His mouth brushed my cheek, making my body go all tingly. He kept going up, teasing me, edging me. Then he reached my ear and whispered, "our first kiss won't be in the middle of a bar and not because you demanded it." My eyes widened in shock.

"So we will kiss? Because clearly that statement is suggesting that we will," I said. He cocked his head, pulling at my hair. I nearly let out a moan.

"We will, when the time is right."

"THAT NIGHT THOUGH," I said out loud, lost in the memory.

"That was the night I made a decision," he said quietly. I felt my heart pounding in my chest. "With my parent's divorce and the curse I figured it would be okay if I never kissed anyone. I was fine with that. There were other things I could do and feel that didn't involve sharing lips with someone."

When Caleb first came to town he really didn't talk much. I didn't have many memories of him from my childhood. He lived in Lavender Falls until he was 12 but we never had the same classes. And then he moved back around the same time I did. In the beginning he was quiet. He wouldn't really hold a conversation with many people.

But the more time Sailor, Lilianna and I came around the grump began making full sentences. My throat tightened. And now we were having emotionally charged conversations.

"Then you plowed straight through my pub four years ago and no matter how hard I tried to keep you away you kept pushing through my barriers," he said. He's been living with this curse for over ten years and because of my loud ass pixie mouth he wanted to break the curse. Me? *Me.*

I sat up, peering over the wall. His eyes were sad, longing. His hand played with the pillow wall as if he was fighting the urge to reach over and grab me.

"You're breaking the curse just to kiss me?" I said in disbelief. His head popped over the pillow fort. His gaze caressed my lips as I felt the ghost of his thumb trace against my bottom lip.

"I want to know how you taste like Eleanor so yes. The sheer temptation of your lips makes me want to get rid of this curse," he said in a low voice. My mouth parted at his words. My tongue swept against his thumb and he slowly brought it to his own mouth. The room felt hot or maybe it was my body reacting to Caleb. "I can't wait to have a taste."

"If you've never been kissed, how the stars are you so good at eating pussy?" I asked, trying to snuff the fire he was brewing within me. Caleb fought back a laugh. I could tell by the way he pursed his lips and his body slightly shook. My heart skipped at the reaction.

"As you've pointed out, those lips don't affect me. Just because I couldn't kiss someone didn't mean I couldn't do other things. An elf has needs Eleanor." His eyes traced around my bra.

"Focus," I said, waving my hand in his face. His eyes snapped back up. "Why do I have the worst luck with men?" I muttered.

"I would rather you not discuss other men while in my bed." His voice deepened. I rolled my eyes.

"I would rather you not tell me what to do," I fired back. He sat up, leaning against my curated pillow wall.

"But you took my orders so well a few minutes ago," he teased. My nose flared in annoyance, remembering how willingly I listened to him while he ravished my body. I pushed him away and got up to get my things, seeking back my control.

"Where are you going?" he asked, following after me. I pulled on the rest of my clothes. I grabbed my bag from the floor and tried not to look at the wall where I finally got a taste for what Caleb could give me.

"I'm going home," I stated. He pulled me away from the door. I turned to face him. My mind was already set on what was going to be happening.

"Eleanor-"

"I'm going home," I said, cutting him off. "I need space to digest everything that happened tonight. Then we are going to meet up so we can figure out how to break your curse," I huffed out. Caleb's mouth was slightly agape in shock.

"You want to help me?" he asked in disbelief. Was he really that shocked that I wanted to help him? We were friends-ish weren't we?

"Yeah. You have kissable lips and it's going to be a problem if I can't kiss you. We won't be proper friends-ish with benefits and that's the agreement," I said. He nodded his head absentmindedly in understanding. I opened the door and stepped into the hallway. Turning back I stared at the incredibly sexy elf.

"But Caleb? This is the last time we will have any sexy time because I don't need you accidentally turning to stone while inside me." And with that I closed the door on him and my vagina.

CHAPTER 4
THE TRUTH SHALL SET YE FREE

First, I got told I would be working with my estranged sister, then a shitty phone call with my asshole of a father, followed by the best orgasm of my life from the man I've been crushing on for years and naturally he had to have some stupid curse on him. Seriously? What was with my luck? Why did we *both* have to have family issues? I sighed.

It was finally Sunday and I was anxiously waiting at Coffin's Coffee Shop for Lola and Lily, my best gal pals. The door chimed and my two soul sisters walked in. Lola's coily dark hair brushed the tips of her shoulders. She had some pieces individually twisted back with golden butterfly clips mimicking a headband. She was dressed in tight denim jeans and a cropped knitted sweater.

Lily strolled in with her wavy hair pulled to the top of her hair in a messy bun. She was wearing acid wash jeans and an oversize men's hoodie that was probably Celestino's.

"Ellie!" Lola squealed, crushing me into a hug. I laughed at her infectious energy. Lily smiled and leaned over to kiss my cheek.

"Ladies, mimosas are on the way and we're going to need a lot," I said, gathering my strength. The girls eyed each other, settling into their seats.

Lola had recently moved back after graduating from vet school. She was working at our local vet clinic since Ms. Heinstein has been wanting to spend time with her grandkids. She was also working with Priscilla and the local community garden to start creating natural remedies for the animals and supernatural creatures around town.

Lily, because of the success of the Full Moon Fall Festival was promoted from marketing assistant to marketing coordinator. Her and her boyfriend/our mutual best friend would be doing another pub crawl for our winter festival called The Frozen Pub Crawl. I was so happy that they finally got together.

They were the cutest couple. Celestino was shorter than her which made them look adorable. They complimented each other well. He kept her grounded while she reminded him to look up at the stars.

A pain shot through my heart. I wasn't jealous of their love. I was just well aware I had never had it. I tried to have serious relationships but they could never handle me. I'm a strong, confident and capable pixie. I didn't need someone with a small dick for a brain thinking he could tame me. I didn't need to be tamed. I needed to be cherished and ravished like the people in my romance books.

My mind wandered to Caleb who I was well aware was the opposite of the men I usually went for. He was assertive yet quiet. Demanding when need be and brooding.

"Earth to Ellie. Mimosas are here so sip and spill," Lily said, waving a glass in my hand. I giggled, hoping to mask the thoughts that were clouding my mind. Taking a sip I let the tartness of my drink soothe my nerves.

"So...I'll be fully in charge of the winter festival. We're going to have an intern at the office. Less work for me in a way," I started. The girls broke out in smiles. *Just wait.*

"My father's company is one of the biggest sponsors which means I have to work with my sister," I continued. Their eyes widened comically.

"Fury fuck," Lily whispered.

"You're kidding," Lola said, clutching her drink. I nodded, taking another sip. I picked at my napkin.

"I am excited to see my sister but also terrified. She probably hates me, you know. And my father called me Friday. He still thinks I'm the same wild child. He told me and I quote, to keep my silly wishy washy antics to myself," I said, annoyed. The girls scoffed.

"Oh please that bastard doesn't know jack shit about you and doesn't deserve to," Lily said, getting heated. She was there through it all. We were roommates in college and she took care of me as I grieved the loss of my family. Pieces of her hair were beginning to float. I could feel her magic in the air. I smiled at her. Always protective. It's the quiet ones you have to worry about, you know.

"Why now?" Lola asked skeptically. I took another gulp and pointed at her in agreement.

"That's the million dollar question. Something isn't adding up. I have a feeling he has something up his sleeve. I just don't know what it is," I said, shrugging my shoulders. My father never made any moves without reason. Everything to him was a game of chess with him as the winner.

"What do you need us to do?" Lily asked. My girl was always ready to back me up. Lola nodded in agreement. This is why I loved them. Ready to talk or claw their way for me.

"Nothing," I said. Lola shook her head.

"As fucking if. We're helping you figure out whatever he's doing. He's not going to hurt you again," Lola said with ruthless conviction. I could see her fangs poking out. I tapped my glass nervously. Lily squinted.

"There's more," Lily stated, sitting back. I downed the rest of my mimosa, before waving for another. Lola raised an eyebrow.

"She's pausing for dramatic effect," Lola whispered loudly. Lily nodded.

"Trust me the effect will be worth it," I said as the waitress brought me another mimosa. "Wait," I told the fairy waitress with blonde hair. I downed the drink again. The girls eyed each other, on the edge of their seats. Once the waitress brought me another, Lily took it away.

"You more than sipped, now spill," Lily said. I took a deep breath and Lola groaned impatiently.

36

"Caleb overheard the phone call with my dad and said he would help me deal with him." I chewed my lip. I was never flustered when it came to talking about sex but I felt my face flushed. Lola motioned for me to continue.

"He suggested having a friends-ish with benefits situation. And I agreed because I have pent up aggression and I'm in desperate need of relaxation. So after he deliciously, mercilessly ate my vagina out and gave me the most explosive orgasm he revealed to me that he is cursed to not be able to kiss anyone on the lips or he'll turn into stone," I said. I grabbed the drink from Lily.

"I threw a pillow at him because I almost kissed him. I've also decided that I'll help him break the curse but there's to be no funny business until the curse is broken because I can't chance us accidentally kissing." I gasped for breath as I finished. The girls were looking at me with jaws dropped.

"Mimosas!" They yelled in union. Madame Coraline looked at us with an arched brow and I guess from the look on our faces brought us an entire bottle of champagne. Once she was out of earshot Lily flicked my shoulder.

"What the *fuck* Ellie?!" Lily hissed.

"Why is it friends-ish?" Lola asked. I shrugged my shoulders.

"Well I'm not friends with him like I am with Sailor. We're friendly with each other but not *that* friendly," I said. Lily snorted.

"You guys are now," Lily said. I groaned.

"He was so fucking good with his mouth I was sure I was going to lose my voice," I confessed. Lola passed around the bottle.

"This is giving me serious Pushing Daisies vibes," Lily said.

"That means you're going to rewatch it, aren't you?" Lola asked before waving her hand. "Wait so that's why he kept his distance. The curse?" Lola said. I nodded. "Why now?" she asked. I chewed the inside of my cheek.

"He said it was because of me," I mumbled.

"Shut the fuck up! That's so romantic," Lola said with hearts in her eyes. I giggled, drinking straight champagne. The need for the tangy dilution of orange juice was gone.

"Sure, but we're not going to have anymore of what we just did. I don't want to risk us kissing while he has some body part inside of me," I said. I regretted that declaration the second it came out of my mouth. Surely we could fool around and be careful right? Lola tsked.

"That's going to be hard for you," Lily said. I groaned.

"I know because he was so fucking good. Literally the best orgasm of my life," I said.

"You won't last a week," Lola snickered. Lily leaned towards Lola.

"They did last four years," Lily pointed out. I scoffed.

"How do you know he won't be the one to cave first after already having a taste?" I arched an eyebrow.

"Should we bet on it?" Lola asked with a smirk. I gave her one back.

"Isn't that your thing with Flynn?" I teased. Lola sipped her drink instead of responding.

"Wait, how are you going to break the curse?" Lily asked. I placed my head in my hands.

"I have no fucking idea. The curse was an accident and the family has tried everything to get rid of it," I said, not wanting to reveal too many details.

"Maybe I can find something in one of my mom's books. She has a shit ton of books from when she was a teacher assistant in the enchantments and curses class at the university," Lola offered. Hope bloomed in my chest. Lola's mom was one of the smartest vampires in all of Lavender Falls. She was a professor in a nearby university.

"I can do some research," Lily offered.

"You guys don't have to do this," I said, grimly. They stared at me in silence.

"Eleanor," Lola said, placing a hand on top of mine. Lily placed hers on top.

"We're your friends and we don't leave friends to handle things on their own. At least I'm still learning that," Lily confessed. My heart grew three sizes. Lily has come a long way in accepting help and with her anxiety.

"We won't let anyone or anything dim your sparkle Ellie. Friends are there when you need to remember to shine," Lola said with a toothy grin. I had a feeling this winter season was going to kick my ass but with these ladies by my side I knew I could tackle anything and anyone. We refilled our glasses and cheered.

"To the winter festival," Lola said.

"To blessings in disguise," Lily said.

"To my poor vagina," I said with a giggle.

CALEB

I was fucked. I was so fucked up the ass. One night with Eleanor and I was craving for more. Her screams replayed in my head. My hands itched to feel her body beneath mine. We were friends-ish with benefits and I needed us to reap more of the benefits.

I was at the tavern before opening hours with Sailor and Celestino who were helping me move in the new tables they made for the place. Tatiana and I came to an agreement to slowly refurbish the tavern to bring it up to date while still keeping the old school Irish pub charm. I poured each of them a glass of beer. It was five in the afternoon somewhere.

"Thanks again for this guys," I said. Sailor the siren grinned madly.

"Who am I to turn down free beer?" Sailor joked. Celestino tapped the back of his head.

"We got paid to do this fish brain," Celestino said. Despite my outward demeanor I was grateful to have Celestino back. We were roommates in college and while I put two and two together about where he was from I never told him who I really was. I've always been quiet and selective of people.

The curse made me retreat further into my cozy shell. Back in college I was just trying to finish school as quickly as possible so I could move back here. My dad and I had an agreement. I studied business and he paid for my schooling.

But after graduating instead of working for his whiskey distillery I came back here to work at the tavern. Luckily Flynn was the one who was into whiskey making so my dad wasn't too upset. Right now they were planning to open a storefront in town seeing how they've been selling out like crazy at the tavern.

Moving back home, to my real home to help run the tavern years ago, slowly opened me up. I stared at the men I was happy to call friends. I told myself all morning that I needed to tell them before Eleanor blabbed to Celestino because I knew she would. Either she would tell him or she would tell Lily who would.

But also I just wanted to tell them. After telling Eleanor the truth I didn't realize how much weight it took off of me.

"Are you going to say something or not?" Sailor asked, interrupting my thoughts. I raised an eyebrow. He waved his hand around me. "Your aura is all troubled. You want to tell us something," he said. I sighed. I forgot the fucker could read emotions. Celestino set his glass down.

"What's wrong?" Celestino asked. I rubbed the back of my neck and braced myself to tell them what happened the other night.

"You mother fucking elf," Sailor yelled, eyes bright with excitement.

"You little introverted shit," Celestino exclaimed. I sighed.

"Thanks guys. Way to make me feel better," I muttered.

"Listen I'm very happy that you and Eleanor are stepping forward in your relationship but I fucking knew it," Sailor said. The siren was practically bouncing in his seat.

"I'm happy for you guys too. Side-note: if you break her heart I'm breaking your face. But also I'm grateful that you were able to share this with us," Celestino said. I began rearranging the bottles, needing to fidget with my hands.

"I'd rather break my heart before breaking hers," I said firmly. Celestino nodded with a smile. Sailor however was still bouncing in his seat. "Why are you so damn excited?" I grunted. Sailor took a quick sip of his beer.

"You know I can read energies right? Well there's always been this black stain around you but I figured maybe it's a part of your brooding attitude. But now that you've mentioned the curse it has to be that." His eyes wandered around my body.

"I'm not always brooding," I said. Both of them stared at me. "Okay well whatever. You can see a mark? Seriously?" I asked. He nodded enthusiastically. No fucking way.

"So you and Eleanor," Celestino said, smirking. I felt my cheeks flushed and I turned away.

"Too bad she has your dick under lock and key," Sailor snorted. I glared at him.

"How are you guys going to break the curse?" Celestino asked. I shrugged my shoulders.

"My family has tried everything, seen everyone. I'm not sure. But maybe with you guys and Eleanor-"

"And Lola and Lily," Sailor interjected. Celestino and I nodded in agreement.

"Yeah with all of you, maybe we could find something," I finished saying. There was a quiet moment before Sailor spoke up.

"I might have some connections from my town who can help," Sailor offered. His grip on the beer bottle tightened.

"You know I love research," Celestino said. I sighed in relief. The weight on my shoulders felt lighter. This is what it was like to have friends. People who liked you, valued you and you could trust to be there for you. I stared at the men I called friends, brothers. I could trust the circle that I've carved for myself. Stars, I wish I had told them all sooner.

"But Caleb…" Celestino's voice wavered. I eyed him suspiciously. "Eleanor's father. He's a major dick and he's a dick with a lot of money. Growing up we never really saw him much but when we did? He was a judgmental prick and controlling," Celestino said carefully. Sailor raised an eyebrow.

"It's that bad?" Sailor asked softly. We both turned to Celestino who stared at his glass.

"He hated that Eleanor went out, partied, and was friends with Lily, Lola and I. He wanted her to be like him," Celestino said. His hand tightened around his beer as recounted. I felt my heart drop to think that Eleanor grew up with such a troll's ass of a father. "You have to be careful around him. I just hope he hasn't twisted Crystal around his golden finger. She was always a sweetheart. A bit shy but nice," he continued. Sailor blew out a breath.

"And I thought I had family problems," Sailor muttered. We both turned to look at the sunshine siren. He gave a wry smile. "If you guys want to hear about my family problems we're going to need a night with stronger alcohol," he said jokingly.

But I could tell there was something below the surface of those words that were true.

"Well this got depressing fast," I said, hoping to break the tension.

"To breaking curses," Celestino said, lifting his glass. I shook my head, a chuckle escaping. I reached for a bottle of whiskey.

"And assholes," I chimed in.

"To Eleanor who holds the key to your dick," Sailor said, laughing.

CHAPTER 5
A MYSTERY IS UNFOLDING

ELEANOR

M y stomach was churning. I couldn't sleep at all last night. Today was the day I would be seeing my sister for the first time in four years and getting Emily the intern situated. However, it would be the first time my sister and I would be speaking in almost ten years.

Did she hate me for leaving her? Did she feel abandoned? Did she feel betrayed? Did my sister still have the same gentle heart or had my father carved it into ice like his?

I stared at my ceiling. For once I didn't feel confident. I felt small, like I was a kid again. Taking a deep breath I made my way over to my closet. Look good, feel good. That was always my motto and I needed my armor to face my sister. *My little sister.*

I pulled on my favorite gingham pink slacks with a cropped, distressed knitted mustard sweater with some booties. I styled my pink hair courtesy of a spell crafted by Lily into blown out waves.

"Look good, feel good." I muttered at my reflection. I could do this. I was going to explain to her what happened and expressed how badly I wanted our relationship back. If she accepted then a part of me that I lost years ago would be back. I bit my lip. But if she didn't, well I understood and would respect to keep our relationship strictly professional.

I WAS SITTING in the meeting room of the town's office waiting. I was a few minutes early. I grabbed coffee from Coffin's Coffee Shop and a few pastries from Godmother's Patisserie. Brownies were her favorite when we were little. But fuck what if she hates them now or thinks that I'm trying too hard? *You are.* I groaned. I opened my laptop, ready to write some notes down. I needed something to do while I waited.

The winter festival included activities like ice sculpture competitions, pie bake offs, sled rides, a snowball fight tournament and a few other things. There were going to be vendors and food trucks. Mayor Kiana said my father's company was one of the biggest sponsors and only agreed if my sister could work side by side with me to ensure the success of the festival. But I couldn't wrap my head around why. Why now?

The door creaked open and my heart faltered. My sister walked in. She was taller than me now, thinner with straight dark hair that fell near her waist. Her hazel eyes were lined with black eyeliner. She wore a black suit. My stomach dipped. She reminded me of our mom with her high cheekbones and sharp eyes. I stood up immediately.

"Cry-Ms. Hale," I corrected myself. She stared at me. Even though she looked like our mom her eyes were calculated like our father. Her mouth was set in a grim line. *Fuck.* She hated me. I stared back at her, trying to keep my cool. And then she did the last thing I expected. She ran up and threw her arms around me.

"Crystal," I whispered, my arms catching her. She held onto me tightly curving her body over mine. She was so much taller now. No longer a lanky young teen but a beautiful woman. Tears threaten to spill. I missed this so much. I missed her so much.

"I'm sorry. I'm so fucking sorry," I repeated, over and over again. She pulled away immediately. She stared at her hands as if in shock of what she did.

"I'm sorry," she said, quietly. I took a step towards her.

"Why the fuck are you sorry? I left," I said. She let out a sniffle, trying to compose herself.

"Dad did push you," she said softly. What the fuck was happening? This is not what I expected. I thought she would either yell at me or give me the cold shoulder. But Crystal was quiet and reserved.

"Don't you hate me?" I asked, my hands shaking. She sighed, taking a seat. She tugged at her hair.

"In the beginning I did. I felt like you abandoned me. That you wanted nothing to do with me anymore." Her voice cracked. I bit the inside of my cheek. That was the furthest thing I wanted. But I made her feel that way.

"What changed those thoughts?" I asked, hesitantly. She took a breath.

"You guys fought all the time. A part of me always knew you would leave. I asked dad about you all the time and he said you made your choice. When you showed up to the office that day after you graduated I could see it in your eyes. I could see how happy and terrified you were. But then dad called security and told them you weren't allowed on the property. I knew that the only reason you couldn't come back was because of him." My heart broke. She wiped her eyes.

"I saw you on social media…but I was scared to connect with you," she said, pausing to take a breath.

"I-I was going to go to your graduation as a surprise. But dad…" she trailed off. My hands tightened in my lap. "He said that he would kick me out of the company and I would lose any chance of taking over…and I like the company," she said, finally meeting my eyes.

"Fuck Crys," I said. How could a man like that be so fucking cruel? "I wanted to talk to you and I should have tried harder," I pleaded. She nodded, her eyes watering. "So…you don't feel like I forced you to be a part of the company?" I asked. She tugged at her hair again.

"In the beginning…yes. But I grew to love what we do," she said. Her eyes brightened in a flash. "I even implemented a program; with any of the lumber that can't be sold we donate to local wood shops. We even host classes once a week for young kids who want to get into carpentry." She beamed brightly and for a second I saw a sliver of the sister I grew up with. I spent so many years worried she would resent me. I took a deep breath.

"I'm hoping to open locations for carpentry stores that supply our wood. At least that's a future idea." She smiled softly in thought.

"That's amazing Crys. I can see how much you love it. But I have to ask. Why the sponsorship and the festival?" I asked. She sat back in her seat.

"I'm not sure. He wanted me to work with you actually," she confessed. Really? I wonder why. I shook my head. Right now what was important was that I had my sister back. My little sister was going to be in my life again. At least I hoped so.

"Is everything okay with the company?" I asked. She picked her nail.

"There is something wrong. You know how we use our magic to cut down the trees and then with the power of the Hollow Tree we nurture the wood that has been cut and help replenish it?" she said, looking at me. I nodded.

The Hollow Tree of Lavender Falls helped provide magic for all pixies and even helped the fairies. We nurtured the tree and the earth and in return it helped our magic stay strong, giving us an extra kick every once in a while.

"I think the tree is sick. Something has been happening to our magic. The trees aren't doing well. But you've always had a special connection with the Hollow Tree," she said. Was this why when I touched her hand her magic felt slow? I cursed. This wasn't fucking good and we were stepping into winter when all of the grounds would be covered in snow. The Hollow Tree kept vegetation alive and well through the brutal winters. I took a deep breath.

"I wonder if his sponsorship has anything to do with it. Either way we have to solve the problem with the tree," I said. She nodded in agreement.

"Also the festival has to be a success," she added. *Right.* Have the winter festival be a success, save the tree and break Caleb's curse. Shouldn't be too hard. Crystal reached for a brownie.

"I definitely still like brownies by the way." She smiled boldly. Before the meeting really began there was something I needed to ask.

"Crys?" I asked, nervously. She looked up at me, mid chew. "Do I have my sister back?" I asked. Her eyes softened as she took another bite.

"I think so," she said quietly.

THE MEETING with my sister went well after we reconnected. Advertisements were beginning and vendors and food trucks were being scouted. Hale's Lumber Industry would be in charge of the ice sculpture contest and donating prize money to the winners of other contests.

Crystal gave me her personal phone number and promised to keep me up to date if our father did anything suspicious and I promised to check out the tree and see if there was anything I could find. She didn't like that.

The Hollow Tree was near the company's land but I needed to see it for myself. I needed to feel what was wrong with it. She said she couldn't figure out what was wrong but maybe I could.

We spent the last thirty minutes of our meeting catching up and I could feel the hole in my heart that kept her close was beginning to close.

My muscles tightened. I hadn't visited the tree in years. It used to be my favorite place in the whole world. Around the Hollow Tree I wasn't Eleanor Silva Hale I was just Eleanor. The power that would surge through me as I walked the grounds was almost intoxicating. Sometimes I swore I heard the tree whisper to me. But would the tree accept me stepping back into its precious circle? My hands clenched into fists.

If the tree was sick this was serious business and I was going to do everything in my pixie power to help save it from whatever the fuck my father did. He was probably the reason the tree was sick. A pain ran through me. Maybe it wasn't his fault. Maybe I just wanted it to be.

But it was our family duty as Hale's to protect it and he was failing. Well I wasn't Hale anymore but I was going to fix this after my meeting with Emily. I still had a to-do list to get through.

EMILY WAS STANDING by my desk, clutching her laptop. I waved at Lily who gave me a thumbs up.

"Emily! How are you?" I asked. Her eyes jumped to me. She had short red hair, with freckles and brown eyes. You could tell she was the granddaughter of Ms. Gladd. I smiled warmly at her. She seemed nervous by the way she kept rocking on her heels.

"Hi Ms. Silva!" she said brightly. I snorted.

"Please, you're making me feel old," I said. She nodded enthusiastically. She seemed young, eager. I remember being like that in the beginning.

When I got into college I went with the major I already had an idea about: business. I would always help my father out with company, not knowing he was trying to groom me to take over. But then I minored in hospitality and fell in love with it. I loved interacting with people and events. When I moved back I needed a job. I couldn't go back to my father. Mayor Kiana offered me one and I couldn't say no.

I looked at Emily who held the same fire I did when I moved away for college. For a second I wondered if I still had my fire. By the stars, maybe I was getting old.

"May I ask why you want to intern under the mayor?" I asked. I could feel Lily's eyes on me. Emily lowered her laptop, the air around us shifting.

"I've always been interested in politics. Mainly having the power to make a real difference. That's what I want to do. I'm not sure if I want to make a big splash but I'm ready to get my feet wet and learn what I can," she said firmly, eyes blazing.

"If I'm honest I'm very glad to have you. The festival takes up a lot of my time. So are you ready to receive all your duties?" I asked, waving my pen like I was about to knight her. She pulled a chair from an empty desk and sat down. With her laptop opened she nodded.

"Let's do this," she said.

CALEB

Eleanor and I hadn't spoken in a few days but according to Celestino today was the day she would be meeting with her sister. I could barely focus on customers. I was worried. After everything she told me about her family there was a possibility that her sister hated her and was working with their father to do stars know what.

"Fucking Caleb!" Flynn bumped my shoulder. My hand was covered in beer. I had overfilled another glass. Flynn glared at me. "What is up with you?" he asked. I ignored him. I didn't need my little brother in my business.

"Just a day," I muttered. He snorted before handing another customer their order. Throwing a rag over his shoulder he crossed his arms over his chest.

"No bro. Something is up. What's wrong?" He arched an eyebrow. He looked so much like our dad. Same stubborn chin, brown eyes and dirty blonde hair. I sighed. "You slept with her," he stated. I choked.

"I didn't sleep with her," I said through gritted teeth. He snorted.

"But you did something," he said. I groaned.

"How the fuck do you know?" I asked, staring at him. He smiled.

"You think I don't know you? Because I do. What you just did was the same thing you did the very first time you saw Eleanor walk in through these doors. So spill. What's up with you two?" he asked, leaning against the bar. I sighed. He was right. The first time Eleanor walked in I lost my demeanor.

The tavern was in full swing and my brother and I finally got into a working rhythm. I was happy to be settling back in Lavender Falls. I was happy to finally be with my siblings. Bridget was at a booth taking orders when she met my eyes with a tentative smile. My heart constricted.

My poor little sister. We had her memory wiped after the incident with the curse. We should have never done that stupid spell. Now she was always hesitant around me. But that was also partly my fault. I kept my distance and we grew up separated. It pained me. I didn't want to be the distant reclusive older brother.

But dad took me away after our parents divorce to see the best curse breakers around the states. I was never around. It didn't mean I didn't care about her. I was worried about triggering her memory. Flynn bumped my shoulder. His brown eyes softened. He knew. Him and Greg, my older brother, knew about the curse. I nodded and went back to work.

The doors of the tavern opened and a hypnotic laughter carried across the room. A zing ran up my body as I snapped up trying to find the owner of the laughter. Peeking through the crowd I caught a glimpse of long auburn hair. I began pouring another glass of beer. The laughter continued to get closer.

Once some vampires moved over a vision stood before me. I felt my heart pound faster than ever. My stomach dropped and the world melted away.

A woman with long hair, two toned eyes and full lips captured me. Freckles danced around her face and her body swayed to the Irish music that was blasting. Her eyes met mine and I swore I felt lightning struck. Her lips tilted up slightly, drinking me in. A new sensation was ripping me apart. I needed to know her. I needed her.

What the fuck was wrong with me? I had no idea who this woman was but something about her drew me in.

"I've never had an elf before," she said. Her voice created friction against my skin that set fire to my blood.

"Caleb!" Flynn shouted. I broke out of my stare to realize I had overfilled the draft. I had beer running down my hand. Fucking stars. I quickly placed the beer down and grabbed a towel to dry my hands.

Meeting the eyes of the goddess I felt something begin to loop around me that led towards her. She held my gaze again. Stars above, her eyes could allure me to my death and I would gladly follow.

"Caleb? What a pleasure to meet you."

THE SOUND OF HER LAUGHTER, one look in her eyes and I became undone. I spent years keeping any sort of romantic feelings at bay. But Eleanor danced her way through my doors and stole my heart in her hands without trying. Since then I did my best to keep her at a distance. But she refused to be held at arm's length. No. Eleanor demanded what she wanted and took it regardless.

I was her challenge and she refused to give up without a fight. I thought I was doing a good job at caging myself. But as the years went on I watched her leave with other men and it slowly began poisoning me. Because she didn't belong with them. She belonged with me and I knew it deep in my bones. I snapped during the Fall Festival. I couldn't take it. I made a stupid promise, cursed be damn. *We will, when the time is right.*

When those words flew out of my mouth I knew it was time to try and break the curse. I finally had a reason. *She* was my reason. And after having her scream my name in my bed there was no fucking way I would live without ever tasting her lips. I groaned into my hands. I was so fucking screwed.

Flynn dragged me to the end of the bar where there weren't many people hanging around. He motioned for me to talk. I sighed. He wasn't going to let this go and so I caved. Compared to Greg who was the oldest I've always been closer to Flynn. Probably because we were less than a year apart. Gotta love Irish twins.

"Fucking finally," Flynn said slapping my back once I told him everything. I was seriously turning into a talker with the way I was telling everyone my business. It was like the second I opened up to Eleanor it broke a dam within me.

He had a big grin on his face before it dropped. "I can help you know," he offered. A silent understanding passed between us. My lips twitched.

"I know. I just need you around the tavern a bit more. I might not be able to cover as many shifts," I said begrudgingly. I didn't like to be pulled away from work but to help Eleanor and break this curse I needed time. Flynn waved me off.

"Please, that's fine." His eyes flickered over my shoulder. "Speak of the pixie," Flynn said with a wide smile. I turned around to see Eleanor and Lola walking towards us. Eleanor blushed and it made my heart trip slightly. Lola sat on the stool and tapped the bar.

"Whiskey neat Rider," Lola said with a smirk. Flynn's smile dropped immediately.

"My name is Flynn. Just Flynn," he said flatly.

"Aw but you're like a real life Flynn Rider," Lola said with a pout. Flynn rolled his eyes and poured her a glass of whiskey. Eleanor snickered, sitting down next to Lola.

"I'm sorry Lola. My brother has seemed to have lost his manners," I said, bumping his shoulder. Lola giggled.

"It's probably because of the garden," Lola said triumphantly. Flynn scoffed. I raised an eyebrow. Lola beamed a smile in retaliation against Flynn. From what I've gathered over the years Flynn and Lola had always held an academic rivalry.

"My plans with Priscilla to start using the vegetation that we grow in the garden to make treats and medicine for the vet clinic got approved. And now, your adorable brother has to share his wonderful garden with me," she said proudly. I choked on what could have been an innuendo and Eleanor let out a giggle.

"I thought you already had a section when you moved back," I said. Lola's eyes brightened more than I thought possible.

"Aye, aye. Alas with this project approved I need more," she said, beaming.

"That's really cool Lola. I guess my brother never learned the meaning of sharing," I said. Flynn scoffed again.

"I know how to share," he grunted. Lola cocked her head, staring at him. I noticed the tips of his ears turning red.

"Do you?" Lola asked skeptically with a smile. Flynn leaned in close as Lola took a sip of whiskey.

"Don't you remember the time I let you win at the science trivia portion of game night last month? I decided to *share* with you the feeling of actually winning," Flynn said. Lola rolled her eyes.

"You didn't *let* me win. You clearly said mitochondria instead of mitochondrion," Lola fired back.

"Did I? Would I really mess up on the fact that mitochondria is the plural form of mitochondrion?" Flynn said with a smirk. Lola opened her mouth to respond.

"So my sister doesn't hate me," Eleanor said, cutting her off.

I SWEAR if I were to ever be in the same room as Eleanor's father I was going to be punching him in the face. Flynn's hands were clenched and Lola looked ready to rip someone's neck off.

"He's a fucking dick," I said.

"I know. But I'm happy I have my sister so that's a good thing… but the Hollow Tree." Eleanor's bottom lip slightly trembled.

"The tree is sacred to you guys right?" Lola asked. Eleanor nodded weakly.

"It's like the beacon for our magic. The tree has been around since the town was founded. The roots are embedded in the ley lines. If the tree is sick then our magic and possibly everyone else's will suffer," Eleanor said. This was bad. The whole town could be in danger. "I have to visit the tree this weekend but…"

"But what?" Flynn asked. Eleanor's eyes flickered to Lola who took a deep breath.

"The tree is near my father's company. I'm technically banned from the premises so I'm going to need to be sneaky."

"Oh I forgot about that!" Lola said. "I can go-"

"I'll go with you." I said. Lol smirked and Eleanor's eyes widened.

"But don't you-" Eleanor began before Flynn cut her off.

"I'll be covering for Caleb for the time being," he said. Lola's eyebrows raised in surprise. Flynn smirked. "See I'm nice," he said, his tone back to its normal flirty state. Lola rolled her eyes, fighting back a smile. Eleanor looked at me with concern.

"Are you sure?" Eleanor asked. She knew how much I loved my job and this tavern. But there were some things Eleanor hadn't realized yet. One of them was that over these past four years she had been showing me that there was more to life than just working. I nodded. Lola clapped her hands.

"Alright. I'm going to look into your curse this weekend. You two do some sneaky shit and see what's wrong with the tree. Maybe Priscilla might know a remedy to help whatever is wrong with it," Lola said confidently. I looked at Eleanor again. While her smile was confident her eyes revealed all. She said we weren't allowed to be intimate but maybe there was another way I could ease her stress.

CHAPTER 6
CALDO VERDE

ELEANOR

After hanging out with Lola at The Drunken Fairy Tale Tavern I headed back to my apartment for some much needed relaxation. I was grateful to have my sister back but this thing with the Hollow Tree could end in disaster. For the whole town no less. During the fall Lily had to solve a mystery and now two months later I had to rescue the town from losing magic. Why was life never easy in Lavender Falls?

I changed into an oversize t-shirt from college and continue to stir the pot of soup I had cooking. I smiled at the smell. When I was sick my mom used to make *caldo verde*; a Portuguese soup with collard greens, potatoes, carrots and *linguiça*. It was always one of my favorite comfort foods and I was so grateful my mom taught me before she passed.

My hand tightened around the spoon as I began stirring in the collards. Crystal didn't get the chance to learn our mom's recipes and I didn't spend much time teaching her.

I took a deep breath, forcing the waves of sadness to back away. That was the past. Now that we were reunited I could pass them down to her. I lowered the heat to a simmer and covered the pot slightly. I opened my fridge and poured myself a glass of wine when there was a knock at the door.

I glanced at my phone. Lily and Lola didn't text me saying they were coming over. I grabbed my glass in case I needed to whack whoever was behind my door as a distraction so I could zapped them with my magic. Would the wine be lost in the process? Yes. However I did have an entire bottle.

But when I opened my door a different kind of zap rushed up and down my spine. Caleb stood there with a bottle of wine, wearing a hoodie and some sweatpants. His hair hung loose around his shoulders. I wanted to run my hands through his hair and feel the soft strands against my skin. *Fuck.* Lola was going to win the stupid bet.

I raised an eyebrow. He rolled his eyes and crossed his arms. I leaned against the doorway and took a sip of my wine. His eyes glided down my body and stopped where my shirt hit the top of my thighs. His eyes darkened. I pushed off the door and turned to walk back towards my kitchen. I heard him step in, slip off his shoes and lock the door. I set my wine on the kitchen island and took a deep breath.

This was no big deal. Caleb was in my apartment. He was in sweatpants with his hair down looking like the last solar star biscuit from Godmother's Patisserie. I had a small one bedroom apartment that was scattered with knick knacks and color. I turned around to see him assessing the trinkets I had on my bookshelf that was next to my tv. I felt my face flushed. He was definitely going to notice the copious amount of smutty titles I had on my shelf.

While his face gave away nothing, the tips of his ears turned red. I reached back for my glass and downed the rest of my wine. He picked up a snow globe that Lily got me when she and Celestino went to Coralia Coast on a weekend vacation after the fall festival.

I turned away to check on my soup. I could feel his eyes on me as he walked around.

"Smells good," he said, finally breaking the silence. I stirred the pot a few times, before covering it again.

"It's called *caldo verde*. It's a Portuguese soup my mom taught me to make," I said. Caleb placed the bottle he brought on the kitchen island and was staring at a picture of my mom that I had on the wall.

"You look like her," he said softly. I leaned against the island.

"You think so? When I was younger people said I looked like my father. Crystal on the other hand definitely looks like her," I said with a smile.

"Your eyes though," he pointed out. I nodded.

"My eyes have always been different colors. Not sure why. My mom used to joke that I was blessed by the Hollow Tree actually." I smiled at the memory from when I was 12.

"I'm cute aren't I?" I told my mom as she braided my hair. Her dark hair was pulled back in a low ponytail. She flicked my head. "Ow!"

"You don't need to be so arrogant," she said. I rolled my eyes and she flicked my head again. "Don't roll your eyes," she said with a smile.

"You can't even see the front of my face," I mumbled. My mom's laugh filled my tiny bedroom. She always dried and braided my hair after a bath. She swore walking around with wet hair would get you sick.

"And you have very pretty eyes, minha estrela," she said, finishing my hair. She pulled me in a tight hug and I squirmed. I turned around to look at her. She had beautiful hazel eyes. She pushed a strand of hair out of my face. "Beautiful eyes, blessed by the Hollow Tree."

"Can we have a picnic by the tree this weekend? With Crystal too?" I asked. Crystal walked into the room, her hair a mess and eyes barely open from her nap. My mom reached a hand towards her.

"Sim meu amor."

CALEB STAYED silent as I grabbed a glass and bottle opener for him. "She loved cooking. I spent the majority of my time watching her cook, soaking up her recipes." Memories began filtering in my mind. He popped open the wine and poured himself a glass.

"This soup is my comfort soup. Collard greens, other veggies and *linguiça*. It's a simple soup. Perfect for when the weather is starting to get cold," I said. He nodded, watching me.

"I didn't know you liked to cook," he said curiously. I smiled as he poured wine to my glass

"I actually do like cooking. It's one of the few times where my brain just focuses on one thing." He slid my glass over to me. "It also makes me feel closer to my mom," I confessed. A pang vibrated through me.

"I was entering high school and Crystal was starting middle school when she passed away. Car accident," I said before pausing. "I-I feel guilty." I bit my lip. Crystal was a full fledged adult. And I missed out on so much because I was scared to stand up to my father. Because I didn't fight hard enough.

"Why?" Caleb asked. I sighed, taking a sip. I didn't know what possessed me to spill my guts but everything felt easy with Caleb. After he opened up to me about his curse I felt like I could or should do the same with him. Which was scary. It must be the wine.

"I missed out on so much. I could have been passing these recipes to her. Who was her first kiss? Did she go to prom? If she did, who helped pick out her dress? What about her first relationship? Has she done the dirty deed? What did she major in?" My heart was cracking open. All the guilt began weighing me down. I missed out on so many memories and fights. Caleb came over and pulled me into his chest. I didn't resist his warmth.

"But you're here now and she's happy you are right?" he asked tentatively.

"I think so," I mumbled as tears threatened to spill. What was wrong with me right now? It must be the stress. And the wine. Definitely the wine.

"Then that's what matters. We can't change the past and we can't live in what ifs. We can only move forward," he said. He pushed my hair back as he continued to soothe my worries. I felt myself slowly fall under his spell.

"She is back in your life and you'll slowly rebuild your relationship," he continued, his fingers slipping into my hair. I leaned my head back into his touch. "And I bet she is happy because you are a wonderful being that fills any space with light. As long as she knows your care and you'll be there then it'll be okay." His thumbs dug into the nape of my neck. Who knew Caleb was capable of being so soft. He made me feel like a cloud, weightless with nothing tying me down. *For now.*

"I'm sorry," I said. He raised an eyebrow.

"For what?" he asked.

"I told Lilianna and Lola about your curse. I didn't give any details but I still told them and I shouldn't have without consulting first," I said. He nodded.

"You told them because you were telling them about that night. A lot happened that day for you. I understand why you told them and I appreciate you keeping out the details. I do plan on telling them though," he said. My eyes widened.

"Really?"

"Well they're my friends. At least I consider them my friends," he said. He looked down at me. I felt a tug in the back of my head. Something whispering to me to push him away. I thought by giving into our four year temptation I wouldn't be tangled with emotions but I was being caught in his web. My heart wasn't ready for this.

"Why are you looking at me like that?" he asked.

"Look at you. Your little icy shell is melting," I teased. I needed to break away from this emotional wave that was building. He rolled his eyes.

"I don't think there's anything little about me," he said, smirking. I shrugged my shoulders.

"I haven't seen anything that proves otherwise," I said, batting my eyes. His lips brushed my ear and my fingers clutched his hoodie. He let out a dark chuckle that made my body shiver. Lola was absolutely winning the bet.

"Do you know what I think we should do?" he said, against my cheek. I tilted my head to the side, wishing for his lips to trail down my neck. One hand slid down my back. *Fuck, please squeeze my ass.* I silently begged.

"Eat," he said. With that one word he pulled back, leaving me with temptation.

CHAPTER 7
IS IT REALLY A SLOW BURN?

CALEB

My heart was stuck in my throat when she opened up to me about her mom. Eleanor has been nothing but sweet fire in all the years I've known her. She has always lent a helping hand to everyone. But she hid her worries from the world.

And to watch her be racked with guilt broke something open within me. I knew what it was like to hold guilt because of family but the difference was I was still a part of mine in a way. Eleanor had been alone for years.

Sure, she had our friends but she didn't have anyone take care of *her*. No one to remind her to breathe, let go, feel. She's been so busy providing for everyone else who provided for her?

I glanced around her apartment again. It was so cozy and full of color just like her. We sat on her couch, enjoying the soup she made. I close my eyes, savoring its simple flavors. She looked at me with wide eyes in anticipation. My lips pulled slightly at the side and I nodded. She sighed happily and we continued eating.

However as my eyes wandered back to her, I couldn't help but notice just how big the shirt she was wearing was. She was sitting on her legs, exposing her bronzed skin. I bit the inside of my cheek, remembering our night together.

"Whose shirt is that?" The question tumbled out of me as I took a sip of wine. She glanced down in surprise, before setting her bowl on the coffee table.

"Just a shirt from a guy," she said nonchalantly. The grip on my glass tightened.

"And you wear it to bed?" I asked, harshly. Her eyes narrowed at me as she crossed her arms.

"Yep. It's comfy," she said. I snorted.

"You're sleeping in another's man's shirt," I forced out. She pulled her legs out and crossed them. I sucked in a breath. She raised an eyebrow as my eyes followed the movement.

"Eyes up Elfie," she teased. I clenched my jaw. I spent that one night claiming her and now she was sitting here in another man's shirt. It pissed me off to no end. And I knew why. *Eleanor was mine.*

She's always been mine and I couldn't stand the idea of her wearing something of someone else's. Especially someone she used to share a bed with. Sure, for four years we skirted around each other. She had seen other people and with my curse and the tavern it was just my hand and I for the most part.

But since the fall festival Eleanor was mine while we had this agreement with each other and she would learn that. Without much thought I took off my hoodie and pulled off my t-shirt. Her eyes widened. I tossed the shirt to her.

"Throw that one out or I'm burning it," I said roughly.

"Aw Caleb. Don't be jealous," she said.

"I want it off," I said. She sat up on her knees before tugging that hideous shirt off her body. My body tightened as she revealed to me a pair of pale pink panties. The shirt continued to go up and I couldn't stop watching. Her skin looked soft.

My fingers gripped my knees as her bare tits came into view. Her nipples puckered and I felt my tongue go heavy. She threw the shirt in my face before pulling mine on, her eyes trained on me.

"Is this better *Mr. Kiernan*?" Her question was laced with lust and my dick responded immediately. Her eyes glanced at my lap. She tugged at her bottom lip. "I suppose it is, now isn't it...*Mr. Kiernan*?"

I needed to break this curse asap. I pull on my hoodie and her eyes follow. I reached for the hem of the shirt, my fingers lightly grazing her thighs and she shivered.

"It is *Ms. Silva*," I responded. She was biting down on her bottom lip as my fingers traced a line below where the shirt ended. "You don't wear an ex's shirt or anything of theirs you got it? I don't care if they're an ex or one night stand," I said, my voice low. "Not while we have this agreement between us." My fingers moved to her inner thigh and I could feel her skin heat up.

"Or what *Mr. Kiernan*?" she asked. I stood up and roughly dragged a finger over her core, up her stomach and in between her breasts until my hand was wrapped around her throat. I pushed her further into the couch. I could feel her pulse jumping beneath my fingers.

"I'll make your ass red, *Ms. Silva*," I said, through gritted teeth, my lips against her ear. She was breathing fast, her hands gripping the couch. She gave me a wicked smile before pointing at the shirt that was now on the floor. With soft whispers the shirt began unraveling until it was nothing but strings. She shrugged her shoulders nonchalantly.

"Understood Mr. Kiernan," she said, teasingly. I chuckled.

If she thought she could last, holding out from what her body was craving, she had another thing coming. I knew for fact after tasting what I could give her she wouldn't be able to resist much longer.

Looked like our little game was going to continue...for now.

ELEANOR

I went to bed after Caleb left with a vibrator in my hand and smelling his shirt; forest and mint. I could still feel his fingers toying with my body, beckoning my will to break. Staring at my ceiling in the morning I recounted what I shared with Caleb.

It was so...boyfriendy. Was that even a word? He came over to check on me. We ate soup and sat on the couch. It was *normal*. I couldn't remember the last time I did something normal with someone I was intimate with. I bit my lip. I had never opened up to anyone about my guilt over my sister. Not even to Lily and Lola. But everything with Caleb felt natural and that was scary.

The beginning was always nice, wasn't it though? You wore rose colored glasses and everything seemed great. The touches, the caresses filled you with excitement. But at some point those glasses would crack. The world is no longer blossoming in pink but filled with shades of gray.

I gripped the soft black shirt in my hands. I had never had someone be so possessive over me. It was usually the opposite. I had a tendency to be clingy and if that didn't send them packing it was my will to never conform myself to what they wanted.

I felt like Caleb could consume me. With him I was easily and eagerly willing to give myself over to him. And I wanted to. I wanted to be possessed, consumed and craved in the most chaotic way. I sighed. I needed to stop reading mafia romances.

I glanced at my alarm clock. Tomorrow I would be heading to the Hollow Tree to uncover whatever the fuck my father was hiding. If he was hiding something. But today I had another meeting with Emily to make sure she had everything she needed before I could fully switch to festival mode.

I also needed to meet with Ben. He was the head of the Cultural Affairs and Special Events department and I would be checking in with him and Celestino to make sure everything was running smoothly. It was now or never.

"WE'VE ALREADY CONFIRMED food trucks and most of the vendors," Ben said in our meeting. I nodded at the burly werewolf with auburn hair and deep set eyes. He was just a few years older than me and a total sweetheart.

"Also the pub crawl is ready to go," Celestino added. I relaxed into my chair as I checked it off my notebook. I knew I could count on these guys to have everything in order. Ben cleared his throat.

"I hope this isn't weird that you're reporting to me," I said to Ben. He snorted.

"Eleanor. With how well we worked together for the fall festival I'm grateful to have you on board for this winter. Plus we grew up together. I heard all about how amazing your parties were," Ben teased. Celestino chuckled.

"She's the queen of parties," Celestino commented. I tossed my hair over my shoulder.

"And this winter will be one to remember. Ticket sales are booming because of the fall festival," I said, beaming. Ben hummed in agreement before his eyes narrowed.

"I heard that Hale's Lumber is one of the major sponsors," Ben said, carefully. He eyed me. I nodded, keeping my face neutral. Everyone in town knew about the strained relationship I had with my father. Perks of living in a small town. Ben also probably knew that it was the big reason I was working with them again.

"They're going to be providing a lot of the prizes for the events that we have planned. By the way don't forget we need to secure the park for the snowball tournament," I said. Ben nodded, tapping on his computer.

"Patty confirmed being in charge of the sleigh ride. She'll be sending a map of the trail soon. She wants to update some parts of it. Let's just say Frosty The Snowman is making a comeback," Ben said, drumming his fingers against his desk. Everything seemed to be on track. Ben stopped tapping and glanced at Celestino. I looked at them both, something silent passing between them.

"What?" I asked, my stomach twisting.

"Mr. Hale is involved…" Ben trailed off. I nodded. He scratched his beard. "He moved out of town long ago, washed his hands of this place and now he's back," he stated. I went rigid.

My dad was once a part of this community. He moved to Lavender Falls when he married my mom. That's why Hale's Lumber Industry was technically within our district and by the Hollow Tree.

But since my mom's passing he's pulled away. It was like being here reminded him of everything he had lost. Celestino placed a hand on my shoulder. Ben's dark eyes glowed a tiny bit.

"You let us know if he tries anything." His voice was rough, his inner wolf bleeding out. I smiled. Celestino squeezed my shoulder.

"Remember if you need anything let us know, okay?" Celestino said, his green eyes filled with concern. I nodded.

I guess my father being back had everyone on their toes and claws.

CHAPTER 8
SEXY SUPERNATURAL SPIES

CALEB

I f you told me one day I would be walking through the Gasping Greenwood forest on a Saturday morning dressed in camouflage to go find a sick magical tree I would have snorted. But here I was spending my Saturday morning trudging through the forest with Eleanor.

My eyes roamed over her body. She said we needed to blend in and showed up to my apartment with a bag. She wore camo cargo pants with a tight olive green cropped hoodie. Her pink hair pulled into a ponytail. Her face was makeup free except for the glossy sheen on her lips. Her freckles were on full display. She had me wearing the same pants with a black hoodie.

Honestly this all felt very extra but Eleanor loved drama and if that meant wearing matching clothes to blend into the forest so be it.

"You still remember the way?" I asked once we passed the clearing most people used for ceremonies and picnics. She looked at me over her shoulder with a smile.

"Do you trust me?" she snickered. I rolled my eyes.

"Are you trying to be Aladdin?" I teased. This time she rolled her eyes. As we walked over tree roots and leaves crunching beneath our feet I did my best to not focus on the way her pants hugged her ass. My hands twitched at my sides. Her body felt divine beneath mine.

This is the last time we have any sexy time. I finally had her and she was shutting us down. I understood why. She didn't want to risk the curse. Fucking stars I should be on the same page. But I wanted another taste.

"Eyes up Elfie," she called out. I let out a chuckle. She knew I was checking her out.

"Hard when you're walking in front of me with pants like those," I grunted. She let out a laugh and I felt my lips quirk up in a smile. I could get drunk on the sound. She had a deep throaty laugh that was carefree like the winter breeze.

"Well you're going to be hard for a while until we can break your curse," she said. Her shoulders tensed. I came up beside her.

"Eleanor," I said, placing a hand on her shoulder. She took a deep breath before looking up at me.

"We're almost there." She pointed off to her left. Between the trees I could make out a wired fence.

"That's where my father's company is. It's the warehouse where they store the wood to be made into firewood and lumber," she said, sounding sad. Her cheeks were rosy from the cold. Winter was slowly arriving in Lavender Falls. I wrapped an arm around her, pulling her into me, drinking in the smell of cinnamon. She shuddered. "I would sneak out from the office over there to come to the tree. I can almost feel it."

We heard the cracking of a branch and I grabbed Eleanor, pressing her behind a tree. I leaned away slightly, hoping to find the source.

When I glanced back at her, her fingers were digging into my hoodie and her eyes were trained on my neck. The heat of her body seeped into mine. She opened her mouth and I tapped her lips with my finger, signaling her to be quiet. She nipped my finger playfully.

"Eleanor," I warned. She looked at me, her two tone eyes swirling with emotions. I glanced away and saw someone heading towards the warehouse. "I think we're safe," I whispered into her ear. She nodded, soundlessly, relaxing into me. I smirked before kissing her cheek.

"Is this how I get you to be quiet?" I asked softly. Her eyes narrowed.

"I'm quiet because I don't want to get caught," she said. I tilted her chin up.

"From the look in your eyes this excited you," I said softly. She blushed, biting into her lip.

"Last I checked you liked hearing me scream," she pointed out. I dragged her arms above her head. "Caleb," she hissed. Her back arched against the tree.

"You're very tempting, Starburst," I said, my lips brushing her neck. "I just need a taste."

"We can't right now," she mumbled, exposing more of her neck. My lips traced up her throat. When I pulled back her eyes were hooded.

"Right now? That's an interesting thing to say," I said, placing a quick kiss on her cheek. She fought back a smile. "I don't have to kiss you to have you scream my name again. Remember that," I said. She stared at my mouth for a second.

"Trust me I'm well aware," she said. She was tempted. I was sure of it. But then the lust I saw in her eyes slowly began to be replaced by confusion.

"What's wrong?" I asked tentatively, letting go of her hands. She shook her head, wiggling her fingers.

"I can almost feel it but something is off," she said. She moved out of my arms and began walking. She paused and turned back to look at me. "Stay close by, please," she said, softly. I followed wordlessly. I would be wherever she needed me to be.

THE TREE WAS FUCKING huge and thick. I cranked my head back to look at how the branches intertwined with the surrounding trees. It was almost like the wilderness was seeking out the Hollow Tree. Flowers traced a circle around it.

I glanced at Eleanor who had a pensive look on her face. I kept my mouth quiet. We were in her territory. I was only a bystander. My hand cradled her elbow.

She looked up at me and nodded. Taking a deep breath she walked into the circle of the tree. I swore I felt the forest sigh as she stepped closer. The fallen leaves rustled beneath our feet as if waking up. Eleanor placed her hand on the tree.

"Hello friend," she said with a sad smile. The air around us dropped in temperature. My eyes widened as I saw vines come around the tree to touch Eleanor's hand. She trembled slightly as the tree hugged her. She glanced at me quickly.

I took a step forward as her eyes flashed gold and she crumpled to the ground.

"Eleanor!"

ELEANOR

I felt warm, safe and nurtured. I remember watching the vines wrap around my hand in an embrace and then there was a bright flash. Next thing I knew everything around the forest froze, including Caleb whose face was painted with worry. But the forest looked different. I saw strings and sparkles of gold everywhere. I gasped.

This was magic.

This was the magic that ran through the forest and connected to everything and everyone. I turned to look back at the Hollow Tree and my heart sank. The tree was dying. I was sure of it. The trunk had darkened, the branches looked weak and typically it would be the only tree that remained lush with leaves during winter. My eyes casted toward the ground where the lines of magic were turning brown, no longer gold.

My child, a voice whispered. My heart rattled against my chest.

"Um...Hollow Tree?" I asked shyly. A breeze caressed my cheek and I felt a surge of warmth.

Yes. My child.

So I could hear the tree. I knew it.

You could always hear me. You just needed to listen.

I smiled, tears welling up in my eyes. Ever since I was little I always found solace at the Hollow Tree. Something about the tree brought deep comfort within. Something about it always had my magic buzzing. A cold began twirling around my legs, a sickness. It felt wrong. It was a plague within the roots.

"What's wrong?" I asked. The vines wrapped around my hand tightened.

I am sick. I am weak.

This couldn't be happening. If the Hollow Tree were to die, who knows what could happen to the town and our magic.

"How can I fix this?" I asked. The wind picked up again. I closed my eyes tightly, pressing my magic into the vines, urging it to provide warmth and peace. The same feelings the tree has always given me.

You can not fix this my sweet youngling.

My body trembled. I needed to fix this. I needed to save the tree. I let more of my magic flow into the Hollow Tree. I imagined it like a flood, filling the branches and roots. I felt the sickness retreat. The breeze wrapped around me tighter.

What once is lost or gone can be found or reborn.

I furrowed my brows in confusion. What did that mean? Lost?

Gone? No, we couldn't lose the Hollow Tree. I felt a tug at my other hand. I needed to stay. I needed to heal it more.

Go. We'll meet again, my child.

And with that gold light flashed once more and I awoke to see familiar pale blue eyes.

"Caleb?" I croaked out. My body felt heavy, sluggish. He sighed, pulling me to his chest.

"Fuck, I was worried Eleanor." His voice was shaky. I was laying in his lap, the vines slipping away from my hand.

"What happened?" I asked. He pushed a strand of hair away from my face.

"The vines came out and wrapped around you. You looked at me and then your eyes flashed gold. You slumped against the tree. I wanted to wake you but…something told me not to," he said, still cradling me.

I looked back at the tree. It didn't want me to save it. But I needed to. I needed to figure out what my father did. The leaves on the branches seemed to have new growth. My magic had worked. But it wasn't enough.

"Now tell me what happened," he said in a stern voice. I shivered, but not from the cold.

"Let's get out of here first and I'll explain. I don't want us getting caught," I said. Instead of helping me up Caleb carried me in his arms and refused to let me back down until we made it out of the forest. I took one more glance back.

I'll save you, no matter what.

CHAPTER 9
COUCH SHENANIGANS

ELEANOR

W alking into the tavern a few people casted glances at us as we made our way up to his apartment. I didn't care what people thought about me personally. I never have even cared when my father would try his hardest to try to keep my adventurous side under lock and key.

And frankly he was the only one who had an issue with it because he was oblivious to everything else I did. I helped out at every town festival. I was a part of the student council in high school, putting on the best events. I took care of Crystal. I helped out with the company on the weekends. I was a cheerleader who won competitions. But nothing was good enough.

Once safely inside of Caleb's apartment he dragged me to his couch and moved to the kitchen to make me a hot cup of chamomile tea. I took a deep breath. I was tired. It took more out of me than I thought to attempt to heal the tree. I needed more magic or something else.

What was causing the tree to decay? Was it a sickness? A curse? I glanced at Caleb as my mind found its way thinking about curses. He was tall, broad, and strong. I shivered.

I don't have to kiss you to scream my name again. Remember that. I had no problem remembering that because it was all I thought about whenever I was left alone with my thoughts. I groaned into my hands. The man was walking temptation. I snuck another glance as he poured the hot water into a cup. We could be careful couldn't we? A pixie has needs…very strong needs.

"We need to talk to Priscilla. Maybe she can whip something up to slow the progression of the sickness," I said, looking up at Caleb as he handed me the mug. He knelt down to adjust the fireplace. The soft glow painted him like a King of Elves. His white blonde hair was tangled in a low bun. His eyes assessed me with a predator's protectiveness. He looked haunting, almost ethereal against the fire.

"Do you know what kind of sickness?" he asked, settling on the floor. My eyes traveled down his long, lean body. He cleared his throat. Fuck I needed to focus. Lola was right. It's been less than a damn week.

"I'm not quite sure but there's some rot happening at the roots that's slowly making its way up the trunk. She'll probably need to see it. I'll text Crys to let her know Priscilla needs to see the tree and she'll make sure my father doesn't find out," I said, pulling out my phone. I sent Crys and the girls an update. Caleb nodded.

What once is lost or gone can be found or reborn. I'm surprised I wasn't freaking out over a talking tree but hey we have a zombie living in this town. Strange things happen all the time. My brain mentally pulled up my to-do list.

"I have to go see Priscilla," I muttered into my tea. It was Saturday afternoon. She was probably at the shop. Caleb grunted. I raised an eyebrow.

"Doth protest?" I asked.

"You need to rest," he said plainly.

"I have to talk to Priscilla and then get some work done," I stated. Caleb stood up and walked over to the couch. My heart picked up as he towered over me. He looked delicious standing over me. I could feel

74

the heat of his body. My eyes wandered down his wide chest to his cock that was perfectly lined up to my face. I bit the bottom of my lip as I glanced back up. What I really needed was to not think.

"You need to rest," he said stubbornly.

"What if I tell you I'm hungry?" I asked, a smirk playing on my lips. Yep. Lola was right. There was no way I could have kept that stupid promise after feeling what Caleb could give me. Screw a slow burn romance. I need it fast, hard and now. His eyes narrowed and there was a tug on his mouth. He was fighting back a grin.

"This is the last time we have any sexy time because I don't need you accidentally turning to stone while inside me," he stated. Of course the bastard remembered word for word what I said. One of my hands gripped the back of his thigh as I leaned over to place the tea on the coffee table. I kept my eyes locked on his blue gaze. There was hesitation with a flicker of hunger. I sat up, shrouded in the blanket and let my hand trace a line up and down the back of his thigh. I sighed dramatically.

"That is true. I did say that. But if you occupy my mouth with your dick there will be no chance of you turning into stone," I said with an innocent smile. Caleb breathed in sharply.

"You have a filthy mouth." His voice was rough and his hand caressed my jaw.

"And how do you plan to shut me up?" I asked.

"You're tired," he stated. My finger traced the outline of his bulge and his chest rose rapidly. I needed a distraction. Just a tiny one. Or a big one if what I was seeing was correct.

"My mouth isn't. Now are you going to deny me something I've been fantasizing about for years? You *did* say you would help me destress," I said. He closed his eyes briefly. "I want to, Caleb."

"You sure?" he asked. I nodded. When he opened his eyes my thighs clenched. "Lose your pants and sit with your legs open," he demanded. I shivered. I enjoyed this side of him. The only reason I let him boss me around was because it always ended in my favor.

"I don't need to lose my pants to suck your cock," I stated. Caleb gave me a devilish smile that went straight to my core. His hand gripped my jaw, tilting my head all the way back until I hit the couch. I gasped at the sudden strength.

"You're going to lose your pants and fuck yourself with your fingers while I fuck your mouth with my cock," he hissed. I couldn't hold back my smile if I tried.

My body trembled and I scrambled to pull my pants and underwear off. My heart was beating erratically against my chest. Caleb began palming himself through his pants as he watched me. I couldn't stop staring at his movement. I fantasized seeing his cock so many times. Would it be long? Slightly curved? Thick?

"Show me," he commanded. Sitting up straight against the couch I opened my legs. I was already wet. I trailed my finger up and down my thigh, teasing myself as I watched his hand unbutton his pants. "Wider, Eleanor."

"Yes," I whimpered as I watched him undress. My fingers slid between my slick folds as his cock sprang forward. He was fucking perfect. Now I knew he was indeed thick in all the right places. I moaned as I played circles around my clit. I opened my mouth, feeling greedy.

"Get your fingers wet," he growled. I tipped my head back against the couch to look at him as he leaned over, one hand on the back of the couch. His face was flushed, pupils blown. I did as he said and my fingers slid inside easily. He licked his lips and his hand on the couch tightened. He rubbed his hand faster on his cock.

"Wrap your hand around my cock and take me in your mouth," he said. I went to reach for his cock but he pulled back with a dark chuckle. His eyes went to the hand between my legs. "That hand Starburst," he said.

I stared at him with wide eyes. *Holy stars.* With a shaky hand I gripped his cock and began running it up and down his length, getting it wet with my arousal. Caleb moaned deeply and it sent a thrill up and down my spine. Our eyes met once again and I leaned forward, running my tongue on the under seam of his cock.

"Fucking shit," he groaned. This time I took the head of his cock in my mouth with a moan, loving the feel of how full he felt. I took him deeper as I sucked and swirled my tongue around. Tasting myself on his cock sent an erotic thrill through me. It made my heart pound harder and edged me closer to an orgasm.

I slid my other hand down between my legs and rubbed my swollen clit. Caleb began rocking slowly, his hand gripping the back of the couch, the other wrapped around my throat.

"I can feel you fucking my cock, Eleanor." His voice caressed me. My fingers worked frantically. I wish it was his fingers inside or a vibrator. I wanted to feel full.

"Fuck. Can you taste yourself on my cock? See how fucking good you taste." His words only made me more wet. I circled my clit again as I continued suck and stroke him harder. I was climbing higher and higher. I moaned deep in my throat and Caleb's body tightened.

"Switch hands. I need you to taste yourself and my cum and swallow every last fucking drop," he groaned out. His hips moved faster and I tried to keep up, mimicking his speed.

My body tensed as we moved faster, in time together. Stars danced around my vision as I tried to focus on us. But it was getting difficult to keep up. My body tightened as I pressed my finger against my clit.

"Come," he said and I fucking did. One word and my body exploded like pixie dust. Caleb came down my throat and I did as I was told, swallowing every last drop as his body trembled. My hand fell away from my clit and I squeezed my thighs, relishing in the after-shocks, trying to catch my breath.

"That's my fucking girl. You suck my cock so good with that dirty mouth," he whispered, pushing my hair back.

I laid against the couch trying to catch my breath. I had a lot of experiences in my life and especially in college but never had I ever done something like that, something so…thrilling. I fucking loved it. I sure as stars didn't expect this from Caleb The Stoic Elf King of Eating Pussy. He pushed his hair back, staring at me with a satisfied smile.

"Good?" he asked, eyebrows raised. While his tone sounded cocky I knew Caleb well enough that he hid the truth in his eyes and in the slight twitches in his shoulders. He wanted to know if I was satisfied.

"That was the hottest thing I've ever done," I confessed with a smile. His shoulders dropped slightly. I giggled.

"Were you worried?" I asked teasingly. He grunted before turning to the kitchen. I bit the inside of my cheek, waiting for his answer. He brought me a glass of water and pressed it to my lips. I took a sip keeping my eyes on him.

"Yes," he finally said.

"You know I still have the cup of tea right?" I asked. He grunted again. Looks like my brooding elf was back. My heart stopped. Did I just say *my elf*? I took his outstretched hand and let him lead me to the bathroom.

"What are you doing?" I asked, tentatively. Instead of answering he kept with his grumpy personality by quietly turning on the shower.

"I'll bring you some clothes. Take a shower before you leave for Priscilla's. Would you like a sandwich?" he asked.

"Who says I was still going to Priscilla's after this?" I asked.

"You're not going to rest today until you do," he said. Fuck, he was right. He grabbed a fresh towel from the cabinet above his toilet. I stared at him wide-eyed. Who was this man? He let out a chuckle before smoothing my hair away from my face.

"I take care of what's mine Eleanor."

"I'm not yours," I stated.

"Keep telling yourself that," he said while smacking my ass. I yelped and with that he left me standing alone in his bathroom. I looked at myself in the mirror, my heart in my throat.

I've gone so many years taking care of myself and others that this was new territory. I didn't know what to do. Was I supposed to just accept this nicety for what it was? This isn't what friends-ish with benefits did. I eyed the towel on the sink.

I began undressing. This didn't mean anything. It didn't. It was just an orgasm, a shower and a sandwich. Nothing more.

CALEB

Going through my closet I knew I had some of Bridget's clothes somewhere. Her and Flynn would sometimes stay over after a long shift and I kept a few clothes for them to use.

I pulled a pair of Bridget's sweatpants and grabbed one of my hoodies. I found myself smiling. I could have just given her one of Bridget's sweaters but I wanted her to be seen wearing something that was *mine*.

I felt a wave of possessiveness over Eleanor. Something inside me kept screaming to take her. To actually make her mine. But it was obvious she wasn't completely comfortable with me taking care of her. I was going to make her a sandwich and she made it seem like a damn proposal. I shook my head with a chuckle. I knocked on the door before entering to place the clothes on top of the sink.

"Do you have a sandwich preference?" I asked, staring at the flimsy curtain that kept her wet naked body hidden from my view. I felt myself getting hard again. I needed to calm down. I was acting like a horny college student.

But I've kept this side of me under lock and key because the damn curse for so long. After pining over Eleanor and having her I couldn't stop craving for more.

"Do you have peanut butter and apples?" she asked.

"Is that the kind of sandwich you want?" I asked.

"Yes please," she confirmed. I heard the squeeze of the soap bottle. I bet she was lathering herself. Soapy. Wet. Fuck I needed to get a grip.

I left temptation in the bathroom and headed to make my pixie her sandwich. I remembered her eyes from when we went to check on the Hollow Tree. They were glowing pure gold. It was like she was possessed. I was so scared something was happening and I had no idea what to do.

I could sense the magic. I could feel Eleanor's magic connecting with the tree, mingling. Her magic felt like sunlight and the scent of cinnamon hung strong in their air. But paying close attention I could also feel something was wrong. She tried her best to heal the tree with her magic but it wasn't enough.

Did her father do something? I also felt like she wasn't telling me something. However, if she was keeping something from me she had her reasons.

I faintly heard the shower turned off as I finished making her a sandwich and reheated her tea. Eleanor stepped out and my ears burned. My black hoodie swallowed her body and she definitely rolled up the sweatpants since Bridget was nearly my height. She looked adorable. I gave her a small grin and her face turned red.

"Thanks for the clothes," she said. Was she being shy? She made her way towards me, avoiding my gaze. I caught her by the waist and pulled her towards me. She looked at my lips before my eyes. I couldn't wait to break this fucking curse.

"Are you being shy Eleanor?" I asked teasingly. Her eyes lit up.

"I've heard some men like it when a woman is coy." Her fingers ran up my chest. I chuckled.

"Coy doesn't suit you, Starburst," I said as my hands squeezed her waist.

"Mhmm so I guess we'll cross role playing out," she said nonchalantly. I shook my head, letting her go. She was going to ruin me.

"Eat your sandwich, Starburst."

WHEN WE MADE it downstairs the tavern was just starting lunch. Crystal was talking animatedly to Lilianna. Celestino had his arm wrapped around Lilianna's waist. I could sense Eleanor's mood brighten. She smiled warmly and her eyes lit up.

"Crys," Eleanor said, happily hugging her sister. Crystal smiled weakly. Lilianna glanced at Eleanor's hoodie before smirking at me. I ignored her and began pouring a drink for Celestino.

"This is Caleb by the way." Eleanor introduced me to her sister. Her sister was thinner, with long dark hair and much taller. Unlike Eleanor who only had one eye the color of hazel her sister had both. She had a light dusting of freckles. They looked similar enough. Her sister gave me a hesitant smile as she fidgeted with her fingers.

"It's so nice to meet you Caleb and thanks so much for helping us with the Hollow Tree. All of you really. It's a relief to have people to rely on," Crystal said shyly. I nodded.

"Of course," I said, handing Celestino a beer. It was the weekend anyway.

"I hope Priscilla can whip something up," Lilianna said.

"I'll make sure to take her to the tree when father isn't around," Crystal confirmed. Lilianna's head popped up.

"Oh by the way everything is set for the pub crawl so you both don't need to worry about that and ticket sales are going up." Lilianna smiled. Eleanor laughed. I groaned inwardly. Lilianna rolled her eyes.

"It'll be fun Caleb. You have Tatiana now," Lilianna said. "The only thing you need to worry about is whether or not you'll have enough tequila," she teased, bumping her shoulders against Eleanor. I nodded solemnly.

"I appreciate that. We should be confirming a few of the events we'll be sponsoring this upcoming week. I'll send you our company's logos once I get back behind my computer," Crystal said. Lilianna placed a hand on hers and Crystal's shoulders eased. It felt like Crystal was much more comfortable around Lilianna than Eleanor.

I wondered if it was because they were both introverts. They probably found peace within each other. I hope Crystal and Eleanor could find that same comfort with each other. And maybe one day Bridget and I as well. A puff of smoke appeared and Fabian settled into Lilianna's lap.

"Oh Crystal! Meet Fabian. He's my familiar," Lilianna said, petting behind his ear. Crystal grinned and let out her hand. Fabian glanced at her before sniffing. He immediately crawled into Crystal's lap who was beaming.

"She smells like Eleanor but nicer," Fabian said. Eleanor scoffed while everyone laughed.

"She smells nicer than me?" Eleanor glared at the little fox. Fabian stuck his tongue out at her. I leaned over the bar.

"No familiars in the pub," I grunted. The fox rolled his eyes.

"We both know that is not a rule," Fabian said. Lilianna bit her lip to keep from laughing. I grimaced.

"Don't get fur on my floor," I warned. Fabian nestled back into Lilianna's lap.

"Sure thing bubble butt," Fabian said, before sneaking a glance at Eleanor. My eyes widened.

"Bubble butt?" I asked, looking at Eleanor.

"Fabian! What is said in our Sip n' Spill sessions stays in our Sip n' Spill sessions," Eleanor hissed. The little fox had the audacity to yawn. Lilianna coughed while I smirked. I gave my full attention to Eleanor.

"So you like my butt?" I asked Eleanor. Her cheeks turned rosy.

"Shut up Elfie," she mumbled, looking away from me.

"So it's really great to see you again Crystal. Maybe we can have you join one of our girls nights," Lilianna suggested, shifting the subject. Eleanor nodded.

"R-really?" Crystal asked in disbelief.

"Duh. You're back in our lives. You can't get rid of us now," Lilianna said confidently. Celestino kissed Lilianna's cheek and she blushed. A part of my heart ached. I wanted this curse to be gone already. I wanted to be with Eleanor. Hold her hand in public, kiss her temple and do all the couple shit. I also wanted her to want that.

But with how she freaked over a damn sandwich I wasn't sure. Crystal's phone rang and her face paled. Eleanor's happy emotion was erased and Lilianna's grip tightened around her glass. It had to be their father for all three ladies to have such a strong reaction.

The smell of the ocean began trickling in. I looked at Lilianna again who was taking deep breaths. Whenever her emotions ran high her magic…flourished.

"Hi daddy," Crystal said in a sickly sweet tone. We all watched her. Looking at her she was picking her nails but her face gave nothing away. The way Eleanor perfected showing no emotion Crystal had clearly practiced being the dutiful daughter.

"I already sent the updated marketing report. Still waiting to hear back from Mr. Calder on the merger with Coralia Coast. I have another meeting with Ms. Silva on Monday morning to finalize a few event details," she said. Eleanor fidgeted with the strings of the hoodie.

"Make sure the festival is appropriate," could be heard through the phone. I felt my hands tightened against the bar.

"Father," Crystal warned. For a split second Crystal's mask fell and was replaced by annoyance. Their father said something else and Crystal eyed her sister. Eleanor raised an eyebrow. "She's good," Crystal said. I looked at Eleanor again. She gave me a smile. How many times had she practiced her detachment from hearing her father? How many times did she feel alone?

"I understand. Bye." Crystal sighed, hanging up.

"Did he ask about me?" Eleanor said in confusion.

"He asked how you seem to be doing," she said softly. Lilianna placed a hand on her shoulder.

"I thought he was going to say something rude which would have made me want to punch him," Lilianna growled. Celestino patted her back.

"Now, now you don't need to hurt your pretty hand. I'm sure Caleb could handle it." Celestino looked at me with a smirk. I nodded.

"Well…that's something of him," Eleanor hesitated. Eleanor was great at taking everyone else's pain. She was great at pretending that nothing bothered her. She deflected with smiles and laughter.

But eyes were windows to the soul and I could see her broken pieces. My fractured soul called to hers. She was slowly healing mine and I was going to do the same for her.

CHAPTER 10
SHIT IS STARTING

ELEANOR

It was Monday afternoon by the time I got to leave my desk and head to the meeting room. I had spent most of the morning finishing training Emily. She was a young witch with a bright future. She was a quick learner and naturally a diplomat. I smiled. She was sweet. She was going to do great things, especially learning from Mayor Kiana. She was fitting in perfectly while it took me some time to get my bearings.

I still remember when Mayor Kiana took me under her wing. I had just moved back with a degree in business and needed any kind of job so I could support myself. I had run into her at Griffin's Groceries and she offered me the position. No questions asking why I wasn't working for my father.

Mayor Kiana taught me balance. She never thought I needed to tone down my colors and I never have. Emily just needed a little fire and while Mayor Kiana taught me when to rein mine in when need be. I'm sure she could help Emily grow hers.

I was meeting my sister again to go over some of the events we had lined up. Crystal was already waiting for me in the meeting room. I could see in her eyes how lost and lonely she was.

"Hey there," I said. Her head popped up with a start. A smile broke out and for a second.

"Ready for this meeting?" she asked, tentatively. I pulled out my notebook with my colored pens and matching sticky notes.

"Of course I am," I said. She turned on her laptop.

"Alright so we'll be making a donation for the prize in the ice sculpture competition along with the others. Lilianna has the pub crawl secure and ready. How are the vendors and food trucks?" she asked, typing away on her laptop.

"According to Ben and Celestino they are secured. Celestino will be sending me a map of where everything is going to be placed like the snowball tournament. Entries for the pie back off are starting this week. We will have a *'Meet Santa'* thing for tourists to come and a small petting zoo where kids can ride the reindeers. Don't worry they'll be grounded," I said, pausing to let her type.

"Ice skating will take place on the swamp. The water fairies will ensure that it's frozen and strong enough to hold people," I said, reading off my list. Crystal nodded along.

"Father wants to add something," she said in a hesitant voice. My jaw clenched.

"What does he want?" I asked. She tugged a piece of her hair.

"The clearing at the Gasping Greenwood? The one you guys tend to use for ceremonies? He wants to hold a bonfire there with a hot chocolate stand and music," she said. I furrowed my eyebrows.

"We have that but that's usually in the center of town," I said. She sighed.

"That's what I said. But he wants there to be inflatable slides for the kids. Add string lights around the trees. He says it makes more sense to host it there since the area is used for events and this an event. Plus more spacing," she said. I paused before answering. He was right.

I hated to admit it but it was a great idea. It would open up the space. Traffic would flow better. Maybe we could add a small stage for performances in the center of town instead. I could see it all unfolding in my head.

"Fine. I'll let Ben and Celestino know. They'll need to look at the area and plan accordingly," I agreed begrudgingly.

"I'm sorry," my sister said. I shook my head.

"You don't have to be sorry, Crys," I said, placing my hand on hers. "And I hate to admit it, but he's right." I could feel the turmoil rolling off of her. I pressed my magic forward in hopes to soothe her. Her magic felt sluggish again as I pushed mine to warm her. She gave me a small smile.

"Thank you." Her eyes softened.

"You're going to show Priscilla the tree on Wednesday right?" I asked. She nodded.

"He's always out of the office that day. It's the perfect day for her," she said. She closed her laptop. Our father was still a creature of habit except for that one time.

"Perfect. You're having dinner with me and the girls after," I stated.

"You want me to join you guys?" she asked. I beamed at her.

"Of course! You're my sister and remember Lily would be sad if you didn't," I said. She stared at her laptop for a few seconds before giving me a small smile.

"I would like that."

IT WAS Wednesday and I was sitting at the usual booth with Lola and Lily, anxiously waiting for Crystal to show up. I got a phone call from Priscilla confirming my worst fear.

"You're right," Priscilla said. My stomach sank. "The tree is dying. I'm still not sure from what but I can definitely come up with a few things to at least slow down whatever is causing it," she continued. I sighed in relief.

"Okay well that's a good thing," I said. Priscilla was silent. "Priscilla?" I asked. She took a deep breath.

"I took a sample with me to study, to figure out the cause. But the roots. They're deeply embedded into the Earth. Like connected to the ley lines. Eleanor if we don't save the tree this…" she trailed off, afraid to finish her sentence. I gulped. This confirmed my worst fear because I could see it affecting my sister. And if she was being affected, who knows how many other pixies and magic users.

"Do whatever you can to slow it down. Let me know if you need anything," I said before hanging up. I took a deep breath. We were in utter deep dragon shit. But Priscilla was one of the best nature fairies in town and there was a reason her shop, Priscilla's Lotions and Potions, was one of the best when it came to natural remedies.

"How are you holding up?" Lola asked. I smiled at her. She had just come from tending the community garden. Apparently Flynn and her argued about the new section she was allowed to plant in.

"I'm okay. The winter festival is going as smoothly as ice. Priscilla is going to see what she can come up with to help the tree," I said. Lily eyed me. Being an anxious witch she read people like a book.

"Anything else?" Lily asked. I was hesitating on the whole, *'I can talk to the tree,'* because I still hadn't fully rationalized it. I've never heard of anyone being able to talk to the Hollow Tree. But what are friends if you can't trust them?

"The tree sort of talked to me," I said quietly.

"It spoke to you?" Lola asked. I nodded.

"Is that a thing that happens with pixies?" Lily asked, eyebrows furrowed. I shook my head.

"I've never ever heard of anyone being able to communicate with the tree. I've always felt a deep connection but this was something else," I confessed.

"Did it say anything that might help?" Lily asked. I took a deep breath.

"That I can't fix whatever this is. And also what once is lost or gone can be found or reborn. Whatever that means," I said. Both girls looked at each other.

"Now that we know you can connect with the tree I can expand research," Lily said, smiling.

"And I'm still researching the curse but I may be onto something!" Lola said. I smiled at the girls and felt my heart constrict. I was once again on the verge of being hit with a big emotion that was a combination of guilt and gratefulness.

"You guys don't have to do this." My voice cracked slightly. They each reached for my hand.

"You don't have to do everything alone. We got your back," Lily said, placing her hand on top of mine.

"Well Caleb may have you *on* your back," Lola snickered. My face flushed. At that moment Crystal walked in. This time she was sporting a gray suit. At least it wasn't black.

"Hi guys," she said, her hand clutching her bag. Lola stuck out her hand.

"I'm Lola. I don't think we really crossed paths in school. I'm one of the local vets here." Lola smiled widely.

"Luna family, right?" Crystal asked. Lola nodded. "You're mom was my English teacher. It's so nice to meet you. I'm Crystal but you can call me Crys," she said, sliding into the seat next to Lola. It was time to commence girls night.

CRYSTAL and I were on our second caipirinha when the boys strolled in. Celestino came and gave Lily a quick kiss before heading to the bar. Caleb waved at us while Flynn brought more drinks to the table.

"Rider," Lola said, smiling up at him. Flynn rolled his eyes before handing her a mojito.

"I'm not a Disney prince," he muttered.

"Too bad," Lola teased.

"Madame Lola, Lilianna, Eleanor. It is such a pleasure to see you all here on this fine evening," Sailor's voice sang through the bar. His eyes landed on Crystal. He held his hand out to her. Crystal blushed adorably.

"I'm Sailor," he said. It took a second for Crystal to respond. She hesitated before placing her hand in his.

"C-Crystal," she stuttered. I felt the corner of my lips twitch.

"A jewel you are indeed," he said softly, before placing a soft kiss on the back of her hand. A giggle escaped from her.

"Aren't you smooth," she said. She playfully squinted her eyes and Sailor smiled wider. He shrugged his shoulders.

"I can be rough," he said. Crystal's face flushed again and Sailor made his way to the bar with the rest of the guys.

"Crystal!" I exclaimed.

"I sense something brewing," Lily said mystically. Crystal rolled her eyes.

"Please he's a siren. I bet he flirts with everyone," she muttered. Lola shook her head. A puff of fog appeared. Fabian scratched his ear on Lily's lap.

"This is girls night. No guys," he said. We all laughed. I glanced over at the bar and caught Sailor looking at my little sister. I raised an eyebrow at him and the siren actually blushed. Well this was an interesting development.

"But doesn't girl's night involve talking about people?" Lola asked, fiddling with the straw of her drink. She glanced at Flynn again.

"I agree with that. Sip n' Spill has been activated," I said.

"What's Sip n' Spill by the way?" Crystal asked. The girls smiled.

"It's when we sip drinks and spill whatever update we have to give. For example Lola has sipped and should absolutely spill about Flynn," Lily said. Lola rolled her eyes.

"Nothing is happening between Flynn and I," Lola stated. Crystal cocked her head.

"But you guys were definitely flirting?" Crystal said. I choked on my drink.

"Damn Crystal," Lily said. Crystal's eyes widened.

"I-I'm sorry," she stammered. Lola shook her head trying not to laugh.

"It's okay. You're technically correct. Flynn is just stubborn. Kind of like a plant," Lola commented. Lily and I looked at each other.

"So Crys, let me catch you up. Flynn and I have been academic rivals since we were kids. Both of us studied science related majors. He runs the community garden along with being one of the product developers at Kiernan's Whiskey Distillery. We've been bickering more because he's a child who doesn't like to share," Lola explained. Crystal nodded and looked over at Flynn.

"May I remind you that you want him to water your garden," I teased. Lola rolled her eyes.

"What about you Crystal? Anyone in your garden?" Lola asked. Crystal blushed.

"Oh…um no," she said, nervously. Lola placed her arm around her shoulders.

"Well since it's just us two at this table we'll have a night out so we can get back out there," Lola said, smiling wide. Lily shook her head, laughing.

"Oh. Actually I've nev-" Flynn came with two baskets of monster-ella sticks, interrupting Crystal.

"Thanks *Rider*," I said, teasingly. Flynn rolled his eyes and glanced at Crystal.

"I'm Flynn by the way. Caleb's younger brother." Flynn held out his hand. Crystal smiled, taking it. My sister's cheeks flushed again.

"What are we talking about?" Sailor said, appearing next to Flynn. I bit my lip to keep from laughing. Fabian growled from Lily's lap.

"This is girls night," Fabian whined. Lily giggled, petting his head. Caleb and Celestino came over and Sailor moved to stand next to Crystal.

I looked around my group of friends that has gotten a tad bigger this season and smiled. No matter the impending doom with these people by my side I had a feeling I would be okay.

THE NEXT DAY Priscilla asked me to stop by her shop. Pushing through the door of the lavender building I was hit with the smell of sage and oranges. Priscilla had her brown hair with streaks of purple piled on top of her head. She wore an orange tunic with a quilted apron. She was currently flipping through an old book while crafting some potions. She glanced at me and her amber eyes melted.

"Ellie!" she squealed. She came around to give me a big hug. I felt my muscles instantly relax.

"Hey there sweetie," I said softly. She squeezed me.

"It'll be okay," she whispered. I pulled away, nodding. She twirled towards her spell book. "I'm whipping off a few different salves that we can try that will slow the progression of the rot," she continued. Her fingertips held a soft glow as herbs began floating in the air.

"However..." she trailed off. My heart dropped. Was something wrong? "There's one spell I would like to try but I need a certain ingredient," she said.

"I'll get it for you," I said immediately. Whatever she needed I would get. Whether it meant climbing a mountain or deep sea diving.

"There's a rare sea moss that is the shade of light cyan," she said, mixing whatever she had in the bowl. So I was going to do some deep sea diving. I knew I should have gotten my scuba diving license in college.

"Where do I find it?" I asked. She chewed her lip. Her cheeks flushed and I felt her magic vibrate in the air, giving me goosebumps.

"Well the thing is I know where to find regular sea moss. But light cyan? It's this particular shade that is pale, almost translucent in the water. From my research it's connected to sirens. I haven't gotten a chance to talk to Sailor about it." She sighed as she poured the concoction into a mason jar. I nodded along.

"I can talk to Sailor for you and get to the bottom of it. Literally," I said as a giggle escaped. Priscilla joined in. She placed the mason jar next to three others. I bit the inside of my cheek. A guilty feeling started to embed itself into my skin the past few weeks and it was growing.

"Thank you again for doing this Priscilla. I know you must be busy," I admitted. She bumped my hip as she began making another mixture.

"It's no biggie Ellie. You're my friend. Of course I was going to help! Plus it's so much fun learning about the tree," she said, easing the tensions off my shoulders. My phone beeped.

TINO

Don't forget to meet me at Greenwood

Shit. I forgot I was meeting Tino at the Gasping Greenwood Forest. He wanted to check out the clearing and sketch out how everything would look. I would be sending the sketches to Crystal afterwards since she was still in the office. I hated that my father's idea was perfect. Lily already put out a post about seeking performers now that the center of town was cleared for a small stage.

"Text me everything about the moss and I'll talk to Sailor," I said, heading towards the door.

"You got this. Everything will work out," Priscilla said with a soothing smile. I hoped she was right.

———— ❄❄❄ ————

"The inflatables will go in that corner. We should have snow by then." Celestino pointed out. I wrapped my coat tighter as the wind picked up.

"That's fine and we can put the bonfire in the middle of the clearing. We don't want it near the trees. We're going to need a few fairies or pixies on deck to monitor the fire. The wind has been picking up lately," I said. Celestino nodded as he took notes.

"We can put the hot chocolate in that corner," he said pointing to the left.

"Oh maybe we could do a caramel apple stand? I can talk to Greg." I smiled. I loved caramel apples and Greg made the best. From caramel apples covered in candies to toasted butterscotch stardust apples.

"That's great. Maybe we can get the Plastered Pixie to have a stand. They make great holiday drinks," he suggested.

As we continued planning out the area I couldn't help but realize how much better this was. This was a big space where everyone could come, relax, and hang.

"We could do a lighting ceremony for the bonfire as a sort of welcome reception," I said absentmindedly.

"That would be awesome," he said as his eyes wandered around. He fidgeted with the pen in his hand.

"What's wrong?" I asked. He shrugged his shoulders.

"I hate that he was right to have it here," he said with a frown. Celestino knew about my father. He had met him a few times and had been the subject of his harsh words. And yet he stayed friends with me.

"Priscilla still isn't sure what's wrong with the tree. She has no idea where the rot came from or what it is," I said, taking a deep breath.

"We'll figure it out. By the way how are you and Caleb?" he asked, smirking. I rolled my eyes.

"He may not be as such of a grump as I thought," I admitted. He threw his head back in laughter. The sky cracked at that moment and we looked up. Rain? I shivered and looked back into the woods. Everything seemed normal.

"Let's go back," I said tentatively. We made our way out of the forest and could see Boogeyman's Swamp. A few sprites were buzzing around.

"Something is off," Celestino stated. I nodded silently. The sprites were flying around haphazardly. One of them noticed us and zipped straight towards us, a frown on their small face. Sprites were like mini fairies, with delicate bodies and wings that glistened in the light.

"What's wrong?" I asked. The young sprite motioned for us to follow. Near the water were a small group of sprites that seemed to be in distress. Celestino and I looked at each other and my heart sank. They were coughing up water. He knelt down for a closer look. The sprites were shivering, their wings hung low and their color was slipping. A tiny sprite grabbed Celestino's finger and pointed to the water. I gasped.

The water was becoming murky and the lily pads were shriveling up. Celestino placed his fingers near the water's edge and closed his eyes.

"Answers are what I seek. Reveal to me what is weak," he whispered as his magic flowed in a deep violet color into the ground. His face contorted in concentration before he let out a curse.

"What's wrong?" I asked, gripping my bag tightly.

"The water. It's wrong…it's starting to feel…" he trailed off.

"What?" I asked, offering my hands to the sprites, letting the warmth of my magic heal them.

"I can feel the lake dying." He looked at me, his green eyes tormented.

"Fury fuck Tino. It has to be the tree. The roots run deep. The rot has to be spreading into town," I said. He nodded solemnly. "We *have* to fix this," I said, staring at the lake that was home to so many.

CHAPTER II
MYSTERY INGREDIENTS

CALEB

Flynn and I were about to close the tavern for the night when Sailor and Lola walked in with giant grins. I raised an eyebrow.

"You know we're about to close right?" Flynn said, his eyes glued to Lola. She only smiled wider.

"Yes, but we have something to tell you," Sailor said, throwing an arm around Lola. She practically jumped with excitement. I raised an eyebrow. Flynn was rigid next to me. I eyed him and Lola.

"Well...out with it," I said, wiping down the bar. The siren and the vampire took a seat.

"Well as you know my mom has a bunch of books about curses and enchantments from the University. And some of them are super old, like Dracula old," Lola began.

"Dracula is real?" Flynn interrupted. She shrugged her shoulders.

"A story for another day. Anyway there is a spell that can break just about any curse. It requires a few ingredients which I already checked with Priscilla. She has all of them but one."

I stopped cleaning. My heart began racing. Was this it? Was it finally happening? My dad contacted everyone he knew in hopes of breaking my curse and nothing worked. Was there something he missed?

"What's the one ingredient?" Flynn asked, leaning against the bar. Sailor cleared his throat.

"That's where I come in. It's a very rare pearl that is found under a waterfall that has been blessed by sirens of the royal bloodline. We have a waterfall in my hometown," Sailor said. Royal bloodline?

"Coralia Coast has a waterfall that was blessed by royal sirens? Wait, royal sirens exist?" Flynn asked in shock. Sailor rolled his eyes.

"Sirens have been around for thousands of years. And yes the royal families still exist. The siren community is very secretive and protective. Some landed in Coralia Coast in order to escape from the pirates that kept terrorizing the seas," Sailor explained, his demeanor shifting.

I turned to look at him. That explains why Sailor was tight-lipped about sirens. He took a deep breath. His fists were clenched, his eyes drawn tight. I had never seen him so serious.

"So I go to Coralia Coast and find this pearl," I asked. Sailor relaxed as he snorted.

"I'm going with you. You need my help to find it and I doubt you can hold your breath longer than a minute," he said, crossing his arms. I shook my head.

"And you're okay with going back?" I asked. He twitched slightly. Sailor didn't like talking about his hometown too much and I never really pressed him on it. None of us ever did.

"For you and Eleanor to be together? Duh," he said. Lola smiled and leaned on his shoulder.

"Aren't you a sweetie," she said.

"The Hollow Tree is starting to affect the town," Flynn said softly. I glanced at him. We were all quiet for a moment. "The community garden? It only continues to thrive in the harsh winter because of the tree. The roots go deep into the Earth. Who knows what's going to happen," Flynn said. Lola tapped his hands that were wringing a towel. He placed the towel on the bar.

"It'll be okay. Eleanor is on the case. She never backs away from a challenge," Lola said confidently. She was right. Eleanor never shied away from anything. When she committed to something she did it wholeheartedly.

"Holy stars are you smiling? Quick, someone take a picture!" Sailor teased. I glared at the siren. The door to the tavern pushed open and Eleanor walked in with Celestino, Lilianna and Fabian. Her cheeks were pink from the cold. She looked adorable in her oversized light pink knitted sweater and jacket in hand.

"It's spreading," Lilianna said. I looked at Celestino who nodded.

"Eleanor and I were at the clearing to go over details for the festival," Celestino said. Eleanor was clenching her hands together. Fabian hopped onto a bar seat.

"The sprites were sick from the water. Something is wrong with the lake," Eleanor said, her voice slightly breaking. Celestino ran a hand through his hair in frustration.

"I could feel death sinking into it," Celestino said. His voice was rough. He belonged to a family of necromancers and I couldn't imagine how he must be feeling. We all let out a curse.

"What about Priscilla?" Flynn asked, hopefully. Eleanor nodded.

"She's coming up with different potions to slow down the rot. One of the potions involves an ingredient she needs," Eleanor explained.

"What is it?" Lola asked. Eleanor looked at Sailor.

"Some special sea moss? It's supposed to be connected to sirens," she continued. Sailor sighed. We all looked at him. His eyes looked like a tormented sea. Lilianna placed a hand on his shoulder.

"Sailor?" Lilianna asked timidly.

"I can help with that too," Sailor said, looking at his hands.

"Too?" Eleanor asked. Lola nodded.

"To break the curse we need a pearl," Lola said, catching everyone up.

"Are you sure? It's okay if you can't," Eleanor said. Sailor was definitely hiding something.

"Road trip to Coralia next weekend?" Sailor suggested with a smile that didn't quite reach his eyes. I glanced at Eleanor who nodded.

"Coralia Coast, here we come," Eleanor said.

"Oh, a road trip! Can I come?" Fabian yelped. I rolled my eyes.

"No fur is allowed in my jeep," I said. Lilianna scratched Fabian behind his left ear.

"I need you here with me. I want you to help Lola with the creatures and make sure they're okay," Lilianna said softly. Fabian turned his big fox eyes to Lola.

"Do I get treats?" Fabian asked. Lola giggled.

"I need you to try my latest recipes," Lola said and Fabian purred.

THINGS WERE TURNING COMPLICATED FAST. We worked together the rest of the night to come up with a game plan. Flynn would be taking over my shifts next weekend. Celestino and Ben had the festival running smoothly and Crystal said she would handle anything that came up. Lilianna and Lola were going to help Priscilla with the potions for both the curse and the tree.

Sailor, Eleanor and I would be heading to Coralia Coast next Friday afternoon. I couldn't help but worry about Sailor. He never really talked about his home and family. They obviously had a strained relationship. I hope whatever he needed to do to help us wasn't anything excruciating.

Everyone left the tavern except Eleanor who was reorganizing the straws for the sixth time. Her eyes nearly matched in color which wasn't a good sign. She looked stressed. I understood. She felt pressure to make sure the festival was a hit, heal the tree and help me break my curse.

I wish I hadn't dragged her into my mess. She didn't need to help me with my problem when she had so many worries. On instinct I began making her favorite drink. A memory replayed as I went through the motions.

ELEANOR SILVA. That was her name. She was a short pixie with long auburn hair, blessed curves and hypnotic eyes. She had come to my tavern after work and made me remake her drink three times.

She wrapped her lips around the straw and took a sip. She swirled the alcohol around, eyes narrowing. The people at the bar watched with curious stares. I watched her throat work and imagined how it would look taking my co-

"This is better, but I need it to be colder with a splash of more lime juice." She gave me a wide grin.

"You know most people just take the drink they're given," I said through gritted teeth, my hands automatically remaking her drink. What the fuck was I doing? I couldn't stop myself from trying to perfect her drink. What I hated was that I wanted to. Something about her compelled me.

Maybe it was her luscious smirk or her two-toned color eyes. For some reason I couldn't fight against her wishes. The patrons snickered around us and I glared at them.

"I'm not most people," she said. I scoffed.

"And what makes you different?" I asked, my eyes flickering back to hers. Her left eye stopped me. I watched in fascination as the hazel color melted into a swirling green. My stomach tightened. What the fuck was happening to me? She leaned forward, trapping me in the scent of cinnamon.

"Make me a decent drink and I'll show you," she said with a wink. And I did, because I needed to know. I needed to know more about this loud mouth flirty pixie.

"You don't have to help me with the curse," my voice woke her from whatever daydream she was having. She rolled her eyes.

"I'm helping you," she stated. I walked over to her, handed her the drink and threw the towel on the other side of the bar.

"No," I said firmly, caging her against the bar. She giggled, her eyes swinging to me.

"I am," she said. I leaned into her.

"No," I said again. She placed a hand on my chest. My heart unwillingly pounded against her touch.

"You're going to lose this fight. I'm helping you whether you want it or not," she said. I clenched my jaw. She was as stubborn as an ogre. Her eyes twinkled playfully. I knew that look. She was up to something. I raised an eyebrow.

"What are you thinking?" I asked. Her luscious lips twisted mischievously, her hands sliding up my body and around my neck. Her scent wrapped around me, pulling me closer into her orbit. She still smelled like cinnamon. It was alluring. Her breath was hot in my ear and my body slowly became alive, aware of how close she was.

"I've never seen a waterfall." Her voice was innocent but her teeth nipped my ear. My eyes flickered close, relishing the feel of her body against mine.

"Waterfalls are nice," I said as evenly as possible. She pulled back with a smile.

"In the romance books I read, they're *very* nice," she said softly. Her left eye began to bleed green. My pixie was back. I pulled her closer to me and pressed her against the bar. She blushed immediately.

"Tell me more," I said.

CHAPTER 12
FAMILY REUNION

Caleb

It was the day before we had to leave for Coralia Coast and Tatiana and I were running through inventory. With the day over we needed to double check we would have enough for the pub crawl.

When Lilianna came up with the idea for a crawl for the fall festival I was a bit hesitant. It would mean the tavern would be over crowded and we would be working double time to get the drinks out. But it was amazing.

Sure, the tavern had a shit ton of people and some spilled their drinks however I found solace in the chaos. Coming up with cocktails was something I hadn't done in awhile. It felt great to do that again.

Back in college I was always bartending at parties as a way to make extra cash and I liked doing it. So coming back to take over the tavern after college just felt right. My father wasn't too happy but it was my decision.

For years we had no idea how my family owned the tavern. My granddad received a letter one day asking if he could watch over it. And we did for years. Lilianna and Celestino discovered the rightful owner when they were digging into the past of each bar for the crawl. Turns out the original owner was living amongst us.

I looked over at Tatiana. She was around my older brother's age with long dark hair that had natural streaks of gray. She had sharp brown eyes. I was ready and willing to hand over the business to her but she wanted a partnership. I was grateful. A part of me didn't want to let this place go. It was great to have someone else help around and she was more into conversing with people than I was.

"Thanks for letting Flynn take over some of my shifts," I said. She looked at me and shrugged her shoulders.

"He's more of a smooth talker with customers anyway," she teased. I rolled my eyes.

"Whatever," I muttered. She pointed at me.

"See like that," she said. I chucked a crumpled piece of paper at her and she swatted it away.

"It's okay. Do whatever it is you have to do," she said. I nodded, staring at another paper in front of me. "I don't know if it's because on my dad's side we have fairies but I feel it Caleb," she said. She looked at me, worried.

It was slowly sinking into the town. The magic was beginning to fade and disrupt things. Pixies and fairies were slowly struggling with the simplest of things like reviving plants, moving water, lighting fires. We needed to hurry before Priscilla was affected and couldn't perform her spells. I nodded.

"We're working on it," I said, hoping to ease her worries.

Crystal and Eleanor with Celestino and Lilianna were going over the crawl and other stuff when I heard the tavern doors slam. Whoever the fuck slammed my doors was going to get kicked in the shin.

"What the hellhound was that?" Tatiana said, standing up.

"I'm going to fucking find out," I said, already making my way out the office.

WHEN I CAME out of our office Crystal was standing by an older gentleman while Lilianna, Celestino and Eleanor were opposite.

"What is happening here?" I called out. Everyone's eyes shifted to me.

"You're supposed to be working not in some hole in the wall drinking," the old man bellowed. He was shorter than me with close cropped gray hair and brown eyes. His skin was a deep tan color, almost like Eleanor's. *Oh fury fuck.* Was this her father?

"We were discussing the pub crawl and other events that Hale's Industry will be a part of." Crystal's voice sounded small as she tried to make eye contact with her father. She was retreating into her shell.

"It's called work drinks. Many companies have those," Eleanor said, crossing her arms. Her father tsked her and my blood began boiling.

"I said to keep your silly wishy washy antics away from your sister," Mr. Hale said. Magic crackled through the air.

"Once again we were working. Not everything needs to be done in an office setting. How many nights were you away having business dinners?" Eleanor raised an eyebrow. That was my fiery pixie.

"Business dinners in a five star restaurant. Not some bar," the asshole said. I walked over to Eleanor.

"This beat up bar is one of the best bars within a 50 mile radius," I said. Eleanor glanced at me with a small smile.

"And who are you?" Mr. Hale asked. I stuck out a hand.

"Caleb Kiernan. One of the owners." He looked at my hand as if I was gum on his leather loafers. Eleanor placed a hand on my arm, pulling me back. Her father looked between us.

"Really?" Mr. Hale said. Eleanor's face flamed.

"Just say why you're here before he kicks you out." She kept her voice even but I could see a light tremor in her hands. He straightened his tie.

"I needed to see if things were running smoothly. The festival must reach the standards of the company." He sounded haughty. It was Eleanor's turn to scoff.

"You don't trust your daughters?" I asked. A flash of almost regret flickered in his eyes.

"The festivals of Lavender Falls have always been a success and bring in tons of tourists. You should know that seeing how you were once a part of this community," Lilianna spat. I glanced over at her and then Celestino who had a hand on the small of her back.

"Still hanging around the Rosario's are you? And how is your mother doing? Still cleaning up people's messes." Lilianna's eyes widened and Celestino was going to say something when Lilianna waved her hand. Eleanor's eyes widened. The air around us shimmered. The smell of the ocean waved in. Everyone's eyes turned to Lilianna.

"I couldn't say this when we were younger because I didn't want to lose my friendship with Eleanor. But you Mr. Hale are a fucking golden spoon asswipe. You were once a part of this small town and now you think because you have money you're better than us? You're not," Lilianna paused, taking a breath.

"You're a lonely shell of a man. If you could open your fucking eyes you would see that Eleanor and Crystal are doing a fantastic job." Lilianna's fingers twitch at her side. I swallowed, watching the event unfold before me. Lilianna was never vocal. She liked to remain in the background but I've always heard about the temper of the Rosario's.

The air around us all grew cold. Lilianna's fingers slowly tightened into a fist and everything from chairs to cups began rattling. Sailor appeared and slid in to stand next to me. He looked at me before glancing at Lilianna.

"*You* wanted to sponsor our festival because you saw something. So don't act like you're doing *us* a favor. We've been putting on these festivals long before you joined, successfully I might add," Lilianna said. Eleanor placed a hand on Lilianna's shoulder and she loosened her fingers. Mr. Hale gasped in a breath and everything began to settle. He took a deep breath before stretching his shoulders. There was a quiet pause.

"I expect updates on every little thing. You change the color? I want to know about it. You add a new event? I need to know. I don't need this town disgracing my name," he said, turning around.

"You did that when mom died," Eleanor called out. Mr. Hale went rigid. We all did. Crystal's eyes widened. Eleanor stared at the back of her father, trembling. Mr. Hale turned back around but instead of acknowledging what Eleanor said he looked at Lilianna.

"I shouldn't have said that about your mother Lilianna," he said. "I apologize and I hope she is doing well." His voice was softer.

"She refuses to stop working but other than that she is fine," Lilianna said. Mr. Hale gave a ghost of a smile as if lost in a memory. Lilianna waved her hand and the tavern doors blew open. "It's time you leave," Lilianna said.

While Mr. Hale entered my pub with a giant chip stuck up his ass he didn't leave that way. His expression was one I easily recognized. I saw an old man who was tired and broken.

"I'm so sorry." Crystal repeated over and over again. Lilianna and Eleanor went to comfort her but Crystal stepped away from them, trembling. Celestino and I looked at each other. Sailor took a step towards Crystal and stopped.

"What the fuck was that magic?" I asked. Eleanor looked at Lilianna who blushed.

"Magic is tied to emotions. My Posey here is an empath," Celestino said, kissing her cheek. Celestino turned his green eyes to me. "I told you he was a dick," he said, wrapping an arm around his witch. He was but he was also broken.

Just like Eleanor was.

106

ELEANOR

The audacity of that man. The only thing that changed was that his auburn hair was now gray. I can't believe he walked into the tavern like that. He stood there and acted as if the tavern was beneath him. Crystal has been dealing with that asshole all by herself. She even still lived with him.

According to her, he's always barging into her meetings and trying to take over. It was like he didn't want her to take over the company. Or he didn't trust her. And the fact he just fucking showed up? Getting angry over a business meeting with drinks as if he didn't miss countless dinners with us doing the same fucking thing was hypocritical.

But I couldn't get the look on his face when he apologized about Lilianna's mom. He looked tired and so lost. It made it harder to hate him. But did I hate him? Honestly, I just felt sorry for him.

He's been in pain since mom died. In the beginning I understood. The fighting, the protectiveness came from losing mom but at some point it just felt like he was using her death as an excuse to be a shit dad.

Crystal stirred in her sleep and I walked over to place a warm cup of coffee by the night stand. She had stayed over after the fight with our father. She looked at me with a small smile.

"That was the best sleep I've had in awhile." Her voice was gravely. I giggled.

"I bet. Are you okay?" I asked. She glanced at the cup.

"Shouldn't I be asking you that?" she said timidly. I took a deep breath. In a way I was okay. My father could say whatever he wanted about me. It made no difference. I spent most of my adolescence letting his harsh words roll off my skin. I brushed her hair down the same way mom always did.

"Nothing he can say or do can hurt me," I said. She sighed, plopping her head back on the pillow.

"Thanks for letting me crash and sorry I lost it in the tavern," she mumbled. I crawled into bed and laid by her side. Seeing my sister try desperately to keep it together sliced through me. How many times did she cry alone? How many times did she need someone to vent to? I wasn't there for her. All these years she's been alone. I squeezed her hand.

"I'm your older sister. There's nothing I wouldn't do for you," I whispered.

"You're leaving today right? I'm going to take Priscilla by the tree later and she's going to try to start healing it," Crystal whispered. I nodded.

"Alone in a car with Caleb and Sailor," I said. She began humming Life Is A Highway. "I wonder how long it'll take for Caleb to snap at Sailor," I thought out loud. My little sister smiled, her cheeks a little flushed. A two hour car ride with a sunshine siren and a grumpy elf. Should be smooth sailing right?

CHAPTER 13
ROAD TRIP TIME

ELEANOR

It took about an hour before Caleb cracked. Sailor was belting out sea shanties, purposefully off key. I was a mess in the front seat laughing. Caleb's eyebrow twitched in annoyance.

"There wasn't any other siren we could have asked?" Caleb grumbled. I wiped a tear from my eye. Sailor scoffed in fake offense.

"Carrie is not going to leave the saloon this close to the festival and I'm the only other siren in Lavender Falls," Sailor pointed out. Caleb rolled his eyes.

"Well that explains why you're such an attention whore," Caleb grumbled. I tried to hold in my laugh.

"I'll have you know my whore days are over," Sailor said, sitting back in his seat. I raised an eyebrow looking at him. His blonde hair was a bit longer, tousled waves coming in. His skin was beginning to lose its golden glow with winter approaching.

"Oh really? Someone caught your eye?" I teased, looking back at him. A blush slowly crept up his face.

"Maybe," Sailor mumbled. He stared out the window, conflict brewing in his eyes. We all sat in silence for a moment.

"Is there something we should know about Coralia Coast?" I asked. Sailor never talked about his hometown much. And according to Caleb he got very touchy around the subject. His hands gripped his knees.

"For the sea moss you're going to talk to an old…friend. The pearl we can find at a waterfall that I'll take you to tomorrow. We'll go early in the morning. There's less chance we'll run into anyone during that time," he said. I didn't point out how he said we would be seeing his friend without him. I turned back in my seat to catch a sign that said, *Coralia Coast 20 miles.*

"Who are we avoiding?" Caleb asked.

"If I can help it, my family," Sailor said.

"Are they like my father?" I asked. His bright blue eyes hardened.

"In certain ways." And that was the end of the conversation. My heart pounded in my chest. My father showing up was a major blow. Guilt washed over me. We were forcing Sailor to possibly confront something and he was doing it for us. If his family was anything like my father I couldn't imagine what we might find.

AFTER NESTLING into Sailor's cottage he gave us directions to a local diner to pick up some food. He wanted to remain hidden which I understood. Coralia Coast was a small seaside town and like Lavender Falls word travels fast. I was already hearing whispers around our town about Caleb and I after my first night with him.

Caleb and I strolled to what appeared to be a small dinner near Calder's Beach. The outside was made of white, weathered wood with big windows and a blue steel roof. The sign above read Calder's Diner. The door dinged as we stepped in. Eyes of the customers turned to look at us. I felt my skin crawl. I stepped closer to Caleb who wrapped an arm around me.

Well this was a nice welcome. I understood that the people in small towns liked to stick together but in Lavender Falls everyone was warm and welcoming. Here though everyone else just continued to eye us suspiciously as we made our way to the front. Lilianna had mentioned to us that most of the young people were very sweet when they had visited for a short vacation.

But it still felt awkward. Were they not used to tourists? The hostess was a young girl with bright red hair and blue eyes. She looked surprised to see us.

"Oh...um just sit anywhere you like," she said politely. Caleb tugged me towards a booth in the back, away from prying eyes. Our waitress came by quickly. She had purple hair, a tattoo on her arm of a trident with a nose piercing. Her hair was cropped short and her brown eyes were outlined in blue eyeliner.

"I'm Mira. Please ignore everyone here. We don't get too many tourists during this time of year. It is winter and all. Summer is where it's at," she said, shrugging her shoulders. I felt myself relax an inch. That made sense. Winter was settling in and it was way too cold for beach activities.

But it was still weird how standoffish they seemed to be. I mean regardless of weather tourists are usually welcomed. It meant money for the town. There seemed to be a melancholy feel that hung in the air. These people seemed...almost sad.

"We're just ordering to go," Caleb said. Mira nodded and handed us some menus.

"I'll be back," she said, walking away. I looked at Caleb.

"This feels weird right?" I asked. Caleb nodded, eyes studying the menu. I looked up and caught the hostess staring at us. She quickly glanced away. After a few minutes Mira came back to take our order.

"Two burgers, hold the pickles on one, both with fries. And then the crab cake mac n' cheese with garlic aioli sauce. A ginger ale and two cokes." Caleb finished ordering for us.

"Garlic aioli on mac n' cheese with ginger ale?" she clarified. Caleb raised an eyebrow back.

"Is that a problem?" he asked. She glanced out into the ocean. She shook her head.

"No, of course not," she said walking away.

"I can see why Sailor wanted to stay in the cottage," I whispered. Caleb nodded, looking out the window. I absentmindedly began rearranging the packets of sugar. I felt anxious. Today we would find the sea moss and tomorrow we were going to find the pearl. Then we could break Caleb's curse and heal the Hollow Tree. Everything felt quick. But there was a feeling in the pit of my stomach; a grim warning.

"It'll be okay." Caleb broke through my thoughts and reached for my hand. His hand was warm and rough. I looked up at his pale blue eyes. He looked determined while I felt like I was losing confidence with every step we took.

I told everyone I had everything under control but to be honest I didn't feel that way at all. We were barely slowing down the rot on the Hollow Tree and its words kept repeating in my head. I couldn't figure it out.

Did it want to die? If it did it would spell disaster for the town? Magic was already acting up all over town.

Mira came by handing us our order. "Here you guys are! You can pay up front with the hostess. Thank you so much for coming by and I hope you enjoy your stay here." Her smile seemed forced. Her eyes were tense as she stared at me. Handing me the bag of food she held a folded paper, facing it towards me. I quickly reached for it and nodded slightly. She relaxed a bit.

It wasn't until we had paid, walked out and were making our way back to the cottage that I opened it. My heart kicked up.

To Mr. Crab Man n' Cheese. It's this year.

I looked at Caleb whose face was scrunched in confusion.

"That's to Sailor," I whispered, afraid that even in the empty streets someone would hear us. Caleb nodded, slipped his hand into mine and tugged us faster on the street. I hope to the stars we could make it out of Coralia Coast without causing trouble for Sailor. He clearly was risking a lot just by being here.

Everyone was working and risking something to help me. Bile

began rising in my throat. People always relied on *me*; it had never been the other way around.

SAILOR DIDN'T SAY anything about the note. Instead he read it, crumpled it and tossed it into the fireplace. I didn't want to pry. I had issues with my own family that I had been keeping a secret and I could see that our sunshine Sailor was clouded by his. My past was coming back to haunt me and at some point Sailor's would too. I just hoped he knew he wasn't alone in whatever he was carrying.

"Do we need to be worried?" Caleb asked, breaking the tension. Well there goes not bringing it up. Sailor scratched the back of his head. He looked at the fireplace one more time before picking up his food.

"You two don't," he said, biting into his food. "Fuck. I've missed this," he whispered.

"But you?" I asked. He stared at his food before giving me a smile I now recognized had been practiced. It was the same smile Lily always gave. The one that was exhaustingly bright. How could I have missed it?

"I'll be okay. Once it gets dark I'll give you an address for a shop you can go to for the moss. I would go with you but..." He pointed to the fireplace where the note had incinerated. "Tomorrow morning I will be able to lead you to the waterfall. I'm sure we'll find the pearl there." He took a sip of his ginger ale. I picked at my fries. Caleb placed a hand on my knee and I felt his warmth blanket my body. A single touch from him and I felt soothed.

He was seriously getting under my skin.

CHAPTER 14
SUSPICIOUS SIRENS

CALEB

Sailor was hiding something from us and I couldn't be mad at him. I hid my curse from people for years. I could tell being back in the place he grew up in was difficult for him. His words from before repeated in my head. *If you guys want to hear about my family problems we're going to need a night with stronger alcohol.*

We would definitely be having a guy's night once everything blew over. Since having Celestino back in town I've learned to lean on my friends more. But I wanted to show them that I could be there for them as well. I should have spoken up about this curse years ago. Maybe we wouldn't have to be dealing with it on top of the Hollow Tree and festival.

Sailor couldn't come with us to the diner and now we were walking the streets of Coralia Coast without him because he couldn't be seen for whatever reason. While it irritated me that we had to do this alone, Sailor had a good soul. He was risking whatever it was just to be here and that was enough.

Also the siren hardly cracked a joke let alone a smile the whole time we've been here. That was worrisome. Sailor reminded me of

Lola. Both of them seemed to fart sunshine out of their asses with quick sarcasm. But ever since we crossed the town's line he's had a permanent rain cloud over his head.

I glanced down at Eleanor. And ever since we crossed into Coralia Coast she's been quiet. Her lips have been pointed down and her eyes have remained hazel. My stomach twisted.

There was nothing I could say that would ease her growing anxiety. I slipped my hand between her soft fingers, enjoying how utterly right it felt. Her eyes widened and she looked up at me. Her cheeks were pink from the cold that had been blowing in.

I nodded silently hoping she could read the look in my eyes. She gave me a hesitant smile and nodded in return. She kept her hand in mine the entire walk. It felt like a silent and small victory.

The building we were standing in front of looked a tad washed up. The store was painted a pale green with a faded yellow door. The shop sign was blinking on its deathbed. *Calder's Apothecary.* According to Sailor the owner might have what we need or know where we could find it.

Stepping in the door chimed. It was warm and cozy inside. The smell of the ocean carried around the store and it was dimly lit. Along the walls were different herbs, teas, and an assortment of books. Tables of seashells, crystals and shark teeth were on display. Priscilla would love this, even Lola.

An old woman was reorganizing some bottles of what looked like potions. She had wild red hair and bright green eyes. She wore crooked glasses and a gray cardigan paired with a patchwork long skirt. She smiled, revealing a golden canine.

"Why hello there," she said. Eleanor pulled away from me and I wished she hadn't. Her warmth followed her, leaving me cold.

"Hi there! My name is Eleanor and this is Caleb. We were hoping to find something very special we need for a potion," Eleanor said, smiling. She turned on her charm, the one that won the hearts of everyone around her. It had won me over. The woman wiped her hands on her skirt.

"My name is Meryl. I'd be happy to help! What do you need?" She walked over to the cash register and pulled out a book.

"You see there is this rare sea moss that's like pale blue. Actually close to the color of Caleb's eyes. We need it because we have a very important tree in our town that's dying," Eleanor explained. My eyes narrowed. Meryl's fingers twitched and her jaw tightened at the mention of the moss. She gave out an awkward laugh.

"Pale blue sea moss? Wow, that is indeed rare. And you thought you could find it here?" She was hiding something and searching for something behind Eleanor's words. I've spent enough time watching people behind a bar to be able to read them. Sailor had mentioned once that sirens were very secretive.

"We were told," I said, cutting in. She looked at me, her fingers tapping on her book.

"Who told you?" she asked. Eleanor took a deep breath and plastered another friendly smile.

"Sirens are very secretive," Eleanor pointed out. Meryl smiled.

"We are. Can't help it," she said, shrugging her shoulders.

"I understand. Our friend told us to come here specifically. Please. This tree...it's connected to our town, the ley lines. Magic is beginning to act up," Eleanor pleaded. Meryl's eyes softened.

"I trust your friend pointed you to my shop for a reason?" she asked tentatively. And he did. Sailor told us that Meryl had a heart of gold and would help us but we weren't allowed to say that he sent us. We nodded. She took a deep breath and closed her book.

"Stop by tomorrow and I'll have it ready for you," she stated. Eleanor nodded.

"Thank you. Thank you so much," Eleanor said, reaching for a handshake. Meryl stared at it for a second before taking it. We were almost out the door when she called our attention.

"I shouldn't have to tell you that your *friend* needs to be careful, right?" she said with a knowing look in her eyes. For a second I wanted to question what she meant but after the interaction at the diner I didn't think it mattered. Eleanor and I looked at each other before she gave Meryl a smile.

ONCE OUT OF the shop I pulled Eleanor towards the beach. She looked at me, curiously. "Where are we going?" she asked. I pointed to the sand. She stopped immediately.

"Do you know how much colder it's going to be once we get close to the water? Also there's sand," she said. I rolled my eyes and grabbed her hand.

"And that's why I have a bag, Starburst."

I tugged her onwards and we walked across the beach until we reached the shoreline. The sun was beginning to set once I found the spot I wanted. Eleanor wrapped herself in her arms and stared into the tumbling waves. The smell of sea salt hung in the air and my body relaxed.

I pulled out two blankets from my bag. One to lay on and one to wrap around each other. There was a container at the bottom of my bag. Pulling it out I couldn't help but grin. It was filled with fruit and a note from Sailor saying to enjoy. I shook my head.

Once everything was settled I tapped Eleanor's shoulder. Her reaction wasn't the one I expected. Instead of giving me a shit eating grin for doing something romantic she looked at our little impromptu picnic with hesitation. I felt my jaw clenched. I knew for Eleanor our relationship was purely to get rid of an itch. But the more we spent time together, getting to know each other a shift began.

There would be a glimmer of moments where it felt real. It felt like the ice between us was melting and I was finally bathing in sunlight. I could see it was that way for her as well. I saw the secret smiles she would give. I noticed the tension easing in her shoulders when I was around.

Then clouds would begin to skirt around our private Eden and she would pull away. Her past had its claws in her. I would fight them off so she could see that with me everything was real. I tugged her hand to sit down. Taking off my boots I moved to take her shoes off. She pulled away.

"I can do that," she said, her voice sounding small. I grunted and grabbed her ankle.

"So can I and I will," I said, firmly. She blushed and nodded. I smirked. "Good girl."

She rolled her eyes but from the way she was biting her lip I could tell she liked it. Slipping off her boots I began kneading her feet. Eleanor closed her eyes, a small sigh escaping her lips. With the sounds of the waves crashing, the caress of the ocean breeze we stayed quiet, enjoying each other's silence. I pointed at the fruit and she nodded.

"This...is nice," she said blushing. One of my favorite things about Eleanor was this quiet softer side she didn't let out often. She offered me a strawberry and I took a bite, my tongue brushing her fingers. I pressed into the center of her foot and she yelped, glaring at me.

"Way to ruin the moment, Elfie," she muttered as she continued to feed both of us. When the container was empty and I was done massaging her feet I pulled her into my arms to lay down. She pulled the blanket tighter around herself.

"This *is* nice," I whispered into her hair. Her fingers dug into my hoodie. My hands traced lines up and down her back. Looking up at the stars she seemed to have gotten lost in her thoughts. The moon hung high in the air. The stars reflected her freckles, scattered magnificently everywhere.

"Tell me," I said.

"I'm worried," she said, softly.

"I am too. You're not alone," I said. She frowned.

"I know that but..." she trailed off. I tilted her head to look at me.

"But what? You can trust me Eleanor," I said. She stared at me with conflict brewing in her eyes.

"I know that I just feel...conflicted," she confessed. I gave her a small smile. My hand slipped under her sweater to feel her heated skin.

"Then how about we just enjoy these moments?" I said, kissing her forehead. We continued to stargaze in silence. Her hand absentmind-edly rubbed above my heart. A strong breeze blew and Eleanor curled herself tighter around me.

"I am enjoying it," she whispered. I pressed my forehead against the side of her face, relishing in the feel of her body against mine. Her scent of cinnamon wrapped around me.

Staring into her eyes I was so dangerously close to claiming those lips. Something must have shifted in our exchange because she pulled away, quietly. My hand wandered down to squeeze her hip. She sighed, turning her face away from me. I pressed a gentle kiss on the side of her neck. The corner of her lips fought back a smile and she reached for my hand. I was going to win over her fears one way or the other.

This was beginning to feel overwhelming. Was this how Lily felt when she was conflicted about Celestino? Fuck I gave her such good advice and here I was eating my words. I trusted Caleb. I did. I do. I always have. Ever since I walked into his tavern four years ago he has never been anything but honestly brooding with me.

I HAD FINALLY CONVINCED Lily to come out with me to The Drunken Fairy Tale Tavern. Ever since we moved back after graduation everyone mentioned how the pub had improved. I wanted to see just

how much my favorite place had changed. And now I could legally drink.

Lily was somewhere waiting for me inside. When I pushed open the door my ears perked up at the music that was playing. Hypnotic strings and a voice that could make a siren jealous echoed. It was Irish I believe. The bar was packed. My eyes widened. I had never seen it filled with so many people having a good time. Cutting through the crowd I decided to head to the bar first.

"Ellie!" Alex exclaimed. I laughed at his infectious smile. Alex and Thalia were here grabbing a few drinks. He had finally proposed to his high school sweetheart. After hugging them both a flash of white blonde hair caught my eye.

I pushed my way through the crowd, catching glimpses of a mysterious blonde man, pouring drinks. And then my eyes connected to a pair of bright blue eyes. I sucked in a breath. He was beautiful. Enchanting. Something about him beckoned me closer. I needed to be closer to him.

Icy blue eyes, hair so soft and blonde that it glittered like twinkling stars in the tavern's lighting. He was tall with broad shoulders. My eyes wandered down, drinking him in.

"I've never had an elf before," I said. The tips of his pointed ears turned pink.

"Caleb!" someone shouted. I bit my lower lip to keep from laughing. Apparently he was just as stunned to see me as I was to see him because he overfilled the glass of beer.

"Caleb? What a pleasure to meet you," I said.

FROM THAT MOMENT Caleb held my attention even when I didn't want him too. Something about him always pulled me. It was like we were connected by a string and it didn't matter how much we pulled away from each other we'd snap right back. I had never experienced something like that.

Now we were exploring each other. I found myself seeking his arms for comfort and his words for solace. Instead of pulling away we were wounding tighter and tighter around each other. Caleb had never been afraid to cut through my bullshit and tell me how it was. Having someone like that hold me was wonderfully terrifying.

I snuck a glance at him. His blue eyes shone brightly against the moonlight. The sound of waves crashed in front of us. It was disgustingly romantic and better than any scene from a romance movie. I never thought I would have a moment like this.

While I read romance books it was always rather difficult to envision myself having these moments. It was hard to trust that moments like these were possible off screen and page. Yet here I was, laying in this grumpy elf's arms.

"Are you just going to stare?" he asked, raising an eyebrow, eyes flickering to me.

"You have a terribly handsome face. I can't help it," I crooned. He grunted.

"Terribly handsome you say? You're devastatingly gorgeous," he said, the tips of ears pink.

"Is this the battle of the compliments?" I teased. In a swift movement, he was on top of me and forced his hips in between my legs. His nose traced a line up my neck and I moved to give him more access.

"As you wish," he said with a slight grin. My heart skipped at his quote. His breath was hot in my ear. I wrapped my legs around his waist. My stomach dipped as my body remembered just how this man made me feel. His lips looked so soft.

Tomorrow we would have what we needed to break the curse. Then I could kiss him. Would kissing him seal something within me? Would it make everything feel real? Did I want it to be real? Maybe.

"You have beautiful eyes," I continued. My fingers moved to trace his jaw and he leaned into it.

"Your freckles remind me of the stars," he whispered. My fingers made it to the tips of his ears and his eyes slightly widened. I smirked.

"You have very sensitive ears," I said softly. His nostrils flared as his pupils dilated.

"Do you know what touching an elf's ear does?" he gritted out, eyes shut. My heart rattled in excitement. I only knew what I read about in books but even then I wasn't sure if those held any truth. I continued stroking his ear. A slow blush crawled up his face. I cocked my head.

"I've taken many lovers but never an elf." My voice was breathy as I felt a bulge against my core. His eyes snapped open with intense heat.

"Eleanor," he warned. I smiled.

"Yes?" I asked, innocently. He shook his head, forcing me to let go.

"Our ears are sensitive," he said, pressing a kiss to my cheek. He continued to gently nip and kiss his way toward my ear. "Stroking my ear is like stroking my dick," he whispered. I giggled as he kissed my neck, his scruff scratching against my skin.

"Mhmm, I guess I'll make sure to remember that," I said as my hand slid down. Caleb lifted off of me before I could reach my destination.

"We should probably head back to Sailor," he said, getting up. I sighed, staring at the stars.

"You're right. I also don't want to get sand in my thong," I said, standing up. Caleb groaned.

"You had to tell me that, didn't you?" he asked, packing up the blankets. I gave him a wink.

"Of course."

CHAPTER 15
STEAMY WATERFALLS

CALEB

It was fucking cold. Like colder than a Yeti's balls. Eleanor trudged on by Sailor's side and I wanted to punch his face. They were both perfectly fine, roaming through this forest with as much energy as a newborn minotaur. Clearly Eleanor had more experience walking through forests in the early morning.

Sailor woke us up at five in the morning and that's when the urge to punch him began. I had Eleanor nestled on top of my chest. My arms were tightly wrapped around her. We were both perfectly asleep when the bastard siren banged on our door, waking us up.

I could still see her face. Her pink hair was falling out of her bun. Her eyes were sleepy and she had a bit of dry drool on the corner of her mouth. She went to bed with my black hoodie. She looked relaxed. And I was going to show her how she would be waking up every day if we shared a bed but then Sailor yelled at us to hurry up.

Eleanor glanced back at me with a smirk. She knew why I was being grumpy. She sat on top of me and grounded into my morning wood with a mischievous smile before jumping off and running into the bathroom. I sighed, irritated. I had plans for the morning. I wanted to finish what we were teasing each other with at the beach. I wanted to make her feel good, ease some stress off of her shoulders.

Walking through the woods of Coralia Coast is not what I wanted to do at almost six in the morning. The ground was covered in light frost. We were getting incredibly close to snow fall. Which made me feel anxious. Because of the town's magic we're able to keep our vegetation thriving.

"We're almost there," Sailor called out after an hour of walking. I could faintly hear the trickle of water. We were getting close. When we found the pearl there was a possibility that my curse could be broken and I could *fully* be with Eleanor. Maybe with the curse broken she could come around to the idea of something genuine.

ELEANOR GASPED and I couldn't blame her. The waterfall was majestic; surreal. The water was tumbling over rocks 25 feet up. It had a beautiful pool at the bottom. I had no idea how deep it was but steam was flowing out. With the sun rising light bounced off the mist from the water painting an eerily enchanting scenery.

I glanced at Eleanor and my heart catapulted forward. Instead of stopping at her beauty my heart raced. Because Eleanor didn't stop me in my tracks. She made me run towards her. Her smile was carefree, her eyes glowing in awe.

For a split second I felt undeserving to witness such peace around her. I was grumpy, quiet and reclusive. Sure the curse made me corner myself more but Eleanor was my opposite. I didn't feel worthy enough to walk in her light. I felt like I was dragging her down with me. She was helping me with my curse but at what cost when I could see how the toll of everything was taking on her.

"It's beautiful," Eleanor said softly, eyes on me. It was and so was she. I swallowed hard, trying to bury the guilt. From the corner of my eye Sailor took a step towards the lake. For the first time since stepping into this town Sailor smiled.

"It is," he said. And I could see why. Something about this place felt different than the town. There was magic here. Magic that felt strong, warm and welcoming as I stared into the blue water. The sound of the waterfall felt like it was humming a lullaby, luring us closer.

Sailor cleared his throat and began stripping. I pulled Eleanor into my arms and covered her eyes. She pushed me away, giggling. Not on my watch was she going to see this man naked.

"Aren't you going to be cold?" Eleanor asked. Sailor pulled off his shirt revealing a tattoo on his chest that looked similar to the one our waitress had back at the diner. He noticed me staring at it and turned his back to us immediately. He reached for his boxers and I forcibly turned Eleanor around who giggled again.

"I'm a siren. I'm never cold in the water. Also the water here is hot. Once the snow lands people tend to use this as a hot spring. Now I'll be back in a bit. Just…stay here," he said. I snorted.

"Where else would we go?" I asked. Sailor chuckled. He stared at the water for a bit, took a deep breath and dived in with a swimmer's grace. For a brief second the water glowed and Sailor popped back up to the surface. His iridescent scales across his cheeks that tended to be hidden, glittered full now and more scales appeared up his arms.

He gave us a wink before diving back down. His tail flicked at us as he disappeared into the depths of the water. Eleanor let out a wow. I had never seen a siren transform in person. His tail was a startling ombré blue that matched his eyes. I could see why humans followed them to their death.

"I guess now we wait. What do you want to do?" Eleanor asked, turning to me. I smirked, pulling her against my body.

"I can think of a few things," I teased. She raised an eyebrow, her left eye transforming in color.

"And by a few things do you mean…" she started as her hands trailed down my back before cupping my ass. I let out a chuckle. "Dipping our feet into the water because mine hurt like a centaur's feet," she finished, giving me a slap before walking towards the water's edge. I sighed.

This pixie.

ELEANOR

My pants were rolled up to my knees as I let the warmth of the water relax me. I laid back against the rocky edge, staring at the cloudy sky. We were close to getting things sorted. *So close.* Caleb laid beside me, his leg pressing against mine.

Falling asleep in his arms felt like a promise. It was a preview of something I was afraid to envision, to hope for. It was like I had this hole inside of me that I never noticed until he crawled his way in making me feel complete.

But while a part of me relished in that feeling the other half wanted to run from it. I spent so long taking care of myself it was hard to give someone else the reins. Control was slipping away from me and I found myself slowly letting it go.

His hand gripped my thigh, melting my thoughts. I turned my head to the side to see him watching, his hand kneading my muscle. I raised an eyebrow.

"Caleb?" I asked. His eyes darkened and I felt my throat closed in understanding. "Sailor could come back any second," I whispered as my heart was beating rapidly. His hand trailed further up, gripping harder. Goosebumps erupted all over my covered skin.

"People could be passing by." My voice came out breathier than I wanted. His lips twitched. He knew what he was doing. I turned to stare back at the sky, willing my body to ignore him. He shifted slightly next to me.

"This is payback." His voice was low, his lips tickling my ear.

"For what?" I asked. What the fuck could he be talking about?

"You teased me this morning and last night," he grumbled. A giggle bubbled out of me.

"All I did was try to get off the bed and in order to do so I needed to climb over you. And I didn't know about the ear thing," I said, knowing it was half a lie. Truth was Sailor didn't wake me up. I was already awake and feeling Caleb's erection. It made me feel hot and bothered. So I wanted to tease him a bit. Also I truly didn't know about the ear thing. At least I didn't know it was true.

He cupped me and I gasped as the heel of his hand pressed into my mound.

"I don't like to be teased, Eleanor," he growled. I bit my bottom lip.

"Are you going to punish me?" I asked, sweetly. My body slowly began to awaken with a fire he was brewing. His eyes captured me and his gorgeous lips tugged into a smirk that had me clenching my thighs. I couldn't fucking wait to kiss him.

"Is that why you did it? Because you wanted to be punished?" His voice had a hard edge to it. I did. I fucking wanted to be punished. I enjoyed the way Caleb took control, told me what to do so my only focus was to feel and enjoy.

He pushed me slightly beyond the box of my experiences and I wanted to see how far he could take my body. I rocked my hips against his hand, begging for him to move, to do something. Looking into his hunger filled eyes I couldn't help but smile.

"Yes," I said truthfully. He groaned and reached for the button of my jeans when there was a giant splashed a few feet from us. I jumped away from Caleb who stood up. Sailor was breathing heavily, his hair in his face. He looked between us and rolled his eyes, swimming closer to the edge. I scrambled to my feet.

"Really? I wasn't even gone that long," Sailor muttered. In the water there was a slight flash and Sailor stood up. My eyes widened and Caleb pulled me against his chest to shield my eyes.

"Really Sailor?" Caleb growled. Sailor chuckled. I could practically feel Caleb rolling his eyes. Once Sailor was fully clothed Caleb let me go.

"It's just a penis Caleb. Don't worry, I'll always prefer yours," I said, petting his chest. He looked down to shoot me a possessive glare but than only made me grin wider. I turned to face Sailor.

"Did you find it?" I asked. Sailor's jaw was tight and he nodded, pulling two small shimmering pearls from his pocket. I sighed in relief. It was crazy how something so small was incredibly valuable in our hopes of breaking Caleb's curse.

"Caleb, do you remember the way back to the cottage?" Sailor asked. Caleb nodded. Sailor pulled his backpack on.

"Perfect. You two enjoy the water. I gotta go back to the cottage," he said.

"Wait what?" I asked. Sailor smiled, his eyes still glowing. Did he use magic down there?

"I gotta make sure I'm not seen, remember?" he said. I nodded. That's right. Sailor was hiding from the town. He turned to walk away. "Plus you guys seem to forget I can see your energies. I can *literally* see the sexual tension between you two," he called out, heading into the woods.

I glanced at Caleb who was watching Sailor's retreating figure. Something fluffy caught my eye.

"Are those towels over there?" I asked. Once Sailor was out of eyesight, Caleb pulled me roughly to him.

"Ever been skinny dipping?" he asked, his eyes were bright. The fire he started inside of me reignited.

"Is this the part where we recreate scenes from my books?" I asked. My hands slid up his shoulder and pulled the bun from his hair, setting his blonde locks free.

"Starburst, it's going to be better than your books." His mouth quickly found my favorite spot on my neck. His teeth sunk into my skin sending shivers down my body. He worked his way up and tugged my earlobe.

"Strip lovely and get your body wet for me," he said. He pulled away leaving my body simmering in the cold air. Keeping his eyes on me he began tugging off his clothes. My body tightened with anticipation. Caleb was long and lean with wide shoulders. He folded his clothes and placed them by the towels. I bit my bottom lip as my eyes traveled south. He truly was captivating. His skin seemed to shine against the backdrop of the water. His hair cascaded down and once again reminded me of starlight. My heart rattled against my chest at his beauty.

"Do I need to repeat myself?" His voice was demanding and made my toes curl. I smiled before slowly reaching for my sweater. Might as well give him the same show he unknowingly gave me. I've always been confident in my body.

But watching Caleb's eyes devour me made me feel ethereal and powerful. I unbutton my pants, shrugging them down along with my lace panties. I tossed him my clothes which he folded. He palmed his dick, his eyes following me as I neared the waters edge.

The cold air stung making my nipples puckered. I stepped into the water and moaned at the feel of the warmth climbing over me. I faintly heard Caleb cursed from behind. I waded further into the water before turning to look at him, standing at the water's edge.

"I'm wet Caleb. What do you plan on doing now?" I asked. He smirked and stepped into the water. As he swam closer I began moving towards the waterfall. The closer I got the louder the crashing of the water became.

"I plan on seeing which is louder. You or the waterfall," he said as he swam towards me like a predator.

We both dove under the waterfall to get to the other side. It was even colder. There was a rocky edge perfect for people to sit or lay down. I felt Caleb's hands grip my hips before lifting me out of the water.

"Lay down," he growled. The rocky ground dug into my back deliciously.

"Caleb," I moaned as he threw my legs over his shoulder and nipped the inside of my thigh. He gripped the edge with one hand, keeping himself anchored. I lifted my hips craving his mouth. I wanted to feel his tongue. His light beard was rough against my thighs. I tugged at his hair, pulling him to where I needed him to be. I glared at him.

"Caleb," I pleaded. He raised an eyebrow before sliding a finger up and down my slit, teasing me.

"Yes," I hissed, gripping his hair tighter.

"Play with your nipples," he said as he still only played with the outside of my lips. I brought my other hand and flicked my nipple back and forth, rocking my hips. His finger parted my lips and he brushed my clit. I sucked in a breath.

"Pinch it," he said. The second I pinched my nipple he slid a finger inside and I whimpered. This is what I wanted. I wanted him to turn me into a mess.

"You're so wet, lovely," he whispered. I moaned as we both toyed with my body. His tongue flicked across my clit and he groaned low in his throat. He added a second finger and curled until he hit a spot that had me choking on air. I tugged on him tighter, not caring if I was suffocating him.

He shrugged off one of my legs and opened me further. I couldn't even stop him if I tried. I was riding high on his mouth sucking my clit and his fingers pumping in and out of me. The sound of me becoming undone and the waterfall echoed around us. I let go of his hair to knead my breasts. With the rocky ground digging into my backside, the mist of the waterfall tickling my skin and Caleb pleasuring me it felt like my nerve endings were set on high.

"Yes! Caleb! Fuck!" I cried out, louder and louder, as I tugged on my nipples. Every muscle in my body was tightening in anticipation to explode into pixie dust. Caleb pulled his fingers out just as I was about to reach my peak. I whined at the loss.

"Fury fuck Caleb," I growled. I sat up, pissed as fuck over him keeping my orgasm away. His eyes were glowing, his mouth glistening.

"Now you know how it feels," he said smirking. This fucking Elf King of Eating Pussy. My eyes hardened before I took matters into my own hands...literally. I dipped my finger inside of myself.

"I don't need you to make me come," I threw out. My head rolled to the side as I felt my fingered glide in and out. Caleb cursed. I slipped two fingers inside. The water was gently moving back and forth beneath my calves and I rocked with it.

"Your hand isn't going to satisfy you the way I can," he growled. I moaned as I moved my fingers faster. With my other hand I pinched my nipple.

"But I'm so close right now," I said, another moan escaping as I stared at Caleb. His body was incredibly tense. I was pushing him and I knew it. Because while I admit that I enjoyed how Caleb allowed me to lose control I also loved it when he did. He moved closer and I opened my legs wider, letting him enjoy the view.

"Eleanor," he groaned, his hands gripping the rocky edge, holding himself in place in the water.

"Don't you want to watch me make myself scream or would you rather be the reason I do?" I asked, breathlessly. I moved my thumb to play with my clit, setting my own heart racing. I was close again. So fucking close. I mewled. I wanted Caleb to touch me. I needed him to satisfy me.

He must have sensed it because he pulled my hand away, gripping my hips. I wrapped my legs around his head and one of his hands came up to massage my breasts. I arched my back and placed one hand down to hold myself up as his tongue caressed my clit. He squeezed my nipple as his tongue flicked against the bundle of nerves.

"C-Caleb yes, fuck. Please," I hissed, rocking against his head. I dug my fingers into the rocks to keep myself upright. His thumbs pressed into my nipples and with a rough suck stars bursted in the corner of my eyes. I cried out his name. Tears rolled down my cheeks as I tried to get air into my lungs.

He pushed me back so I was laying down and my body trembled. He lifted himself from the water, knees digging into the rocks. Water splattered across my hot skin and I hissed as he took my nipple in his mouth. Once he was done ravishing my chest he made his way up my throat.

"I can't wait to fucking kiss you," his whispered into my ear. He pressed his body against me, his cock digging into my stomach.

"My turn," I panted as I exposed more of my neck to him.

CHAPTER 16
WATERFALLS ARE STILL STEAMY

CALEB

She was breathing heavily and her voice was hoarse from screaming my name. She was wet, a mixture of sweat and water. Her left eye was bright green. I smiled knowing I was the reason for her euphoric feeling. Her chest had splotches of pink that matched her hair from where I bruised her skin with my mouth.

"My turn," she repeated with a grin. Her eyes were no longer looking at me but on my dick.

"Sailor is probably waiting for us," I said which in part was probably true.

"Your cock says otherwise," she said, lifting her hips. I pressed into her on instinct with a groan.

"It's my turn to take care of you," she said pleading. I clenched my jaw. My hands dug into the earth on either side of her head as she took me in her hand.

"Do you get turned on by making me come?" she asked. I pulled my head back to look at her and nodded. She began stroking me, slow and hard.

"Eleanor," I said, grounding into her hand. Fuck, I loved having her hands on me. Every stroke, every touch was filled with confidence.

"I want to make you feel good the way you always make me feel good," she said. She didn't need to touch me to make me feel good. She just needed to be around me, smile with me, laugh at and with me. She, herself was more than enough to fill the empty pages in my life with sonnets and poetry. I now understood why some shanties were dedicated to lovers. I grasped the meaning of why sailors sung songs of deep longing for the ones who made their heart a home.

Stars, there was no way I could resist her.

"Get in the water," I growled. She smiled wickedly. We switched positions and I sat on the edge of the rocks. I didn't give a shit that the gravel was digging into my ass. My hand gripped the back of her neck to anchor her to the edge. With one hand on the ledge and the other hand on my dick she began stroking me again. She kept her eyes on me, following every breath I took.

"I want to hear you," she said as the waterfall raged on as if urging us. She licked her lips. I needed my cock in her mouth. I pushed my thumb in her mouth and groaned as her tongue teased me.

"You want my cock my sweet pixie?" I asked. She nodded eagerly. *Fucking gorgeous.* She pulled herself closer taking me in her mouth and I closed my eyes, losing myself in the sensation of her tongue licking around my head. She pulled me further into her mouth and I took in a sharp breath. Fucking stars, this pixie. I glanced down watching my cock disappear in and out from between her lips.

"I can't wait to fucking take you," I hissed as she began to suck and it took every once of self control to not buck my hips.

"Can you take me deeper?" I choke out. She giggled. She fucking giggled as her head bobbed deeper, taking me to where I nearly hit the back of her throat. I groaned loudly like she wanted me to. My hand tightened in her hair, maneuvering her faster as I felt my climax on the edge. She moaned deeply and I could feel the vibration around my cock. *She's fucking perfect.* My thighs began to shake. I felt a tingle at the base of my spine.

This was happening way too fast but I couldn't stop it. Next time I would make sure to take my time, to savor her mouth. But she's had me on edge since last night. Warmth began spreading in my lower belly and my head fell back.

"I'm going to come in your pretty pixie mouth," I growled. She pumped faster, her hand tightening at the base, thumb stroking the under seam and her tongue swirling. "Fucking shit Eleanor," I choked out.

The warmth quickly burned a trail up my body until I exploded in her mouth. My eyes squeezed shut as I lost myself in her hot wet mouth. She continued to suck and swallow every last drop, making me tremble. She released me with a loud pop and a mischievous smirk.

"That was quick, Elfie," she teased with a smile.

"You're going to be the death of me," I said, still trying to catch my breath. She shrugged her shoulders.

"No better way to go don't you think?" she said. I let out a chuckle. "By the way we were both laying down in some sandy dirt so can you make sure my ass is clean before we change?" she said with a twinkle in her eyes.

Dammit Eleanor.

---- ❄ ❄ ❄ ----

IT WAS ALMOST the afternoon by the time we made it back to the cottage. Sailor was on the couch by the fireplace reading a book. His eyes flickered between us. He smiled.

"I take it you had fun?" he said, smirking. Eleanor blushed, kicking off her shoes.

"Water can do wonders for stress," she said. I bit back a smile. *Wonders for sure.*

"We have to pick up the moss at Meryl's," I said. Sailor twitched.

"And then we'll head out," he said, jaw tight.

"The sooner the better?" Eleanor asked. She posed it as a question.

We both could tell being here was hard on Sailor. He looked at us, his eyes broken.

"Yes," he said softly.

"Do you need anything?" I asked. I had never seen a siren transformed before. I wonder if it took much out of him. Sailor had mentioned sirens were very secretive about things and honestly my knowledge of them was limited. He nodded.

"It takes a lot out of me to transform," he said. Eleanor curled up on the couch and I sat beside her, pulling her close.

"If you don't mind me asking, is it always exhausting?" she asked tentatively. Sailor gave a lopsided smile.

"I don't mind. So technically no it's not. But I haven't transformed in a long time so it's kind of like riding a bike in a way," he explained.

"You don't...transform in Lavender Falls? We have Boogeyman's Swamp," Eleanor said. Sailor continued to look into the fire.

"I know that. It's just not the same. Being with my tail...just brings back memories," he said. Eleanor tensed.

"I'm sorry we had you transform," she said softly. Sailor shook his head.

"For you guys I did it. Don't feel bad. I would do it again if you asked." He grinned even though it didn't quite reach his eyes. "I also missed it," he said softly. I bit the inside of my cheek.

"Sailor?" I called out. He finally turned away from the fire.

"Carrie is a siren too," I said. He tensed up immediately again.

"Yes," he kept his tone even.

"Is she from here?" I asked, tentatively. Carrie arrived a year before Sailor but we don't know much about her except her ancestors owned Sailor's Saloon. Sailor took a deep breath.

"Yes," he confessed, placing his book on the cofee table.

"Was it hard to get the pearl?" I asked, changing the subject. He clearly didn't want to talk about her or this place. Something flickered in his eyes.

"No it wasn't," he said.

"I'm surprised the waterfall had pearls blessed by the royal blood-line," Eleanor said. Sailor stretched.

"The waterfall has a channel that connects to the ocean. So things from the ocean end up there. There's also a cave there too. But you have to be able to hold your breath a long time to get there," Sailor spoke plainly. Eleanor looked at me. We both had a feeling about Sailor and his family. And if we were thinking the correct thing, Sailor needed to leave town asap.

"Let's go check on Meryl," I said, pulling Eleanor up. Sailor needed space. I would give him what he needed. And if he wanted to talk I would be there too. Despite his constant sunshine there was more to him. I felt stupid for never noticing. Sometimes those with the most clouds shine the brightest to keep them away.

"I'm going to take a nap and then pack up," he said, leaning his head back and closing his eyes.

CHAPTER 17
WE'RE BACK

ELEANOR

The door to Calder's Apothecary chimed. This time we weren't the only ones in the store. Meryl was talking to a tall older woman with pale blonde hair and brown eyes. She looked elegant, regal. She glanced at us and smiled warmly.

"You must be the tourists," she said kindly. I smiled, slipping into my deputy mayor persona.

"Hello! I'm Eleanor and this is Caleb. We came by to pick up something we needed for our town," I said, politely.

"Lavender Falls was it?" she asked. I glanced at Meryl who looked away quickly. Gotta love small towns.

"Yes. My friend owns a potion shop and she needed some special sea moss for a remedy," Caleb interjected. The beautiful woman's eyes glittered with disappointment.

"Ah, she did?" she asked. I nodded.

"Well my name is Marina. Thank you so much for coming to our town. I believe you're the second couple to have visited from Lavender Falls," she said. I blushed. I was going to deny Caleb and I being a couple when he spoke up.

138

"Our friends spoke highly of your town. Hopefully next time we can visit for fun." His hand slid around my hip and he pulled me close. My heart leaped. He didn't deny it.

But we haven't even discussed the terms and conditions of our relationship. We started the whole thing as a way to help each other, to scratch an itch. My stomach tightened. I felt nauseous all of a sudden. I don't think I was ready to think about the definition of *us*.

"You should visit in the summer. That's when Coralia Coast is at its best. We even have a special festival," she said. Dammit. I love festivals.

"I love a good festival. That sounds amazing! Maybe we can bring our whole friend group," I said, nodding.

"Please do! And apologies if the towns folk seemed a bit off. It's been a rough year," she said, still managing a smile. I nodded along.

"Understandable," I said. Marina waved us off and exited the shop. I glanced out the window shop and watched her shoulders sag in sadness. Something told me she knew Sailor. But it wasn't my place to say anything. Everyone had secrets for a reason.

"I'm sorry but the sea moss isn't ready yet," Meryl said sadly. I looked at Caleb. Kraken crap. We needed to leave here asap.

"That's fine we can come back later," I said and tugged Caleb out the door.

OUTSIDE WE GOT SLAPPED with an icy breeze. The town felt like a ghost town with no one in the streets. But I couldn't blame them. It was fucking freezing. Sure it was winter but being near the ocean made things feel even colder. I was annoyed that we were even out here. We walked along the sidewalk that bordered the beach again. Despite the weirdness of the town it was quite beautiful. The ocean raged on as if angry and the shops were all colorful.

"It seems like the Calder Family owns nearly every place here,"

Caleb commented. I nodded along. He tugged me closer, cocooning me in his warmth. Even though we were here on saving the town kind of business I could almost fool myself into thinking we were on a couples vacation.

Almost. We weren't a couple. I wasn't even sure what we were. We've been using our time, our bodies together to destress but the more time we spent together the more I wanted to do normal couple things.

My heart skipped with fear. The past began rearing its ugly head, filling my thoughts. *Can't you just be less? Can't you tone it down? Do you always have to be this extra?* I swallowed the lump in my throat as I snuck a glance at Caleb. His light blonde hair was pulled into a low bun and even his cheeks were a little pink from the cold.

"Caleb?" I said, getting his attention. His eyes softened when he looked at me which only made my fear grow.

"Yes, Starburst?" he asked. But before I could open my mouth someone interrupted us.

"You guys are still here?" We turned to see Mira bundled up in a cozy sweater. She looked around us.

"Um yeah we're still here but should be leaving soon," I said. I slipped my hand to grip Caleb's. Mira's eyes kept looking around.

"Is…your *friend* still here?" she asked, her eyes wide with worry. My stomach dropped. "Is he…is he okay?" she asked. I sucked in a breath. She did know.

"How do you know who our friend might be?" Caleb asked with narrowed eyes. She took a deep breath, tucking a rogue strand of hair behind her ear.

"I'm family. That's all I want to say. Just tell me if he's happy?" she asked. I nodded slightly. She gave a wobbly smile. She looked at her hands.

"That's good. Good," she said weakly. "Could you tell him one thing?" she asked. I pulled away from Caleb to step closer to her. Something in her tone pulled me.

"Of course," I said, gently placing a hand on her arm. She smiled slightly.

"Tell him I miss him."

CALEB and I once again didn't speak until we were safely back in the cottage. Sailor had just brought his bag to the front door. He glanced at our empty hands.

"It wasn't ready yet?" he asked disappointedly. I shook my head. He cursed, running a hand through his hair.

"Um..Sailor?" I needed to bring up Mira. We needed to bring up all the weird encounters we've been having. There was a knock at the door and we all froze. Sailor stared at me with wide eyes. By the stars, who was that? I looked at Caleb who began dragging Sailor into the kitchen. Taking a deep breath I opened the door.

Meryl stood before me, out of breath with a big bag. Her eyes were filled with worry and her red hair was falling out of her bun.

"Here. I'm giving you three jars just so your friend can have extra. Inside the bag is my business card. If she ever needs anything else she can ring us. Despite what you might think about the town and how sirens tend to keep to themselves we would love to establish a relationship with Lavender Falls." She smiled brightly, cheek flushed. I took the bag wordlessly.

"As deputy mayor of Lavender Falls I think that would be a wonderful idea. Supernatural towns should support each other," I said.

Which was true. Relationships between supernatural towns were valuable and important. We needed to stick together in this world. And I couldn't figure out why but I felt like this town needed us. She stared at me although her eyes were searching for someone else. I think she was fighting the urge to look around the house.

"Promise me you'll get out of here asap. *All of you,*" she whispered. I nodded, feeling my heart break but not understanding why. This time she turned away from me and looked towards the wall behind me that hid the kitchen.

"We miss you," she said before walking away. I closed the door and turned to see Sailor and Caleb walking out from the kitchen. Sailor's brows were furrowed. The sky outside darkened.

"Sailor?" I asked tentatively. He clenched his fist and the cup of water that was on top of the coffee table exploded. I jumped back.

"Let's go," he said with gritted teeth.

WE DIDN'T BRING up the blonde woman until we were an hour away from Coralia Coast. I wanted to make sure we had distance between us. Sailor didn't say anything when we mentioned her.

"There's something else," I started to say. I turned to my seat to look at him. His eyes were still filled with pain. He nodded for me to continue. "Our waitress Mira…" I trailed off. Recognition glinted in his eyes and softened a bit.

"My cousin," he said softly.

"She said she misses you," I said gently. Sailor rubbed his chest and nodded solemnly.

"Thank you for telling me and thank you for not asking too many questions," he said. I nodded.

"We all have secrets Sailor. Just know we're here for you," Caleb chimed in. Sailor laid his head against the window.

"I'll tell you guys everything one day. Just not today," he said, closing his eyes. We all stayed quiet the whole drive back to town.

AFTER ARRIVING in Lavender Falls we each went our separate ways. Sailor went back to his apartment. Caleb went to take the moss and pearl to Priscilla and I met Crystal at Coffin's Coffee Shop.

She was in dark jeans and a Hale's Lumber Industry sweatshirt. Her hair was pulled back into a ponytail. She looked more relaxed. I sat across from her and she smiled.

"I ordered you lavender lemon tea," she said. I smiled. She still remembered.

"Just what I needed," I said, pulling out my laptop.

"How was Coralia?" she asked. I thought about it for a moment.

"Despite the chilly welcome, the town itself is beautiful. Rustic and beachy," I said and then giggled. Crystal raised an eyebrow. "Remember how you were obsessed with the small town from Mystic Pizza?" I asked.

"Despite how they pronounced Portuguese and portrayed us, yes," she said with a wrinkled nose.

"The town reminded me of that location," I said. The movie was about a Portuguese woman who worked at a pizzeria and fell for the rich white guy. His family considered Portuguese people beneath them. But they did end up happily ever after.

Crystal loved and hated that movie as a kid. We both enjoyed it because we got to see a bit of our culture but hated the stereotypical references. I would often ask her why she wanted to watch it and she said she loved the coastal town. Her eyes softened.

"That sounds lovely," she said. I nodded.

"We also got everything we needed. So now it's up to Priscilla," I said as my tea arrived. I took a sip, sighing at the flavors. Crystal cleared her throat.

"Let's get down to business," she said and then started to sing the song from Mulan. I rolled my eyes.

"I see you still like to recite lyrics from music." I said, giggling.

"Habit. Anyway, Celestino has the clearing in the forest squared away. We have some performers confirmed. Lilianna created the sign up for all the competitions this week and she'll post it tomorrow. We wanted to confirm the prize money for the ice sculpture, pie bake off and snowball fight tournament," she rattled off. I nodded along.

"How much is Hale's willing to donate?" I asked. She tapped away on her laptop.

"Alright so we're offering a thousand dollars per competition along with a year's supply of firewood and I'm assuming the other sponsors are offering something as well?" she asked.

"They'll be offering new state of the art tools for the ice sculpture competition and the bake off. For the snowball fight tournament it's certificates that can be used for the year from each sponsor's respective businesses," I said adding everything into my notes.

"That works for us," she said, closing her laptop. Her hazel eyes were drawn in.

"The swamp is getting worse and people are starting to talk," she said tensely. I took a deep breath.

"They should know it's connected to the tree," I suggested carefully. She nodded.

"*He's* afraid they'll connect the company to the tree." She stared into her tea. I took a deep breath.

"If he has nothing to hide then he wouldn't be worried about it," I stated, an edge to my voice. Crys bit her bottom lip.

"You want to set up a meeting with him?" she asked tentatively. Taking a deep breath I thought about it for a moment. Did I want to be in the same room as my father especially after he barged his way into the tavern? No.

But I also needed to confront him on what the fuck was happening with the tree. I was almost 29 and this man who disowned me years ago still thought he had some control over me. I hated it. I needed to show him he couldn't push me around. I wasn't one of his employees and I sure as a hellhound on a mission to bring back a soul didn't need him underestimating me. It was time someone put him in his place.

"Set up the meeting Crystal," I said. She nodded and began typing. She paused and looked up from her screen with a smile. I couldn't help but smile back.

"What's with that look, Crys?"I asked. She leaned forward.

"Does Lily still sing?" she asked. I nodded. Crystal squeezed her hands together to contain her excitement.

"Do you think we could convince her to sing a *fado* song at the festival?" she asked. My eyes widened.

"Oh she is so going to!"

CALEB

"How was the trip?" Flynn asked once the tavern began winding down for the night. I glanced up to see where Bridget was. She was closing out a customer in the back corner. I wiped down the bar.

"Coralia Coast was...interesting. Sailor was right about sirens being secretive," I said. Flynn nodded. "It was weird though. Sailor had to stay in hiding. I wanted to ask but it was obvious he didn't want to talk about it," I said as I rearranged the alcohol. Flynn began putting the glasses back in their place.

"Yeah, he's always been quiet about his town ever since he moved here. But you guys got the pearl right and the moss?" he asked. His brown eyes looked so much like our dad's. I haven't even told our dad about the possibility of the curse being broken. Both my parents felt so much guilt after the accident happened I was afraid of giving them hope.

"Yeah. Hopefully it breaks the curse," I said.

"What curse?" Bridget asked. I froze. *Fucking stars.* I didn't hear her walking. I looked at her. She was around my height, same white blonde hair as me but with honey brown eyes. They were wide with curiosity.

"Don't worry about it," Flynn said, interjecting. She rolled her eyes.

"I'm not six anymore. Telling me to not worry about it isn't going to make me worry less," she said, crossing her arms. Which was true. We were a stubborn ass family. And if Bridget sniffed out an issue, especially involving one of us she was ready to lift a sword to help out.

"It's nothing Bridget," I said. She raised an eyebrow.

"You know secrets have a way of coming out right?" she said, leaning against the bar. I glanced at Flynn whose hands were gripping the glasses. I know for a fact he was remembering four year old Bridget. The pain in her cries were forever etched into our brains. Our poor little sister made a mistake. And while I forgave her the second it happened she couldn't forgive herself.

BRIDGET WOULDN'T GO near me. Every time I walked into a room she scurried away. At dinner she refused to meet my eyes. I tried so hard to talk to her but every time I uttered a syllable she began shaking. And what was worse was she would wake up in the middle of the night crying out loud.

"I'm sorry. I'm sorry." She would repeat over and over again as our mom held her in her arms, trying to rock her back to sleep.

My parents couldn't take it anymore. And so once the divorce papers were signed they sat my brothers and I down and came up with an idea.

"As you know boys I'll be moving out. We think for the sake of your sister's mental well being we erase her memories of the incident," dad said. His voice was like steel, hardened in resolve. They weren't asking us our opinion. They were telling us what was going to happen.

"That's serious dad. Are you sure?" Greg asked. I had a sour taste in my mouth. I didn't like this idea.

"Afterwards Caleb you'll be living with me," he said.

"What?! No!" Flynn shouted.

"Flynn, do not raise your voice," mom scolded.

"You can't take Caleb away from us," Greg pleaded. Mom wiped the tears from her face.

"It's not forever. We're going to try and get the curse removed. That involves a lot of travel," mom explained. I looked at dad. He had shadows under his eyes and his face creased with worry. I bet it was the stress; the ache of what happened. He probably felt like it was his fault. Both my parents probably felt that way. I took a deep breath.

"Maybe it's for the best. We need to see if we can break the curse and with erasing Bridget's memories I should be away. I don't want to trigger anything for her," I said quietly.

Everyone looked at me in surprise. I heard Flynn, Greg and my mom sniffle. They were probably crying. But I refused to look at them. If I did I would crack. I needed to be strong for them. I stared at my dad. He nodded silently. And that's when the weight began nestling itself on my shoulders. The weight of wanting to take care of my family, to not be a burden. And that was the same time my heart began to close.

"I'M GOING to find out at some point," Bridget pointed out. Flynn turned away. If he stayed a part of this conversation he would crack. I knew he would. But I've been practicing this façade for years. I was the one that created the icy wall between us while Flynn and Greg had a nice relationship with her.

"I'm your big brother. If I tell you not to worry, don't," I said firmly, narrowing my eyes. She bawled her hands into fist and I could see the hurt in her eyes. The wall I built up between us was back up higher. Ever since I moved back into town I've been careful with my relationship with her, terrified that the spell we casted on her years ago would break somehow.

But would that be so bad? For her to know the truth? If I broke this curse then she would never have to find out. She wouldn't have to feel that pain again. Biting the inside of my cheek I continue to do what I've taught myself to be good at; burying my emotions and work.

CHAPTER 18
DANCE THE NIGHT AWAY

ELEANOR

LILY

Today is Throwback Thursday at the tavern...

LOLA

Is Lily suggesting a night out on a weekday??

The magic going off must be affecting Lily's brainwaves

LILY

HAHA I can have fun you know. Maybe we should do a dance night?

LOLA

Yes! We all deserve a break

Don't let me drink tequila tonight

LOLA

You could always curl up in Caleb's bed upstairs

LILY

You've done it already...

I'll be sleeping in my own bed

LOLA

...with Caleb

Flynn might be working tonight

LOLA

How dare you bring my rival in this?!

LILY

Well why not?

LOLA

He is the enemy.

The rival.

The man who has always gotten under my skin

You could let him get under you

LILY

or over you if that's what you like

LOLA

I think we've finally corrupted Lily

What has Tino taught you?

LILY

We literally read smut...I know things okay?

The question is have you've done any of them

After spending the afternoon with Ben going over vendors I was happy to be back in my apartment with Crystal getting ready. I stared at myself in the mirror. I had a few bags under my eyes and my skin was slowly losing its glow.

A part of me wanted to think it was because of the colder weather but I could feel my magic slipping. I bit the inside of my cheek. Not tonight. Tonight I was going to have fun. No worries, just my friends and I.

"Is this appropriate?" Crystal called out, stepping out of the bathroom. She wore black tights with a black skirt and slightly cropped olive green sweater. She fidgeted with the hem of her sweater. I glanced at her feet.

"Are you a size eight?" I asked her, walking towards my closet.

"I am," she said. I rummaged through my closet until I found the box I was looking for.

"Wear these! Cute and comfy." I handed her my pair of black knee high boots. Her face brightened.

"These are beautiful!" My heart squeezed. I learned very quickly it was rare to see Crystal smile so freely. As much as I was looking forward to this night, I really wanted it to be a night for her to let loose and enjoy.

THE TAVERN WAS BUSTLING with people as music blasted through speakers reminding me of clubbing during college. Lola was dressed in a beige tight knit dress that had a slit revealing burgundy faux leather boots. She had her arm looped through mine as we made our way towards the bar.

Lily waved and reached for Crystal's hand. Glancing quickly at them I noticed how much Crystal leaned towards Lily. Maybe it was because Lily was an introvert that Crystal felt more comfortable. Whatever the reason, I was happy that Crystal was with us.

"Rider!" Lola called out in a singsong voice. Flynn was behind the bar with Caleb and visibly groaned. I stifled a giggle.

"Why are you here?" Flynn asked. Lola rolled her eyes.

"We came to have alcoholic beverages while shaking our asses on the dance floor," Lola said. Flynn's eyes trailed up and down Lola's body. Her grip on my arm tightened. I tried not to flinch at her vampire strength.

"Try not to flash anyone," he asked. She gave him a toothy grin.

"Why not? Maybe I want to get lucky tonight," she said. Flynn clenched his jaw before turning to Lily who was standing behind us.

"The usual?" he asked Lily who nodded. I finally looked at Caleb. I could feel his eyes on me during the entire conversation. He raised a single eyebrow before holding out my signature night out shot. I reached over to grab it and he pulled away. I leaned over the bar to grab it from him again. When my hand reached the glass Caleb leaned in, pressing a kiss to my neck. Heat curled up my face.

"You're not ignoring me are you?" he whispered in my ear. I rolled my eyes, quickly downing the shot. Lola smirked at us. Flynn handed each of the girls a shot. Crystal eyed it for a second before accepting.

"Where is-" Lily began but an arm around her waist cut her off. Celestino smiled widely at his girlfriend.

"Hey there Posey," Celestino said, kissing her cheek. Lily blushed a deep red, clearly embarrassed by the public affection. Sailor appeared next to Crystal. I watched as my sister gave him a small smile. I bit the inside of my cheek to stop from grinning. Sailor mouthed hello and she nodded back in hello.

We formed a tiny circle, eyes wide with excitement. I grabbed two more shots to hand to Celestino and Sailor. Now we were ready to start the night.

"Let's just have fun tonight," I said sincerely. I looked around my group of friends, smiling. This is definitely what we needed. Lily patted Sailor's shoulder after everyone took a shot.

"How are you?" Lily asked. Sailor looked between us and shrugged his shoulders.

"I'm okay guys," he said. Lola crossed her arms and Celestino squeezed Sailor's shoulder. Crystal looked at all of us slightly confused. "I promise to tell you when I'm ready. For now let's just have fun," Sailor said, giving us his infamous princely smile. I reached for his hand and Crystal's and dragged them to the dance floor. It was time to dance the night away.

I SAID I didn't want to drink tequila but that was three shots ago. Crystal was like an awkward guppy on the dance floor. She would slightly flinch anytime someone who wasn't us would dance too close to her. Sailor was dancing with a fairy while Lilianna and Celestino were lost to each other. I smiled at Lola who was trying not to laugh at Crystal.

I grabbed my sister's hands and we swayed to the music together. She relaxed slightly with a grateful smile. From the corner of my eye I saw Lola slip into a grind with someone. Crystal's eyes wandered around. I leaned towards her ear.

"You can sit down if you like," I said. She let out a giant sigh of relief that had me throwing back my head in laughter. "Go sit Crys," I said, giving her a slight shove. At least she tried. I watched her head back to the bar when I felt a hand on my shoulder.

A man taller than me with short brown hair held out his hand for a dance. On any other night I would have gladly taken it but for the first time I hesitated. I quickly glanced at Caleb who was busy manning the bar. Why did I care if he saw me dance with someone? It's not like he hasn't seen me go home with plenty of guys. We weren't an item.

We were just two people using intimacy as a way to destress from our current situation. And I was probably saying this as an excuse to ignore my emotions. It was also just a dance. With that final thought I slipped my hand into the stranger's and let him help me forget all about the man behind the bar and the Hollow Tree.

CALEB

"May I have some water please," Crystal asked Flynn. It was strange to see that even though Crystal and Eleanor looked like sisters they were the opposite in personalities. Eleanor was vibrant and made herself known while Crystal seemed comfortable blending into the background. Flynn smiled and I could tell his flirty charm was flipped on.

"Of course darling. Anything else? Want me to add some lime or lemon?" he asked, leaning against the bar. I rolled my eyes. I was a witness to Flynn's shameless flirting for the past few years. Crystal blushed.

"May I have some water too?" Sailor asked. Crystal jumped at his voice and Sailor reached to grab her shoulders before she could fall off the seat. She turned around to look at him.

"T-thanks," she stuttered. He offered her a sweet smile before snatching the water out of Flynn's hands and handing it to her. She nodded in thanks. Sailor blue eyes turned to me. He seemed more at ease now that we've been back in Lavender Falls.

"Your girl is dancing with some guy," Sailor pointed out. My mouth twisted. On the dance floor grinding on some stranger was my pixie. Some other man had their greasy hands all over her. Flynn slapped my shoulder.

"Could you not send death glares to our paying customers," he said. Crystal snorted, hiding her laugh with her hand.

"He won't be a customer for long if he gets any closer to grabbing her ass," I said, wrapping my hand around a towel.

"Lola is also dancing with someone," Crystal pointed out. Flynn shrugged his shoulders. Why he might have looked like he didn't care I noticed the way his eyes wandered around, seeking the vampire.

"Would you like to dance?" Sailor asked Crystal, hand outstretched. She stared at it for a second.

"I'm fine here," she said nervously. Sailor's shoulders slightly dropped.

"Are you sure?" he asked. She nodded, turning to stare at the people having fun. Sailor nodded, turning away.

"Sailor!" I called out. He turned around, raising an eyebrow. I waved him over.

"Tell Eleanor if that guy doesn't take his hands off of her I'm kicking her out," I said with a smirk. Sailor grinned, happy to oblige. He walked over, disrupting their grinding. Eleanor's eyes widened in anger as Sailor whispered in her ear.

"Why did you do that?" Crystal asked.

"Because now she's coming here," I said. Eleanor marched her way towards the bar, cheeks red, eyes glaring.

"Are you serious?" Eleanor said. Crystal's eyes widened at her sister's anger. "Kick me out? For dancing with someone?" she asked, her voice getting higher. I crossed my arms over my chest.

"Yes," I said.

"Why?" she asked.

"His hands were all over you," I said.

"And that gives you a right to kick me out?" she asked, mimicking my pose.

"His hands shouldn't be on you," I said. She scoffed loudly before leaning towards me.

"He can have his hands all over me if I let him," she hissed. My blood boiled. No he fucking couldn't. In fact no one could. I looked at Flynn who nodded, reaching for the remote that controlled the music volume. Coming around the bar I grabbed Eleanor's wrist and began dragging her away. She tugged her arm backwards but that made my grip on her wrist tighten.

"Where are we going?" she practically yelled over the music. Instead of heading upstairs I turned to the side and opened the storage room, pushing her inside. I could feel my heartbeat pounding in my ears. In the lowlight of the closet I could barely make out her flushed cheeks.

"Caleb," she stated, anger barely on the surface of her voice as it was replaced by something else. The music outside grew louder. "Why does Flynn keep turning up the music?"

I stepped towards her and her back hit the shelf piled with cleaning supplies.

"Because I need to remind you who you belong to and I don't need anyone else knowing what you sound like when you scream my name," I said before reaching under her tights. She squeezed her thighs, trapping my hands before I had a chance to rip them.

"I don't belong to anyone," she said. I leaned down to graze my lips against her neck. She sucked in a deep breath and her thighs squeezed again. I kissed up her neck and let my tongue trace the shell of her ear. Her hands gripped my shoulders as she turned her head to give me more access to her neck.

Slowly her legs gave away and my fingers lazily traced up and down on the inside of her thighs.

"So you're telling me I won't find you wet if I slip my fingers inside of your panties?" I asked, nipping her ear. She shivered.

"If I'm wet it's only because I got sweaty from dancing," she said. I chuckled, my fingers digging into her thigh as I pressed her against the shelf. She moaned softly.

"From dancing with another guy," I stated.

"Guess you're not the only guy who can make me wet," she said nonchalantly. I chuckled darkly.

"You're going to regret saying that, Starburst," I hissed, before dropping to my knees. I quickly ripped her tights and Eleanor gasped. Instead of tugging her underwear down I ripped them as well. Eleanor shoved my shoulder.

"What the fuck? I have to walk home Caleb," she exclaimed.

"Shit. Looks like you'll stay here tonight," I said as I kissed up her thigh. Her hand slipped into my hair.

"If I don't see stars I'll walk home with my freezing ass hanging out Caleb Kiernan," she stated. *Challenge accepted.* "But can I lean against the door and not against the bleach? I'm not a fan of the idea of accidentally bleaching my pubic hair."

We quickly switched and I had my finger swiping up and down between her folds. Eleanor's body tightened in anticipation. I kissed the inside of her thigh, nudging her legs further apart. She widened her stance, anchoring her hand on my head as she pressed her shoulders against the door and her hips forward.

"You smell delicious. So wet for me," I said and her fingers tightened as my tongue barely grazed her clit.

"Stop playing Caleb," she hissed. I smirked before plunging a finger inside. Eleanor gasped.

"You sure you're soaking wet for him and not for me," I said as I worked two fingers in and out of her, my mouth sucking her clit. Eleanor let out a deep moan as she rocked her hips against my face.

"Is this for me?" I asked as I scissored my fingers and I felt her pussy clench. I flicked her clit with my tongue and she rocked faster, chasing the high I was giving her. My other hand dug into her thigh, eliciting another moan.

"Fuck Caleb," she yelped as I slapped the side of her ass.

"Answer me Eleanor," I demanded. I leaned back to look up at her. She was biting down on her lower lip. I slid my fingers out, gently rubbing her clit. "Eleanor."

"It's only for you," she confessed. I grinned, slamming my fingers back inside of her. Eleanor let out a delicious gasp. She was becoming undone and soon she would learn I was the only one who could make her fall apart.

I twisted my fingers, pumping faster and Eleanor moaned loudly. Her legs were shaking as she got lost in the rhythm. I slipped my other hand under her sweater to squeeze her nipple.

Eleanor mewled, banging the door with her hand as she tugged my hair harder. She tasted delicious and I continued my feast until she screamed my name. Her legs wobbled slightly and I slid her down to settle on my lap, knowing I would have to grab a new apron after. She was still trying to get a hold of her breathing when I tapped my fingers on her lips.

"Suck my fingers clean and see how wet I made you," I growled, gripping her jaw. Eleanor took a deep breath before doing what she was told. Her eyes rolled to the back of her head in a moan. I slipped my hand under her sweater and played with the lace edge of her bra. She began rocking again, ready for another round. Music was still blaring outside. I pressed my forehead against hers enjoying the smell of her arousal mixing with her sweet perfume.

"You're going to eventually learn that I don't share Eleanor. Now let's get cleaned up. I expect you to be in my bed after my shift."

FLYNN SMIRKED at us as we made our way back to the bar. I looked over at Eleanor who was busy fixing her hair. Her other hand clutched my plaid shirt that laid over her lap as she sat at the bar. A pretty blush stained her cheeks. Fuck, she was beautiful. She was like a warm summer day. Everything she touched turned into light, including myself. Not only did she brighten my day but she made me want to be in the sun with her.

"You can turn the music down now," Lola bellowed at the bar. Flynn rolled his eyes.

"I'm not sure what you mean," he said as he poured a beer. Lola gave him a mischievous smile.

"Aw Rider. So innocent are you," she teased. The tips of Flynn's ears turned red. This man was on his way to being a goner for the vampire. Crystal and Lilianna giggled as Flynn leaned against the bar. His eyes narrowed at Lola.

"I can assure you I'm not," he said. I handed Eleanor a glass of water which she gulped down.

"Why don't you show me one day?" Lola gave him a toothy smile. Crystal coughed into her hand.

"So does everyone in Lavender Falls have sexual tension?" Crystal asked. Eleanor choked on her water and we all laughed. Crystal looked around us, wide eyed with a pink face. Sailor leaned towards her.

"More like sexual frustrations," Sailor said. Flynn gave a beer to Celestino who couldn't stop smiling.

"Frustrations?" Crystal questioned, innocently. I looked over at Eleanor who was smiling at the interaction. A part of me felt jealous. I was happy that Eleanor reunited with her sister. You could see their bond slowly rebuilding. I glanced at Bridget who was handing a table their beers. I wish my relationship with Bridget was different.

But as an older brother I wanted to protect her from pain. That pain she went through as a child cut her deep but also me. I didn't want her to relive that.

"Some people just need to give in," Sailor said, glancing at Flynn. Crystal took a sip of water and wrinkled her nose.

"To their sexual frustrations in a bar? That's not sanitary," Crystal said. Lily snorted out her drink and Sailor barked out a laugh. I couldn't help but join in the laughter.

"The closet has cleaning supplies," Eleanor said, blushing.

CHAPTER 19
GIRLS NIGHT IN A DARK FOREST

ELEANOR

"Yes I understand that the water in the apartment building is turning green."

"So you casted a clean up spell and instead of cleaning your shop it made everything dirtier?"

"You tried sprinkling pixie dust to keep your flowers fresh and instead they began throwing dirt at you?"

"The heat spell you use that keeps your oven at the perfect temperature has burned everything at Godmother's Patisserie?"

I dug my fingers into my shoulder muscle, hoping it would relieve some tension. I had been dealing with calls all day with things going wrong around town. At first Emily was handling them but the more that came in the more overwhelmed she became. And while I loved Lavender Falls some of the folks here had a quick fuse.

Spells and incantations had been doing the opposite of what they were supposed to be doing and when they tried doing the opposite spells it just made things ten times worse. I chewed my bottom lip. I was worried that if things were beginning to go wrong then what about Priscilla? How much time did she have until her magic was disrupted?

I took a deep breath dialing the phone number for Priscilla's Lotions and Potions. She picked up on the third ring, still sounding chipper. Hope bloomed in my chest.

"Eleanor hi!" she said enthusiastically. The tensions in my shoulders relaxed a fraction.

"How is everything?" I asked. She sighed. *Fury fuck.*

"So far everything is still working. I'm trying to make as many potions as I can while my magic is functioning. Everything is still relatively okay," she said. I nodded along. That was good. That was smart. "Do you think tonight we could go over to the tree and try some of the new concoctions?" she asked. I drummed my fingers against my desk, the clock staring at me. It was almost time to leave for the day.

After dealing with calls I just wanted to be home and soak in my bathtub. I'm forever thankful to the stars that we hired an intern. There was no way in hellhounds' lair I would have been able to do everything.

"Sure. Meet at the Gasping Greenwood around seven?" I asked. She agreed and I hung up the phone, sighing. Lily popped up over her cubicle.

"Need help?" she asked, her brown eyes filled with determination. There was no way I could tell her no. I sighed again and she smiled.

"I'll text Lola," she said, ducking away.

"This is going to be the most interesting girl's night," I muttered.

I LEAD LILY, Lola and Priscilla through the Gasping Greenwood Forest. The forest had never been something I feared. In fact I always felt at peace walking under the overgrown branches and feeling the grass smooth beneath my feet. But now the grass was covered in snow. We had a few creatures who darted in and out but they always kept their distance.

The moon was high in the sky and the temperature had dropped significantly. Lily shuddered beneath her coat. Lola's eyes glowed as she watched our surroundings carefully. Priscilla clung to her bag tightly, afraid of the potions cracking. Staring up ahead I could feel that we were getting close. But something was off. Something about the whole forest felt off and it made me want to lose my dinner.

"You all feel that right?" Priscilla asked, breaking the silence. Lola and Lily nodded.

"It feels sick," I whispered. We didn't speak until we were standing in front of the Hollow Tree. The branches looked brittled and hardly any leaves clung to it. I had never seen the tree look so barren. Tears welled up in my eyes. I couldn't let the tree die. Too much was at stake.

We all watched as Priscilla knelt before the tree and began pulling things out of her bag. Lily and Lola stood on guard behind us.

"You have a connection to the tree right?" Priscilla asked. I nodded solemnly. She smiled softly.

"I can sense it," she said, holding out her hand. Taking it I crouched next to her. I placed my hand on the root, closing my eyes. I reached with my magic trying to find some bit of warmth. It was there, tiny like an ember.

"We're going to try the first potion I made. The one without the moss to see if it's something internal," she said softly.

"What do you mean by internal?" Lola asked from behind us, her eyes narrowing at something. Priscilla crossed her legs, getting comfortable.

"Well if it's internal it's like taking medicine when you have a cold. The potion involving the moss is powerful and is used when an outside force is involved," she explained.

"Like my father," I muttered. Priscilla placed a hand on me, her eyes softening.

"We don't know that," she said. She was right. I took a deep breath, mustering my magic, calling it to the surface. Priscilla took my hands.

"Since you have a connection your magic might be stronger. I'm going to pour the potion into your hands, rub them together before placing it on the exposed roots. Then you'll repeat these words:

flowers bloom and grow. Roots sink deep below. Fix what is sick by my power and will," she said.

Taking a deep breath, she poured the potion into my hands. It was slightly sticky and smelt of sage, lemon balm, and ginseng. I closed my eyes and placed my hands on the root. My magic slowly trudged through, securing my connection as the words poured out of me.

My sweet child

A shiver went down me as the Hollow Tree spoke to me.

This is only temporary.

"We can help you," I said out loud. I could faintly hear Lola and Lily stepping closer.

You can not control everything my dear.

I felt my hands trembling.

"We *can* help you," I emphasized. The remaining leaves rustled in the air as if the tree was laughing.

For now my child. What once is lost or gone can be found or reborn.

Tears pricked my eyes. And once again the sickness, the darkness I felt around the tree retreated. I opened my eyes to see all the girls staring at me.

"What?" I asked, wiping my nose with the back of my hand. I really didn't want to cry. I had too much to do.

"Your eyes," Lily began. I looked over at Priscilla, her eyebrows were furrowed.

"They're glowing," Lola said. Glowing? That's what Caleb said. Priscilla looked conflicted as she cleaned everything up.

"What is it?" I asked her. Priscilla looked at all of us before settling back to the tree. The branches seemed to have moved up higher, as if it gained strength. Well I hope it did.

"I think you're more connected to the tree than you think," Priscilla said. Lola wrapped an arm around me.

"What does that mean?" Lola asked with concern. Lily helped Priscilla stand up. She shrugged her shoulders.

"I'm not quite sure. But you can hear the tree talk which means you must be connected somehow. Maybe that's why the potions work better with your hands," she said. I stared at the tree and the falling leaves that continue to crash into the snow.

"Snow is sticking. Things are dying at a faster rate without the tree to support them," Lily pointed out. I nodded.

"It'll be okay Ellie. You have all of us," Lola said, squeezing me. I looked at her and she smiled, her canines slightly pointy.

"Absolutely!" Priscilla joined in.

"Alright ladies. Let's get out of here," I suggested.

PRISCILLA'S WORDS played again and again as I walked down the street. *I think you're more connected to the tree than you think.* I had to be. I've always felt drawn to the tree ever since I was a little girl. I found solace under its shade. I felt protected and at peace. *Like with Caleb.*

I hadn't realized I unconsciously walked towards The Drunken Fairy Tale Tavern until I saw Bridget walking up the street. She spotted me and gave me a warm smile.

Bridget's light blonde hair reminded me of Caleb but her eyes were like Flynn's. She walked up to me with a cheeky smile.

"Yes?" I asked nervously. She hummed.

"So do I need to give you the break my brother's heart and I'll break your face talk?" she teased. I giggled. It warmed my heart that even though they didn't have the closest relationship she cared deeply for Caleb.

"I think your brother has a stronger chance of breaking my heart first," I confessed. Bridget's eyebrow twitched.

"I doubt that. He's been practically in love with you for four years," she said nonchalantly. My face burned and I coughed. Love was a big word with heavy implications attached. Was he in love with me? Was I with him? My heart hammered in my chest.

No. I could not be thinking these thoughts. I couldn't even play with the idea with so much happening around us.

"Can I ask you something?" Bridget broke my snowball of thoughts. I nodded. She tugged at her blonde hair, her eyes conflicted. "Does my brother talk about me?" she asked, carefully. I cocked my head.

"What do you mean?" I asked. She sighed.

"It's just that…I feel like there's a wall between us. I know we didn't exactly grow up together but he seems closer to Greg and Flynn. Is it because they're guys? I just…don't understand why he keeps me away." She said the last part quietly, almost to herself. *Oh stars.* My heart bled. Being away from Crystal destroyed me and now that she was back in my life I refused to give her up. But Bridget has had Caleb her whole life but not really *in* her life.

"Have you told him how you feel?" I asked. She huffed out a laugh.

"No. I just always get the feeling he doesn't want to hang around me for long. You know what, just forget I said anything. Anyway I'm really happy you guys are together." Her smile brightened for a second. I blushed again.

"Oh we're not together," I said. She snorted.

"Keep telling yourself that," she said as she walked away, leaving me standing in the middle of the street, echoing the same words Caleb told me.

I continued walking, head in the clouds and my heart in my hands until I was standing in front of the tavern. Caleb was inside, stacking a few chairs. He looked relaxed and I felt a whirlwind of emotions. It was almost the day for the meeting with my father. Crystal was worried about it, things in the town were going wrong, we still hadn't found a permanent solution to curing the tree and I felt responsible for everything.

On top of that I could feel myself falling for Caleb. With him I felt safe. I felt like I could let go. I was a tempest—wild and free and Caleb was a safe harbor, calm and warm.

Would he always be there or would he slowly erode as my waves crashed? It's what always happened and what I always expected. Which is why I only did one night stands. Emotions were never involved, just pure adult fun. I didn't have to worry about fitting into the role of a girlfriend. I didn't have to tone myself down.

But Caleb and I had repeat performances with each one exceeding the last. Could *we* last? I shook my head, turning away to head back to my apartment. I couldn't be around Caleb. He was so worried about the curse, about his sister finding out and now helping me. I couldn't bother him with my issues. I couldn't be anymore of a burden to him. I turned to walk away when I faintly heard the opening of a door.

"Starburst?" Caleb called out. I froze. I didn't want him to see me. "Is everything okay?" he asked. I turned around, plastering a smile.

"Yeah! We just got back from the tree. We tried one of the potions Priscilla made. It didn't cure the tree but it did slow down whatever is happening to it." I forced my body to relax. I didn't need him worrying. His blue eyes narrowed, watching me carefully. He flicked his head to the side.

"Inside," he said, opening the door wider. I shook my head.

"I'm fine. I should head home," I said, taking a step back. An invisible force seemed to wrap around me, forcing me to walk forward. The smell of mint was heavy in the air. He raised an eyebrow, eyes glowing. Fuck, this was hot.

"It wasn't a question. Get inside or I'll make you." His voice was deep, demanding and I wanted to bite back but instead I listened. With Caleb I relinquished control and as much as I wanted to fight him it was easier to give him the reins.

As I stepped inside the warmth of the tavern blanketed me. Caleb locked the door.

"See how easier it is when you listen?" he said, smirking.

166

"Shut up," I said, rolling my eyes, fighting back a smile. His hand caressed my jaw, and my eyes fluttered close. My worries began melting away.

"Go upstairs and draw a hot bath. I'll join you in a few minutes," he said. His eyes softened and my heart rattled against my chest. I wasn't used to this soft side of Caleb. Honestly it scared me more. I needed quiet brooding Caleb, not this version that filled my stomach with butterflies and my head with rainbows.

"You just want to see me wet and naked," I said, hoping we could fall back into our banter. He let out a chuckle.

"I always want to see that, lovely. Now get up there," he said. My smile wobbled as I headed up the stairs. Before I could reach the door knob there was a breeze of mint and a soft click.

My hand slightly shook as I opened his door. His apartment was clean, organized. The opposite of my apartment which was a splash of clashing colors and random knick knacks.

I was still trembling. Something inside me was on the verge of breaking. What the fuck was wrong with me? Why was I freaking out about this?

He was helping me with dealing with my father and I'm helping him break his curse. We use hooking up as a way to destress from these tasks. No feelings. Just pure adult fun as life smacks us in the face.

On top of the sink in the bathroom Caleb had a bottle of lavender bubbles and some epsom salt. My heart twisted. Did he buy this for me? My fingers shook as I took off my clothes. I turned on the shower needing to scrub the forest off of my skin.

Once I was showered I cleaned the bathtub with some products I found under the sink. I could never take a relaxing bath if both the tub and I were dirty. I decided to play some music, in hopes of easing my nerves. However my mind and my heart were in a silent battle as I watched bubbles form under the running water.

This wasn't just hooking up. Every moment with Caleb I felt myself sinking into a rhythm that matched a relationship. A *serious* relationship. Was I even ready for that? Did he even want that? Oh stars, was I turning to Lily and becoming an over thinker? With the click of the front door I hurried into the tub. I hissed as the hot water deliciously burned my skin.

There was a soft knock on the door as I settled beneath the bubbles.

"Yes," I called out. My voice sounded small.

"I brought you something. May I come in?" I blushed at his question. He's seen me naked plenty of times at this point but still asked permission.

"Yes," I said. Caleb walked in, already shirtless with a glass of wine. His skin was smoothed, beauty marks danced across his chest and my eyes traveled to wear his jeans hung low on his hips.

"I brought you some wine," he said, handing me a glass of what looked like white wine. I smiled.

"Thank you. I wasn't expecting that." I said, taking a sip. The wine was dry with hints of citrus. Just what I needed today.

"I'm going to make some dinner. Here are some clothes you can change out of once you're ready," he said, leaning over to kiss my forehead. This was beginning to be too much.

A bath, wine, and dinner? What was he doing? Trying to be the best fuck buddy? Win a prize for best situationship? He must have noticed the hesitation in my eyes because he cupped my face, pulling me in close. I tried to move back, afraid of our lips brushing but he kept me in place. My heart stopped at his next words.

"You're not just some fuck to me Eleanor and I'm going to prove it to you. So when you're done soaking in my bathtub you're going to eat the food I'm making. Then I'm going to have you screaming my name while my face is buried between your legs. After that you'll be too tired to go back home so you'll have to spend the night sleeping in my arms. Where. You. Belong. Got it?"

I nodded helplessly. This fucking elf was going to own me.

CHAPTER 20
NAKED PROMISES

CALEB

She hadn't noticed that I saw her through the window. She looked exhausted and sad. I thought she was going to come inside but then it was as if she woke up from whatever trance she was in and began walking off. There was no way I was going to let her be alone in that state.

Lately anytime I showed subtle affections she would clamp up. I needed to prove to her that we could be more than fuck buddies. She brought me out of my shell and I think I brought her peace. We were good together. We *are* good together. Her heart called to mine. She just needed to trust what it was telling her.

That's why she was soaking in my tub. A part of her knew that with me she could relax. Her skin was glistening pink when I walked in to give her a glass of wine. It took every ounce of self control to not strip and climb in there with her. But I doubted Eleanor wanted my work day sweat mixing in with her relaxing bath. So I left to cook dinner.

I cooked one of the few dishes I knew how. Irish beef stew, a classic. I still had some bread that Greg made and figured she needed something hearty after being at the tree. I wondered how much magic she used. Her eyes were still glowing a bit like the last time. Her skin didn't hold its usual warmth. She was pushing her magic, herself.

I shook my head, choosing to focus on cooking. I began feeling myself relax into the rhythm of chopping, stirring and sprinkling herbs into the pot.

After about 30 minutes I heard the tub draining. The door creaked a few minutes later and Eleanor came out in one of my long sleeves. I felt my throat constrict. She looked devastatingly gorgeous in my clothes. My shirt was a dress on her and stretched over her hips. Her pink hair was tossed into a messy bun, wet pieces clinging to her flushed face. Her nipples pebbled against the fabric. She poured herself another glass of wine.

"The food is almost done. I'm going to shower quickly. Just make yourself comfortable," I said, kissing the side of her temple. She didn't say anything, just nodded. I hurried and took the quickest shower of my life wanting nothing more than to hold Eleanor on my couch.

When I finished showering Eleanor was peeking into the pot, stirring. My lips twitched. She looked at home in my apartment. I could see us doing this. Cooking together, holding each other, bickering, making up. Definitely making up.

"Is it good?" I asked. She jumped, a hand clutching her heart.

"You scared the pixie dust off of me," she said, eyes wide. I chuckled. I wrapped my arms around her.

"It should be done by now. Go and sit on the couch. I'll bring you a bowl," I said, pulling her close to me. She breathed in sharply, her eyes focused on my collarbone. But I knew she could feel my dick pressing against her.

"Maybe we should skip and go straight to dessert," she teased, fluttering her eyelashes. She slowly pulled her full lips into a mischievous smile. I tucked a finger under her chin, forcing her to look into my eyes.

"Didn't I tell you food first and then I would make you scream my name?" I said. She rolled her eyes. I lightly smacked her ass and pushed her towards the couch.

170

"Hey Caleb?" Eleanor called out. She was nestling into my couch while I poured us each a bowl.

"Yes, Starburst?" I said. I quickly glanced at her. My shirt had rolled up slightly as she sat criss-crossed.

"Next time you spank me, put some muscle into it," she said as her eyes twinkled. My lips twitched.

This fucking pixie was my undoing.

SHE COULDN'T STOP MOANING with every bite she took. At first I thought maybe she really liked my cooking. I couldn't help but feel a swell of pride knowing my pixie liked my cooking. But after about four moans I could tell she was trying to break me. Her eyes would meet mine between bites and I would shake my head at her.

"Someone's impatient," I said. She bit back a smile before showing me her empty bowl.

"Want seconds?" I asked, knowing what she would say.

"I want my dessert," she pouted. I took her bowl and placed it on the coffee table. Ignoring her request I continued taking my time eating. She needed to learn patience.

"What was that music you were playing earlier? It was beautiful," I said, taking a bite and redirecting our conversation. Her whole face lit up and it was almost painful to look at. Her cheeks were still a little pink and she brushed a hair out of her eye.

"It's called *Fado*. It's like Portuguese bluesy jazz. The music uses a Portuguese guitar that has twelve strings. Sailors always sang *fado* a lot. It was my mom's favorite genre of music. I play it when I need to feel warm...safe. It also helps me to feel closer to her, to where she was from," she said softly.

"Can you play me a song?" I asked, quietly. She looked at me, eyes slightly wide in shock.

"I-I would love to," she said, reaching for her phone. "This was one of my favorites. It's called *Quem Me Dara* by Mariza," she said. A slight shiver went down my spine, hearing her tongue roll off in her language.

The sound of a guitar began filling the space. A strong female voice sang out and my heart was hit with a sense of pain and longing even though I didn't understand the words. The melody wrapped around me, breaking the cage that held back my emotions. I set my bowl on the table and pulled Eleanor into my arms.

"Can you tell me what she's saying?" I whispered. She snuggled herself deeper into my chest.

"What flower has to bloom to win over your love. For this love, my God, I'll do anything. I'll recite the most beautiful poems in the universe to see if I can convince you that my soul was born for you."

The words echoed the way my heart rattled for Eleanor. They gave words to the feelings she made me feel. My throat tightened with a swell of emotions I wasn't used to.

She stopped translating and we enjoyed the song until the last line. I looked down at Eleanor. Her eyes glistened with unshed tears. My finger absentmindedly began tracing lines up and down her cheek. Her eyes fluttered closed briefly.

"Thank you for all of this," she murmured, looking up at me.

"Could you tell me more about her?" I asked, carefully. Her eyes widened in shock. She nodded, blinking away tears.

"My mom comes from a really tiny village in Portugal. I remember as a kid people would make funny faces when I would say village but it really is," she started. My finger continued to trace the freckles that were on her cheeks. "I haven't been back in awhile but it's my favorite place. So many trees and mountains. I think that's why she came here. Pieces of Lavender Falls reminded her of her home. There's not many people left in her village which breaks my heart, you know?" Tears gathered in her eyes again as I continued to listen.

"People talk about villages and towns ceasing to exist and that has always made me sad. Some of those places were ripped away from them and some died out slowly. There's a reason passing languages and traditions are so important. Because even if you're far from home you can keep it alive within yourself. It's important not only to your people but to yourself that you keep that fire burning inside you," she took a deep breath before continuing.

"My mom tried her best before passing away and I plan on passing what I can to Crystal now." A tear escaped her eye and I wiped it away.

"You have Lilianna and her mom though right?" I asked. She nodded, eyes still glistening.

"I do. They're from a neighboring village actually. Our moms were friends since they were kids and when I moved back after college I had her mom teach me as much as she could. I don't want to forget who I am or where I came from but I feel like Crystal might have." I kissed her temple.

"You have each other again," I whispered against her head. She leaned her head back to look at me.

"Caleb?" she said. I nodded at her, slipping my hand to cup her cheek. "Can it be time for dessert now?" she asked. I couldn't resist her. I couldn't and wouldn't deny her. *Ever.*

"Meet me in bed," I said. She smiled and I felt my body buzz. That's what Eleanor did. One look, one word, one touch and I was more than ready to take her. I cleaned up the kitchen quickly, and ran to the bathroom to rinse my mouth.

I opened the bedroom door, the sight of her made me pause. She had my shirt pulled up, exposing her thighs and her dripping cunt. She was playing with herself. She arched her back, moaning my name. I should punish her for starting what I had planned on doing. I raised an eyebrow.

"Someone is definitely impatient," I tsked. She smirked as two of her fingers dipped inside. She threw her head to the side, gasping. I leaned against the doorframe watching her take her own pleasure.

"Aren't you going to help?" she asked, breathlessly. I shrugged my shoulders.

"You seem to be doing a very good job," I said. She rolled her eyes at me. The glow in her eyes had faded through dinner. With her other hand, she slipped it under the shirt, playing with her nipple. My dick was straining against my sweatpants.

"Caleb," she pleaded, her eyes closed, head thrown back in bliss. I couldn't stand on the side lines anymore. I tossed my shirt to the side and crawled up the bed, kissing my way up her body. She twitched and squirmed as my tongue licked her soft skin. I grabbed her hand that was just inside of her and pulled them out.

"Eyes on me," I growled. Her eyes flashed with excitement as she watched me suck her arousal off her fingers. One second Eleanor wanted to defy me and in the next she gave in. It was constant back and forth for dominance and it set my body on fire to see how far I could push her.

"My turn," I whispered, biting the inside of her thigh. She moaned as I roughly sucked at her skin. I needed to mark her. I forced her to keep her leg down as I attacked her thigh. She kept thrashing, trying to move me into place. Apparently she still hadn't learned that in these kinds of situations *I'm* the one who was in control.

I left a bruising kiss on the inside of her thigh. She slipped her fingers into my hair, tugging. The smell of her filled my senses.

"All of this for me. Just me. Right, Eleanor?" I said as my finger slid between her folds.

"Yes," she hissed. A gasp escaped between her pretty lips as I rubbed a lazy circle around her clit. Her hand in my hair tightened.

"I fucking love dessert," I groaned. Her eyes were locked on my mouth as I brought it down to her pussy. I gave her clit a rough suck and she fought to squeeze my head with her thighs. I wouldn't mind dying between her legs, mouth on her cunt. I teased her clit with my tongue as my finger dipped inside of her. She immediately tightened and I groaned. I couldn't fucking wait to feel her take my cock.

I added a second finger, needing to stretch her. She moaned as I dragged them in and out of her. Her hips began rocking faster, wilder. I glanced up quickly. She was watching me, mouth hanging open, panting. She looked breathtaking.

"More," she cried out.

"As you wish," I said. She hissed when I added a third finger. She was squeezing my fingers so tight I could tell she was close and so I slowed my pace. I ran my tongue from where my fingers were up to her clit, careful with the pressure. I didn't want her to finish quite yet. Eleanor's eyes were heated.

She wanted to chase her orgasm but I arched an eyebrow, enjoying the way she kept trying to manipulate the rhythm. I gave her clit a playful lick and her body spasmed again. She blew out a harsh breath, eyes still on me.

"Out there, Eleanor Silva, I'm at your beck and call," I said as I twisted my fingers. Eleanor's whimpers cut straight through me. "You have me wrapped around your pretty polish pixie pinky." My other hand wandered up her body to pinched her nipple until she was gasping for air. "But behind close doors and *especially* fucking naked you're at *my* mercy," I growled.

Curling my fingers, I pumped faster, harder as my tongue went back to torture her clit. I squeezed her breast. I owned her body. She was mine.

"Just enjoy the ride, lovely," I said.

"C-C-Caleb!" Her voice echoed in my bedroom. I was definitely going to need to invest in a way to soundproof this room. Eleanor detangled her fingers from my hair to chuck one of my pillows across the room as my name was torn from her lips. She was beautiful when she came. I kissed her clit gently which made her twitch. Eleanor covered her eyes with her arm, hiding from me. I sat up on my knees and cleaned my fingers of my victory.

"Fucking griffin shit Caleb," she whispered, staring at the ceiling, still struggling to breathe. I hummed with a smirk, crawling on top of her. Her eyes blinked heavily. One hazel, one green. She bit her bottom lip and I tugged it free. I couldn't fucking wait to kiss her. "When can I have your dick?" she asked breathlessly. I paused and then laughter poured out of me.

"I didn't expect you to say that," I said, placing a kiss on her neck. She wiggled underneath me.

"It's a perfectly good question. We've messed around quite a bit and yet we haven't officially had sex," she said with a slight pout. I cupped the side of her face and ran my thumb over her lips. She froze, eyes watching me, hesitantly.

"Our first time Eleanor Silva will be when I can finally kiss you," I said, placing a gentle kiss on her forehead.

"You make a lot of promises," she muttered, looking away. I turned her head back to look at me.

"I will always keep my promises," I said firmly. Her eyes gave away her hesitation.

"You better," she said softly, turning away from me. I pulled her against me where she belonged. She snuggled in tightly. I smiled. Slowly but surely I was winning over her fears.

CHAPTER 21
RULE BREAKER

ELEANOR

I had slipped out of Caleb's bed early in the morning to get back to my place. While last night wasn't the first time we've been sweaty and naked it felt different. The whole time we were at his place felt different. He bathed me, fed me, let me talk about my mom and held me. I knew what he was doing. He was trying to prove something to me. He wanted to show me that we could be more than fuck buddies.

But my instinct was to run away from that. I spent years content with myself. I was fine with doing this on my own. I was bullheaded, wild, carefree and I spent my whole life with men trying to control me.

Sure Caleb was fine with how I am now but what if later on he couldn't stand my stubbornness and impulsiveness?

I smiled, remembering how he traced my freckles. I touched my lips briefly. I could feel our relationship transforming into something possibly worthwhile.

Opening the doors to the office I pushed those thoughts to the back of my head. There was no sense in worrying about this now. I had shit to do today. We were getting closer and closer to the festival and I

177

needed to stay on top of things. I set my bag down in my chair and Lily smiled at me from over her desk. I waved back.

In front of my computer was a cup of coffee from Coffin's Coffee Shop. I mouthed thank you to her as she continued to talk to whoever was on the phone. I sat in my seat with a sigh.

Taking a sip of coffee I let the bitter sweetness flow through my body, fueling my thoughts. I had a checklist for the festival to go over. My phone pinged with an email from Mayor Kiana. *Kraken crap,* I thought. I powered on my computer and opened the email.

It was a meeting notification. She wanted to meet with me to discuss a few things pertaining to the festival. *Fuck.* My stomach began twisting. She probably knew about the things going wrong in town. There's been a few complaints but Emily and I have been putting out the fires. I glanced at my phone.

Taking a deep breath I called Priscilla to see how she was feeling. With more things going wrong I was worried about her hurting herself with her spells.

"Good morning Eleanor," Priscilla said, brightly. There was something in the bottom layer of her tone that pricked my senses.

"What's wrong?" I asked. There was a rustle on the other side.

"Well…" she trailed off. My fingers tapped on my desk.

"Priscilla just say it please," I pleaded. Whatever it was, I needed to know if I could fix it and how soon I needed to.

"We did slow down the tree's decay. I still can't figure out what's wrong with the tree. I don't think there's anything wrong magic wise. It also doesn't look like the tree was tampered with," she said. I furrowed my eyebrows.

"So it's just…dying?" I asked, trepidation bleeding into my voice.

"Honestly? Yeah. There might not be a way to save it. Sometimes plants, creatures, things just pass." She sounded bleak. I felt tears in my eyes. *No.* This could not be happening. We had to save the tree. All of our magic depended on it. I had to do something.

"Isn't there another potion we could try?" I pleaded.

"I mean…yeah. I can do some things but I'm going to have to act fast. The tree's death is still affecting our crops. The temperature is also dropping and it's snowing." I could hear her rummaging around her shop.

"Get whatever it is that you can. All we have to do is stall the decay long enough to figure out a solution to stop the town from being affected," I said.

"Of course Ellie. We got this," she said, confidently.

"Thank you Priscilla," I said before hanging up. I stared at my computer, the weight of the town's magic resting heavy on my shoulders. Lily threw a note at me like we were back in fifth grade potion making class.

Do you need anything?

I shook my head, doing my best to smile at her. She was already helping me enough as it is so I couldn't burden her with more. Pulling out my list for the festival I did what I did best. I got to work. One thing at a time I told myself.

———— ❄ ❄ ❄ ————

IT WAS FINALLY time for my meeting with Mayor Kiana. I was standing outside her door, willing myself to go in but I felt frozen to my feet. I wasn't sure how this meeting was going to go. Logically everything was in order festival wise. But town wise? It was becoming a mess and fast.

"Are you going to stand there all day or come in?" Her voice rang out. I sighed. Better now than never.

Opening the door Mayor Kiana was typing away at her computer and Emily was sitting across with her laptop open. Emily was a sweetheart and had been a lifesaver throughout this whole thing. She no doubt had a bright future ahead of her.

Throughout this whole season I had found myself enjoying working for the events way more than being Mayor Kiana's second in command. Maybe I was in the wrong field? Was that wrong? Mayor Kiana had helped me so much since moving back. To find something else, feel something for another career felt almost like a betrayal. But could I even explore that realization right now when I had so many other things to worry about? Emily gave me a big smile.

"Hi Ms. Silva!" she said sweetly. I settled in the chair next to her.

"You can call me Eleanor, Emily. Don't make me feel old," I teased. Mayor Kiana snorted.

"And how do you think I feel?" Mayor Kiana smirked. In the fall season Mayor Kiana had the tips of her hair lightened to a beautiful caramel color but now that it was winter she lightened them to an almost icy blonde.

Today she was sporting a green power suit with a floral printed blouse. Mayor Kiana was one of the chicest people I knew which is why I loved working for her. She never demanded I wear boring black suits like my internships back in college did.

"How are you Eleanor?" Mayor Kiana asked. I smiled.

"I'm good. How are things going? I feel like it's been awhile since we've seen each other." My stomach twisted as I lied through my teeth. She arched an eyebrow and just stared at me. All of a sudden I was back in chemistry class when she would scold me about being almost late or decorating my reports with doodles. She waited. I could feel Emily's eyes fly between us. I sighed, giving up.

"Tiring. Stressful but I'm okay honestly," I said. Mayor Kiana straightened her keyboard.

"And your father?" she asked. My fingers twitched at my side.

"He's just as difficult as you remember him to be. I can't deny his ideas have been decent. Working with my sister has been nice," I said. I smiled softly. "If there's one thing I'm grateful for this festival season is being able to be with her again," I said truthfully. She smiled at me and I felt myself relax a centimeter.

"I've heard things…" she trailed off. I bit the inside of my cheek, ready to spill the herbs.

"As you know the Hollow Tree which is sacred to us pixie's has

LUST, LOVE & PIXIE DUST

roots embedded deep into the town's soil. The tree was planted when the town was first settled," I started off, recounting the history I was taught at a young age which she already knew. She nodded for me to continue.

"The roots are deep enough they hit the ley lines of the town's magic. The tree is dying. I suspected my father had something to do with it. But Priscilla assures me that it's simply the tree's time. I do, however, believe my father knows something," I said. "Hale's Industry is in close proximity to the tree for magical reasons. We help the earth and the tree repays us. It's a give and take situation."

The we slipped out easily. No matter how much I separated myself from being a Hale it was still something a piece of me. I took a deep breath before continuing.

"Because the tree is dying and the roots are hitting the ley lines, magic is acting a bit on the fritz. I've been putting out the fires and Priscilla and I are trying every potion and spell possible to help the tree," I finished off. Mayor Kiana took a deep breath, scratching her chin.

"I wish you would have told me sooner Eleanor. Maybe there's something in my spell book that Priscilla can use. I have one of the oldest books you know. Maybe the elders of the founding families can help since their magic feeds the ley lines," she pointed out. I nodded. That was true. I never thought of severing the connection between the ley lines and the tree. I figured I could save the tree and we wouldn't have to worry.

"I understand. I just wanted to be able to handle this on my own. We've slowed down the decay which should buy us some time," I said confidently, which was the truth. She nodded.

"As precaution I'll let the founding families know we might have to separate the connection between the lines and the tree. In the meantime I'll send my spell book to Priscilla. She's probably working double time making potions," Mayor Kiana said. Emily cleared her throat.

"The community garden isn't doing well. Just a few limp greens here and there. We're getting snowfall which means everything is

getting covered. We usually rely on magic to keep vegetation growing," Emily pointed out. I nodded.

"Flynn has a greenhouse. Ask Priscilla what her most important
herbs needed are and have Flynn move it to his greenhouse," Mayor
Kiana told Emily. She typed away on her laptop. I felt a well of
emotion. Mayor Kiana turned to look at me. "Don't you remind
Lilianna to ask for help all the time?" she teased. I rolled my eyes
dramatically.

"Listen, I'm great at giving advice. It's the following part I have
trouble with." We all laughed together and another weight was off my
shoulders.

CHAPTER 22
TIGHTROPE TENSIONS

ELEANOR

The meeting with Mayor Kiana had me feeling lighter but now I had to call my sister to confirm my meeting with my father later on in the week. Lily had left to go grab us a late lunch when I decided to call Crystal. She picked up on the sixth ring which was unusual.

"Hello?" Her voice was slightly annoyed. Something was wrong.

"Hey Crystal I'm just calling to confirm the meeting with Mr. Hale this week," I said slowly. She cursed and I could hear her tapping away on her computer.

"Yeah. I just have to move some of his things around," she muttered.

"Doesn't he have a secretary for that?" I asked.

"If he did, you would be calling them and not me," she mumbled. Oh, that was right. But something was definitely wrong with her tone.

"You're right. I should have checked first. So you're also his secretary?" I asked.

"Secretary, marketing manager, finance reporter, everything and anything," she said. I shook my head.

"That doesn't make sense. Don't you guys have people for that?" I asked. I chewed my bottom lip.

"We do. But I have to double check everything and learn how every department runs if I want to run his damn company." Annoyance dripped into her voice. My stomach twisted. She was only in this position because of me. Because I failed to take on the family company. She sighed deeply.

"Listen I got a million other things to do but we're set for a meeting this Friday morning. I sent you the invite," Crystal said.

"Thanks Crys," I said weakly.

"Also ignore my tone. It's not at you. It's been a long day of putting out fires. Not real fires! Like because of the magic," she rushed out. I smiled in relief. "I'll chat with you soon, promise. I-i love you," she said.

I stared at my phone. Naturally when one area of my life improved another went down the drain. I just got my sister back but it looks like I was going to have to fight my father to keep her there.

LOLA AND LILY sat on my couch with a bowl of popcorn for an actual girls night that involved trashy movies and not walking through the woods at night.

"Mayor Kiana sent her book to Priscilla and she may have found something," Lola said. I leaned my head against the couch and stared at the ceiling.

"That's good," I said. Fabian nestled into my lap. I felt Lily's hand on my shoulder. Her hair was loose and frizzy around her face.

"We haven't had a chance to talk about Coralia Coast or Caleb," Lily said. I bit my cheek. Lola leaned over to hand me a margarita.

"That's damn right. Sip n' Spill is on," Lola said. I smiled and took a sip.

"Alright. Well Sailor's town isn't too bad. A little strange but apparently they warm up to people during the summer," I started. Lily giggled.

"Yeah they were a little quiet but the area is beautiful and that diner had the best burger I've ever had," Lily said. Lola sighed.

"I don't need a vacation just yet since I just started working at the clinic but I wouldn't mind a little trip," Lola said.

"Okay but hear me out. Girls trip?" I suggested. The girls nodded.

"With Crystal!" Lola said. I smiled. Yes. A girls vacation once everything was settled was what we all needed. And it would be the perfect thing to help Crystal and I settle back into our sisterly relationship.

"Alright, I will begin planning for something in the summer then. Anyway Caleb..." I trailed off, taking another sip. Lily nodded, poking my shoulder. "He's great in bed," I pointed out. Lola rolled her eyes.

"We both remember the story from Coffin's Coffee Shop. But how is it going between you two?" Lily asked. I fidgeted with the glass in my hands. They both turned to face me.

"Ellie this is a Sip n' Spill session so spill," Lola stated. I sighed.

"Imightbedevelopingfeelings," I mumbled quickly. Lily smiled big.

"I knew this would happen," Lily said, crossing her arms.

"What do you mean?" I asked. Lola scoffed.

"Please, it's romance book plot 101. Our main characters *swear* they won't get feelings involved but then feelings happen the more orgasms they get," Lola said. Lily began laughing as I groaned.

"I don't do feelings," I stated. Lola tsked.

"You didn't do feelings before Caleb," Lola pointed out. I shook my head.

"I don't *want* to do feelings," I said. Lily took the margarita from my hand and placed it on the coffee table.

"What's wrong with feelings?" Lily asked. I gave her a look.

"Feelings make things messy," I said. She narrowed her eyes on me.

"Should I repeat the advice you gave me about Celestino?" She arched an eyebrow. I pouted. I definitely didn't need to hear what I said to get those together.

"But that was different. That was you and Celestino! You've been in love with each other for years. It was disgustingly obvious," I pointed out.

"W-well you guys have been giving each other sex eyes for years!" Lily stammered, her cheeks blazing.

"You can dish the advice but not take it? Come on Eleanor. You like him. He likes you. What's the big deal?" Lola asked. I bit the inside of my cheek. In reality they were right. There was nothing wrong with Caleb and I confirming our relationship I think.

Honestly, I was just afraid of how we would change if we explored something deeper. I was afraid *I* would change into someone else and it would be without me even realizing it was happening. I didn't want to lose myself in someone.

"You can't let the past control your future. I know that more than anyone," Lily said softly, leaning her head on my shoulder.

"Plus think how much hotter things will be when he's officially yours," Lola snickered, leaning her head on my other shoulder.

"So how does one express their feelings?" I mumbled.

"I confessed in a haunted house," Lily said, still blushing.

"Mine was in a study hall in college before my finals. Got the guy and aced the test," Lola said. "It was kinda boring honestly; the relationship and the confession. The next time it happens I want it to be romantic," Lola finished. Fabian scratched his ear.

"I don't think Caleb cares how you confess as long as you get naked afterwards," Fabian said. I flicked his ear and the girls laughed.

"I'll wear something lacy," I said in contemplation. Lola handed me back my margarita. I turned to Lily who stared at me from above her drink.

"I don't like that look," Lily said.

"You just need to say yes," I said. Lola began scratching Fabian's head.

"I would like to hear what you have to say before agreeing," Lily said. Lola giggled.

"It was Crystal's idea!" I said, defensively. Lola bumped Lily's shoulder.

"Now you have to say yes," Lola said. I rolled my eyes.

"Can you sing a *fado* song at the festival?" I asked, batting my eyelashes. Lily's face turned red.

"I only sing at karaoke!" Lily said.

"Have a shot," Lola said.

"Of port! Get you in the zone," I said with a smile. Lily glared at us.

"We all know that you don't drink a shot of port like a shot of tequila," Lily said. "But if Crystal requested I guess I have to say yes."

Fabian yawned. "Can we move onto a more interesting topic? Like Mr. Bubble Butt and his yummy brother," he said.

IT WAS ALMOST Friday which meant it was almost time for the dreaded meeting with the boogie monster. No offense to the real boogie monster. I heard he was vacationing in Niue this winter season.

I was sitting at the bar with Caleb pouring me a drink when Flynn bursted through the doors. Lola was hot on his heels with a worried look.

"What's wrong?" I asked. Flynn had dark circles under his eyes and his shirt was covered in dirt. Lola's hands were caked in dirt as well and she had a sweaty sheen on her face.

"It's the garden," Lola said, catching her breath. I took a sip of my caipirinha, preparing myself for some shitty news. I looked over at Flynn.

"I was going to say that," Flynn said, glaring at her. She rolled her eyes. "I moved what I could to the greenhouse. I had to get all new dirt because *our* dirt, as in the dirt of the town's ground, is making every-thing worse," he continued. I let out a string of curses. The tree was getting worse.

"I wanted to let you know," he said, settling into a bar stool.

"We think it's best you both hurry up and get whatever you need for Priscilla. Who knows how long her supplies will last," Lola said, looking between Caleb and I. I glanced over at him. His face was stoic but his eyes were far away. We needed to act fast.

"Call Priscilla and see if she can stay open late. Once I'm down with my shift we can head on over," Caleb said to me. I nodded.

"I'm going to go home to wash up and I'll meet you guys there later," Lola said before leaving.

"I'll be the one to call Priscilla and ask her what she needs me to bring," Flynn confirmed. I threw back my drink and looked at Caleb.

"This is not how I pictured the evening," I mumbled. His lips twitched.

"Who knows, maybe by tonight we'll be making out. I hear it's a great way to relax," he said, smirking. I rolled my eyes.

"Well I hope so Elfie."

CALEB

I glanced at Eleanor who sat at the end of the bar nursing her drink. She was lost in her own thoughts. Ever since she walked in something had been bothering her. She had so much on her plate. Between her father, her sister, the Hollow Tree, the festival and me it's been perplexing to watch her retain her smile. I don't know how she was doing it. She just kept pushing herself. I was trying my best to be there for her.

But maybe I was making things worse for her? Maybe pushing us was causing more stress instead of easing her burden.

"Do you want to talk about it?" I asked once I was finished cleaning up the bar. She shook her head silently. My jaw clenched. "You don't have to come tonight," I managed to get out. Her eyes snapped to me.

"Why?" she asked. I took a deep breath and leaned on the bar.

"Because you've had a long day. You don't need to come tonight. I'll be fine with Flynn and Lola." Even though I sounded sure I wanted to stuff the words back in my mouth. Eleanor searched my eyes. She was probably looking to see if it was a lie. It was. I wanted her there. I needed her by my side.

"I'm going to go. I promised I'd help you and I will. I keep my promises, Caleb," she said with a small smile. Of course she was going to be stubborn.

"I understand that Eleanor but you have a lot going on. I don't want to be causing you stress. This thing between us shouldn't be stressful and with the curse hanging above our heads it feels that way." My heart pounded at my confession.

Eleanor came around the bar and brought her glass to me. I took it and began washing it instinctively. My chest tightened. From the corner of my eye she had a determined gleam. Once I set the glass to dry I turned back around.

"I do have a lot going on. But you have been there for me. You even dealt with my father. So let me be there for you," she said, cheeks slightly pink.

"On one condition," I said. I offered my hand to her. She raised an eyebrow, placing her soft hand in mine. I pulled her towards me until we were inches apart. Her hazel eye was a swirl of warm honey with flecks of blue and green. Her left eye was the same shade as a cactus.

Which in reality was a good way to describe Eleanor. Prickly on the outside, warm and sweet on the inside. She was enchanting, even without trying. She simply exuded an air about her that people were instantly drawn to. She was a flame and I was a moth willing to burn.

"You sleep at my place tonight," I said. She let out a soft giggle that melted my heart.

"Caleb…" she started. I squeezed her hand, stopping her before she could say anymore.

"Just sleep. I have a feeling about tonight and I just want to finish the night with you in my arms. That's all," I said. She chewed her bottom lip and pulled her hand away.

"How can I say no to those baby blues," she muttered. I leaned forward and placed a tender kiss on her cheek. She fought back a smile. I felt the thread that had been winding around ua for years slowly tightened. We were getting somewhere.

I was on pins and needles as we entered the shop. Flynn was standing behind Lola who sat on a stool across from Priscilla. Priscilla had an assortment of jars and bottles scattered across the table with herbs and random colored liquids. Her eyes were glowing as she mixed a concoction in a bowl. Eleanor pulled me closer. I nodded to Flynn who had a pensive look. I raised an eyebrow at him and he shook his head silently. Whatever was up with him I would find out later.

"Hey Priscilla," Eleanor said softly, not wanting to disturb her too much. With a swirl of her hand the contents in the bowl began to glow. After a few minutes of us all silently watching, Priscilla closed her eyes and yawned.

"Alrighty guys! It is done!" she said with a giant smile. The lavender in her hair was fading and she had circles under her eyes. I couldn't even begin to imagine the toll of using all her magic during this time. And like Eleanor she kept a smile on her face.

"I'm sorry," I said automatically. My chest felt tight. So many people were trying to break this damn curse for me during the worst time. I should have kept my mouth closed. Maybe I could have told them later. Maybe-

I felt a slap against my chest. Eleanor scowled at me and waved her finger.

"Stop thinking like that," Eleanor said.

"Thinking what?" I asked. She scoffed.

"You know that I know what you're thinking about and I'm telling you to stop it." Eleanor crossed her arms over her chest. I grinned and squeezed her hip.

"Alright lovebirds are we ready?" Lola asked with a grin. I rolled my eyes knowing if I said anything Lola would probably make kissy faces. But it didn't escape my attention that Eleanor didn't deny what she said. I turned my attention to Priscilla. She pulled a stool in front of the bowl and began separating it between two bottles.

"Made an extra just in case," Priscilla said nonchalantly.

"So what do we have to do?" I asked. My fingers drummed at my side as the nerves began to kick in.

"Well according to this spell Lola found from one of her mother's old books you drink this and I say the words and BOOM curse should be broken," Priscilla explained. The door opened. At that moment Lilianna, Fabian, Celestino and Sailor walked in.

"Great, a party," I grunted. Sailor smirked and Celestino patted my back.

"Lily?" Eleanor seemed surprised by her best friend's arrival. Lilianna placed her hand on her hips.

"Did you think you were going to go through this alone? Both of you? Plus shouldn't a decently powerful witch cast the spell?" she asked. Eleanor glanced at me. Priscilla clapped her hands.

"Perfect. Lily's the strongest witch other than her mom and Celestino's," Priscilla said. I looked at Celestino.

"She was very close to bringing down the tavern when Eleanor's father showed up," he pointed out. That was true. I had never seen Lilianna so mad. The air was crackling with magic that night. I nodded in agreement. Lilianna stepped around the table and peered at the open book.

"We all know I get anxious. But this isn't about me. This is about the people I care about. So I *will* do this," she said, reading through the book. "Looks like you drink that and I say the spell," Lilianna said. I glanced at Sailor.

"I can see if the curse is still there," he pointed out. I nodded again. I looked around the room again. In college I mostly kept to myself with the exception of Celestino. In this town that held my childhood I was surrounded by warmth. I had people who would fight for me and with me.

My heart pounded as Priscilla handed me the bottle. The liquid was blue with bubbles. I hope it tasted good at least. Lilianna scanned the book again. She nodded at me and while pointing at the bottle and began reciting the words.

"A mistake was made so let the past fade. Fix what has been broken. Through love, let light be awoken," she said.

The inventory around us began rattling. The air became thick with the smell of the ocean. The bottle glowed and I quickly downed it. I tried not to blanch. There was a strong seaweed taste. I felt a deep rumble in my chest and warmth began spreading.

"Caleb?" Eleanor looked at me with wide eyes. I cupped her cheek as the warmth continued to spread across my body. Was this it? This felt different. I think. I felt a pang in my heart and moved to grip the table.

"Caleb!" Eleanor exclaimed, latching onto my side. Everyone moved closer. I waved them off, regaining my breathing.

"Did it work?" I asked, clutching Eleanor's hand. We all turned to look at Sailor. His blue eyes glowed slightly as he stared at me. He sighed, shaking his head. We all let out a curse. *Fuck.*

"We'll find a way," Eleanor whispered softly. Lilianna let out a noise. I looked up quickly. Her face was nose deep into the spell book, literally.

"There's some writing at the bottom but I can't make it out," she mumbled. Lola hopped off the chair.

"Maybe I can help!" Lola offered. Lola stared at the book intently and chewed her bottom lip.

"What is it?" I asked a bit harshly. She looked between Flynn and I.

"Um…it says the original caster has to say the spell," Lola said, hesitantly. Flynn and I both looked at each other.

There was no fucking way.

No fucking way I was breaking Bridget's memory spell. Flynn's eyes were tormented. I knew it. I knew deep down that this would happen. That we would need Bridget but I wanted to hope that it wouldn't come to it.

"I guess we have some thinking to do," Flynn said, breaking the tension. I shook my head. The answer was no. No discussion needed.

"Thanks guys. I really appreciate all of this." With those few words and my head down, I left Priscilla's and headed back home. I needed to be away from everyone to think. They all wasted their time, energy and resources for nothing. I could hear Eleanor walking behind me. She didn't say anything until we walked into the tavern.

"Caleb," she huffed. I closed the door behind her.

"What?" I asked, annoyance sipping into my voice. My shoulders tensed in anticipation of whatever truth she was going to say.

"Do you want to talk about it?" she asked, crossing her arms.

"There's nothing to talk about," I said, walking over to the bar to pour myself a glass of whiskey. She scoffed.

"I think there is," she said, sitting in one of the bar stools. I took a sip of the whiskey, closing my eyes. It slid down smoothly. As the taste of honey and sage coated my throat the burn kicked in at the last second. It was delicious. This must have been one of Flynn's latest batches. "There isn't Eleanor," I said through gritted teeth.

"Do you not want to break the curse?" she asked softly.

"Of course I want to but not if that means telling my sister the truth," I said.

"Don't you think this could be a good thing?" she asked. My eyes widened.

"A good thing? Are you serious? You think having my sister be reminded of that time is a good thing? It broke her, Eleanor. *Broke. Her.* I'm not going to break my sister just so we could make out," I lashed out. Her eyes hardened. Fuck. That wasn't supposed to come out like that. Before I could attempt to recover Eleanor spoke.

"I wasn't thinking that the reason this could be a good thing was so that we could make out but the fact that these past four years Bridget has been wanting to get close to you. She doesn't know why you keep her at a distance," she said, taking my glass of whiskey. She took a sip, nose twitching.

"She came up to me. Asking me if I knew anything. She hates the wall you have up with her, Caleb. Telling her, breaking the curse could rebuild your relationship," she said. I took the glass back and stared into the amber liquid that was left.

"And what do you know about sisterly relationships? You stayed away from your sister for years." I regretted the words the instant they left my mouth. Her cheeks flamed and she glared at me. I was completely fucking this up. "Fuck, Eleanor I-"

"I know what it's like to not have your sibling around just like you. And I regret those years away from her. I should have fought back then which is why I'm fighting for her now," she said, placing a hand on mine. Her warmth seeped into my skin. "Bridget is going to get tired of the wall you have with her and I suggest you knock it down. Don't keep her at a distance," she said gently. "You have people around you Caleb that support you."

"You keep me at a distance," I said, leaning towards her. My stomach twisted in knots. This wasn't how I planned our evening going. I was saying all the wrong words. Her eyes softened.

"A-and I'm trying to work through that Caleb. I'm trying to trust what you've been showing me because you seem worth it. And my sister is worth fighting my father for. This town and everyone in it is worth fighting for," she said.

I stared at her silently, at a loss for words. Eleanor Silva was everything I wanted to be. Confident, kind, courageous. I spent my entire life hiding, thinking it was better to stay in the shadows. But I craved sunlight. Eleanor on the other hand walked in daylight and attempted to keep her shadows at bay. She sighed, getting up.

"Where are you going?" I asked, making my way around the bar. She smiled softly.

"I want to give you some time to think. If you never break the curse

I'm fine with it. But do you honestly want to keep Bridget in the dark for the rest of your life? There will always be a piece of you holding back from her."

"You said you would stay," I said, quietly. Her smile faltered for a second.

"It might be best for us to cool down tonight. Can I come over tomorrow after my meeting with my father?" she asked. She had a meeting with her father? Dammit. She was probably anxious as a dragon trying to nest. She was probably worried about the meeting and still decided to come with me tonight. Why the fuck was this pixie so fucking giving?

"Food and bubble bath?" I asked. Eleanor, stood on her tiptoes to kiss my cheek.

"How about a bubble bath for two?"

CHAPTER 23
HALE VS SILVA

ELEANOR

I couldn't sleep all night. It wasn't just because Caleb and I had our first disagreement. I understood where he was coming from and I meant it when I said if he never wanted to break the curse I would be okay with it. I knew what he said wasn't on purpose. I couldn't begin to imagine the burden he must feel over his sister. I have my own but it was different.

In the end we sort of settled our emotions. I also couldn't sleep because today was the day I would be confronting my father about the Hollow Tree.

I was sitting in the meeting room with my laptop and notebook spread before me as a shield. I wore a pink power suit that I knew would piss him off. There was coffee and croissants from Coffin's Coffee Shop sitting in the center. The door creaked open and I stood up immediately. My father walked in, eyeing me up and down and grimaced.

"Mr. Hale," I said emotionlessly. Crystal walked in with bags under her eyes looking slightly red. Did something happen? I clamped down on my protective thoughts. I would ask her about it later, once he was

196

gone. My father grunted, taking my outstretched hand in a firm grip. He took the seat across from me and pulled out his laptop. Crystal sat between us.

"Let's get this over with," he said in a rough voice. I bit back a sassy remark. I needed to get through this meeting as painlessly as possible.

"Let's go over the final details for each of the events," I said, pulling up the documents.

SURPRISINGLY THE MEETING WENT WELL. Crystal hardly said a word. My father was on par with everything that we've been doing so far.

"Well this went surprisingly smooth," my father said, closing his laptop. I raised an eyebrow.

"Surprisingly?" I asked, noticing his tone. I could see Crystal's eyes go back and forth between us. He shrugged his shoulders.

"If only you were more like this when you were younger," he said. I scowled.

"The difference is I *chose* this job," I said firmly. He narrowed his eyes. I could feel the tension building up. Before he could respond I cut him off. "We have one more thing to discuss," I stated. He raised an eyebrow. Crystal shifted in her seat next to me.

"Do you know what's wrong with the Hollow Tree?" I asked, crossing my arms. His eyes widened slightly and his ear twitched.

"Nothing," he stated. He was lying.

"You can't lie to me Mr. Hale. One I know you and two the Hollow Tree's decay is affecting the magic of this town. So tell me what you know so that I can come up with a solution and save the tree," I said.

"Are you accusing me?" he asked. That was a good question. Was I accusing him? I easily could. But with what Priscilla said no one was behind the tree dying. It was natural.

"I asked you what was wrong. I didn't accuse you. The reason I'm asking you is because Hale's Lumber Industry works closely with the Hollow Tree in maintaining the forest's preservation. So once again, do you know anything that could be useful?" I asked, calmly.

"You *want* to accuse me," he said, eyeing me.

"And why would I want that?" I asked. His jaw ticked.

"You hate me," he stated. For some reason those words coming out of him hurt. He even looked hurt saying them. The truth was I didn't hate him. I felt sorry for him. He was half a man, wandering through life like a lost spirit. Hate was a strong and exhausting emotion and I stopped letting him exhaust me a long time ago.

"I don't *hate* you. Do I want to believe that you would do something since you're clearly capable of dismantling our family? Naturally. But I'm trying to work with you in order to save the tree and this town. A town you used to be a part of," I said. I bit the inside of my cheek. I needed to feel something to calm myself down. My patience was waning. My father shook his head and began packing his things.

"Do you know anything?" I asked. He ignored me, standing up. My temper snapped. "Do you know something father?!" I said, raising my voice. His body froze. He looked back at me.

"I don't need you handling something you don't understand." His voice was like ice and I hated that it carved out a piece of my heart.

"Then help me understand," I pleaded. He turned around leaning a hand against the table.

"Stay away from the tree," he said.

"Why?" I asked. He was keeping something from me.

"I don't want you near the tree Eleanor. Stay away," he said, hand turning into a fist on the table. His shoulders trembled.

"I won't," I said. From the corner of my eye I could see Crystal looking down with her jaw set. My father tapped the table lightly.

"You've never listened to me in your entire life. But this time I need you to stay away from," he took a breath. "The. Tree," he punctuated. He finally turned around to look at me.

I dug my nails into the palm of my hands. I didn't see my stubborn, cold father. Instead I saw an old man who looked nearly defeated. A tiny piece of my heart that he always held regardless of our relationship squeezed. No matter how many years I spent building myself emotionally away from this man, there was always a part of me that broke for him.

"Please," he said softer. Something passed across his face quickly before I could read into it "Good bye," he said, walking out. Crystal finally looked up with tears in her eyes. She always hated when we fought and I always did my best to not have her around when it happened. I failed her again.

"I'm sorry," I said, sitting back down. I shouldn't have raised my voice with her in the room. "I shouldn't have yelled like that in front of you," I said. She shrugged her shoulders.

"It's fine," she said, her eyes wincing.

"But it's not. It wasn't right back then and it's not now," I said, wrapping my arms around her. She sagged into my embrace. "Are you okay?" I asked.

"I had a migraine last night so my senses are still sensitive," she said. I cupped her cheek. There was a tap on the door.

"Crystal," My father said from outside.

"I have to go," she said quietly.

I stared at the door. It took a few sentences and I felt like a teenager again fighting with my father. My body sank into the chair. A few tears slipped past my face and I let it. I let myself cry for my sister, cry for the father I used to have and missed. I especially cried for myself.

I was going to find out what he was hiding. He was right that I never listened to him growing up and I wasn't going to start now. My father was one of the most stubborn people I knew and as much as I hated to admit it, that was a Hale trait. With or without him I was saving my town and my tree.

I WAITED for the tavern to be nearly close to head inside. I didn't want to see any familiar faces after the day I had. Honestly? I just wanted to be with Caleb. As much as my brain hated to admit my heart and body felt more at ease around him. Tatiana let me inside.

"I'm going to lock up. He's already upstairs," she said, pulling on her coat. "Snow is coming down harder tonight," she pointed out. I nodded. More snow falling meant my timeline was getting close. I nodded silently. Tatiana squeezed my shoulder.

"It'll be okay. This is Lavender Falls. Now get up there," she said, walking out the door and locking it. I closed the lights before heading up the stairs.

With each step I felt my body getting heavier and heavier. There was a familiar smell floating through the air. The door was slightly ajar and I let myself in. Caleb was kneeling on the ground, staring into his oven. I bit back my laughter. His eyebrows were furrowed in concentration and he was wearing oven mitts. He looked absolutely adorable.

"Caleb?" I called out, taking off my coat. His head snapped in my direction.

"Oh hey," he said, getting up. I smiled.

"You know this smells very familiar," I said. He tossed the oven mitts on the counter and headed towards his fridge.

"Beer or wine?" he asked.

"It depends on what's in the oven," I said, crossing my arms. He glanced at the oven hesitantly when my phone buzzed.

LILY

> If you end up with food poisoning it's not my fault.

I snorted and showed Caleb my phone. He sighed, settling on grabbing two beers. He then reached for his phone and showed me a text exchange with Lily.

> So if one were to cook a Portuguese dish what should it be?

LILIANNA

> Is one cooking a Portuguese dish for a someone with pink hair

200

> One might be doing so

LILIANNA

> Porco Assada com batatas. I'll send you the recipe and instructions. You're going to need beer or wine.

My eyes widened as I stared up at Caleb. The tips of his ears were the same color as my hair. My heart pounded in my chest. No one had ever bothered to do something like this for me. He texted Lily asking what would make my stomach happy. He made me one of my favorite childhood dishes.

"You didn't need to do this," I said. He opened one of the beers and handed it to me.

"Tonight is just about us. No family drama, no magic and no curse," he said, opening his own. I took a step towards him and wrapped an arm around his waist. My body melted into his.

"Sure about no magic? I had a few ideas," I said, smirking against his chest. He took a sip of beer as his other hand slipped into my back pocket.

"And risk your magic going haywire and losing a ball? No thanks," he said. I threw my head back in laughter. Caleb grinned down at me and fuck was it beautiful. His features softened and the crinkle around his eyes appeared more prominent. His light blonde beard was beginning to fill out, cutting the angles of his face. His eyes were brighter today.

"Isn't that why you have two?" I teased.

AFTER SURVIVING dinner and telling Caleb he needed to buy smoked paprika because it does add flavor compared to regular paprika we quickly showered and settled into a nice relaxing bubble bath. He opened another bottle of beer that we decided to share together. Caleb's legs cradled my body and I leaned against his chest. The water was hot to the point of steamy and the bubbles smelled like eucalyptus and mint.

"This is nice," Caleb said into my ear. I leaned my head on his shoulder giving him access to my neck. He kissed up my neck with gentle bites. I sighed happily.

However, something nagged in the back of my head. I could still feel the remnants of our argument hanging in the outskirts.

"Can we talk about yesterday?" I asked quietly. I felt his chest rise and fall in a deep breath.

"Yes," he said, handing me the beer. I took a gulp to settle my nerves. I've always been known for being confrontational, which I was. But when it came to topics that involved my heart I wanted to run.

"I was telling the truth when I said I'm okay if we never break the curse. Our whatever this is has been going well without kissing. I'm just worried about this secret between your family and Bridget. Put yourself in her shoes," I said. His arms came to wrap around my belly. The water sloshed dangerously close to the edge of the tub.

"My sister was in so much pain as a child I just don't want to see her hurt. I'm the source of her pain. I feel like our relationship might worsen if the truth is out," he said quietly. I nodded.

"You know my father and I got into an argument in front of Crystal today. Growing up I tried my hardest to keep our arguments from reaching her. But seeing her reaction today I realized trying to keep the animosity my father and I held away from her was just as bad. Because whether she heard us or not she could *feel* it," I said, handing him the beer.

"You should talk to your family. See what they think and remember you have no idea how Bridget is going to react. You can't speak for her." I tiled my head to look into his eyes. He took a long sip of his beer.

"I'll talk to my family," he said. "Also I'm sorry. I took my frustrations out on you and I shouldn't have when you were only trying to help me." My heart leapt. He placed the beer on the floor and he cupped the side of my neck. I shivered at the feel of his cold hand against my heated skin.

"What I said about you and your sister was inexcusable. I am sorry for hurting you. We both have delicate relationships with our families but it doesn't mean one is worse than the other," he continued. I nodded, tears filling my vision. "From now on I will always hear you out and you will hear me out. We'll talk to each other with the respect we deserve," he said.

"Okay." My voice sounded shallow in my ears. I was beginning to feel overwhelmed. These emotions felt like a tidal wave crashing against my heart. I wanted to run and hide but Caleb's hand held me in place.

Because with him there was no running away, only running towards something marvelous. He swiped his thumb across my cheek before letting go. Fuck, everything was feeling too real.

"This friends-ish with benefits agreement isn't so bad is it?" I said awkwardly, trying to bring up the wall that was crumbling around my heart. I was retreating. Caleb's hands came to run up and down my thighs.

"I'm gonna wipe the ish out of friends and then I'm going to put boy in front of it," he said. His lips brushed against my ear and I shivered.

"Doesn't that make it boyfriends. Will I have more than one?" I asked as his hands continued their path up my body. I leaned my head back against his shoulder, too weak to fight against the sensations he was supplying. A chuckle poured out of Caleb.

"It'll never be easy with you will it?" he asked. I froze. I closed my eyes and willed the past to stay out of my head. I forced myself to not think about my exes and their comments on how I was always too stubborn and loud. Caleb must have felt the shift because he gripped my chin and forced me to look at him again. His eyes were beautifully concerned.

"Hey, hey, I didn't mean it that way. I meant we're always going to bicker like this which I do like," he explained. I nodded weakly, eyes still closed and he placed a gentle kiss on my forehead. The kiss crumbled another layer of bricks that kept my heart safe. "Look at me and let me rephrase," he said. I opened my eyes.

"I'm going to subtract and add so that friends-ish turns into boyfriend and I will prove it to you every day," he said with conviction. My bottom lip trembled.

Did I want that? Did I want something real? So far everything Caleb has done for me has shown me what it's truly like to be with someone who respects and admires me.

And this is what I've always secretly wanted and craved; someone to care for me and let me fly. I've yearned for someone to be my safe place to land. I was scared to trust that feeling when I've been fine on my own this entire time. But being on my own was lonely and I was tired of holding everything together.

"Is this another promise?" I whispered. Caleb gave me a lazy smile, a pretty pink flush on his cheeks. My heart rattled strongly against the wall.

"One that will last a very long time," he said, mimicking the same soft voice I gave him.

"I-I might be open to the idea," I said looking away.

"Let me start now," he said. He gently tapped my head and I stared at the elf before me again. "Now that I've used my words may I show you just how much I adore you, Eleanor Silva?" he asked, softly stroking my cheek.

"Adore me, Caleb Kiernan."

CHAPTER 24
NEW RELATIONSHIPS

CALEB

I t had been a few days since Eleanor and I shared a bed together. Snow had covered the grounds and the town was being filled with winter decorations. While half of me was torn between wanting to solidify my relationship with Eleanor the other half was worried about Bridget. She spoke to Eleanor asking her why I had a wall between us. It broke my heart. This family secret should have never been a secret from Bridget.

A headache was beginning to form. This wasn't supposed to be complicated. I just needed to break the curse and help Eleanor out. But now feelings about everyone were exploding. I wanted to officially be with Eleanor. I wanted her father to eat griffin shit. I needed the town to be saved, not just for Eleanor's sake but for the people here.

Even though I spent most of my life away, everyone here made me feel like I belonged. Because I did. This was my home and so were the people in it.

"You're an idiot." A voice called out. I looked up to see Lilianna and Lola, sliding into the seats in front of me.

"Excused me?" I asked. Lilianna shook her head.

"We're all just trying to help," Lilianna said. I rolled my eyes and began drying glasses.

"Of course I know that," I said. Lola cocked her head.

"Then what are you afraid of?" Lola asked. I snorted.

"What makes you think I'm afraid?" I asked. She continued to stare.

"Your heart rate picked up throughout this whole conversation and that cup has been dry the entire time," she said. I cursed. She's a vampire, of course she could tell.

"You care for her right?" Lilianna asked. Her brown eyes were filled with concern.

"Of course I care for Eleanor," I said. The tips of my ears became warm.

"Did I say Eleanor, Lola?" Lilianna smirked. Lola shook her head.

"You definitely did not," Lola said, placing an arm around Lilianna's shoulders. I set the glass and towel down with a sigh.

"Listen, we understand why you might be hesitant to tell Bridget the truth. But remember memory wipes, no matter how good it might seem, have repercussions. Look at her," Lilianna said softly. I turn to see my little sister smiling at Flynn. My heart cracked.

Bridget had never smiled at me that way. We never laughed or even had a non-work related conversation. But my brothers and everyone else had a relationship with her. Stars, even my dad.

Growing up I was always the more quiet one. I liked keeping to myself in the corner. I was an observer and I enjoyed being one. Greg and Flynn would kick the ball in the backyard with Bridget trailing behind them and I would sit on the sidelines with cards or a book.

I cracked a smile as I remembered my attempt to teach Bridget how to play blackjack. She was quick with numbers and always managed to beat me. She was too smart for her own good and she had no problem letting us know.

I watched Bridget turn to take a customer's order without a notepad. She had a sharp memory. Now that I think about it she was a lot like me. I felt my heart tightened. Good with numbers, grumpy occasionally, quick memory. All of those things were like me. We were more similar than I thought despite our distance.

Maybe Eleanor was right. She needed to know the truth. Stars, the fact she asked Eleanor about us broke me up. I turned to Lilianna and Lola.

"You know Bridget is one of the most confident and sharp people we know. But when she's around you she's lost, hesitant, unsure," Lilianna pointed out. I sighed.

"I'm tired of the walls. All of them," I confessed. The women held their hands out. I stared at them confused until they both huffed and grabbed my hand.

Fuck these past few months have been such an emotional roller coaster. First I had Celestino back in my life. Sailor managed to worm his way in and we became a trio. Kinda like the three musketeers although Sailor effectively named us *Magic Men*.

Now these two ladies were joining the group along with Eleanor. Although respectfully Eleanor wasn't *just* a friend.

"Friends are there for each other," Lola said as if reading my mind.

"We're your friends and will always be there for you," Lilianna said. Lilianna smiled easily these days. No doubt because of Celestino. Lola's grip on my hand tightened and I flinched.

"Friends unless you hurt Eleanor. She hurts, you hurt," Lola said with a bright smile. Lilianna giggled.

"How about we toast to our official friendship with some whiskey?" Lilianna said, bumping shoulders with Lola. Flynn clapped my back.

"Did someone say whiskey?" Flynn said, eyes bright with excitement. "I have a new batch you can try." Flynn reached underneath the bar and pulled out a dark amber glass bottle. I set out four glasses for each of us.

"I hope it's good," Lola said. Flynn snorted.

"I made it. Why wouldn't it be good?" Flynn said, pouring us each a glass. This was the same one Eleanor and I had shared the other night.

Although I wasn't involved in Kiernan's Whiskey Distillery much, it was a big part of Flynn. Like my older brother Greg, Flynn loved creating recipes. His were just the alcoholic kind. He's the main one in the company coming up with new batches yearly. It's why he studied horticulture. He wanted to discover just how many ways he could transform whiskey.

"There's a possibility of it not tasting good considering your gardening skills," Lola said, smiling. Flynn snorted.

"Really because last time I checked you had a tendency to over-water the mint," he said, leaning against the bar. Lola scoffed.

"It's *water* mint. They love being *wet*," she said with an irritated voice. "You know what else likes to be wet?" she asked, her tone switching. Flynn's ears turned pink. Lilianna choked on her drink and mine nearly poured out of my nose. That would have burned like drag-on's breath.

"Catnip, cattail, water parsley," Flynn listed with a clenched jaw. Lola threw back the rest of her drink. She handed me the glass and leaned against the bar. Flynn stood his ground despite a flush crawling up his neck. Lola batted her eyes and gave a cheeky smile.

"Swamp *sunflowers*."

ELEANOR

Adore me, Caleb Kiernan.

Adore me?! What the hellfire was wrong with me? I rubbed my chest where my heart was beating rapidly. That was single handedly the most adorable moment in my entire life and it was with *Caleb*. I must have been way too tired, drunk on beer and low on my monster-ella cheese sticks intake for that to happen.

I stared into my kitchen sink. I liked it. I liked it a lot. I bit my lip. Fuck, this was really scary. It was at these moments where I wished I had my mom. I wish I could talk about this with her.

The men in my life, the ones who were supposed to love me and support me had only ever disappointed me and yet Caleb has shown me what I've been missing. He's shown me what I've always deserved. Maybe I just needed to say yes. I squeezed my eyes shut. *Yes.*

Caleb allowed me to let go and I truly loved that. I hadn't realized how tightly I'd been holding onto life until he offered to help. Caleb was like my personal lighthouse; someone who guided me towards safety and that safety was in his arms.

"Alright bitch. You're basically in love with a grumpy elf and everyone saw it coming but you," I said out loud. I shook my head, laughing. *Focus.* What was I doing prior to having happy sexy thoughts of Caleb? My phone caught my eye.

I was walking back and forth in my kitchen, trying to muster the courage to call Crystal. I snorted at myself. I gave Caleb grief about his sister and yet here I was nervous to call mine. I needed to check in on her. She had mentioned quickly she had a migraine. I wasn't too versed in them but I knew people who suffered. My thoughts turned to my father briefly.

He was so animated about me staying away from the tree, it didn't add up. It was almost like he was worried. Like he was worried about me being near the tree. But why? It's not like anything ever happened...besides me now having the ability to communicate with it. Did he know about that? I sighed against my kitchen island. Fuck it. I dialed her number.

"Is everything okay?" Crystal's voice was timid. I smiled. Always a worrier, kinda like Lilianna.

"The more important question is, is everything okay with *you*? How's your head?" I asked. She let out a tired laugh.

"I'm okay. I know how to handle them. But are *you* okay? That meeting was...intense," she said. I curled up on the couch.

"Well the festival part of the meeting went smoother than expected," I said jokingly.

"It did," she said quietly. I waited for her to say something but she stayed quiet. Awkwardness filled the silence and I was itching to break it.

"Do you think father had anything to do with the tree?" I asked. She's been with him the past few years. She now had better insight on how he thought and worked. I reached for a pillow, clutching it to my chest.

"Honestly? No. He's been checking on the tree the past few weeks. He's been concerned. I even caught him going through spell books. I think he's trying to help," she said. My eyes widened in response.

"Well what the fury fuck? He could have said that and we could be working together!" I exclaimed. Crystal let out a giant laugh.

"What?!" I asked.

"Ellie. You do realize stubbornness runs in this family right? We each have issues asking for help," she pointed out. I groaned. She was annoyingly right.

"We do," I agreed, begrudgingly.

"How's Caleb by the way?" she asked. I hesitated.

"He's being Caleb. Stoic. Quiet. Stubborn. Hot," I began rattling off. Crystal choked. "What?" I asked.

"He is pretty hot with those baby blues," she said.

"Crys!" I shouted into the phone. We broke out into fits of laughter. It was amazing to have my sister back. I felt a piece of myself I thought I lost a long time ago, slowly come back.

"He makes me happy," I admitted.

"Good. Anyway, are you ready for the festival?" she asked.

"Ready as I'll ever be," I confessed. My sister began humming a tune. "Are you singing Tangled?" I said with a smile.

"Habit," she muttered.

CHAPTER 25
THE FESTIVAL BEGINS

CALEB

A few days had gone by since that night I surprised Eleanor with her favorite dish. That night I saw something in Eleanor's eyes. She allowed me to see just how far the possibility of us scared her. And yet she stayed by my side. I needed to fight for her, us and our future.

I was preparing for the pub crawl and the festival while she was out handling the festival. I was still wrestling with the fact that I needed to tell Bridget the truth. I just wasn't sure when or even how to approach the subject. I also needed to talk to my family about it first.

"I double checked the stock and I think we should get more tequila. We had that college crowd during the fall festival plus Eleanor. They nearly wiped us out," Bridget said, handing me the list. I had her focusing on stock this afternoon since she was great with numbers. I nodded. She drummed her fingers against the bar. I stole a glance at her. Her mouth was set in a hard line and her eyebrows were cinched. My stomach twisted.

"Anything else?" I asked. She continued to tap her fingers.

"How are you?" she asked, tentatively. My eyes widened at her question.

"How am I?" I repeated. She rolled her eyes at me.

"Yeah. How are you? It's what a person asks another person," she said coldly. I swallowed. It was a simple question but I felt my throat tightened. For so many years I was afraid of holding a normal conversation for the fear something would trigger a break in the memory spell that was casted.

"A little stressed because of the festival and that the magic is kind of going off," I said. She nodded along.

"Yeah, same here. I think a flower came alive and bit Flynn's finger," she said. We shared a chuckle before descending into an awkward silence. The door ding as customers strolled in.

"Want me to pour you a beer while you finalize the inventory list?" I offered. This time her eyes widened at me. Her lips attempted to twitch into a smile.

"Yeah but no dark beer please," she said, hopping onto the bar stool.

"Excuse me?" I said jokingly. This time she smiled and it reminded me of Flynn's; all teeth.

"Dark beer is bitter," she said. I rolled my eyes.

"It's an acquired taste, Bridge," I said, pouring her a sour cider. Her smile turned shy.

"I haven't heard you call me that in a long time," she said softly, looking down at the bar.

"I know...I'm sorry," I said, handing her the cider. She nodded, taking a sip. For a quick second her eyes brightened and I stood frozen. Did the spell break?

"You know this would taste amazing with mead," she said, staring into the glass. I chuckled.

"You know thinking like that is how Flynn ended up wanting to work at the distillery," I said. Which was true. Once we were 16 my dad allowed us to try whiskey during events. Flynn didn't like the taste at first but then immediately thought of how to improve it so he could like it.

"I prefer mead over whiskey," Bridget confessed.

"Someone said mead?" Sailor appeared with Celestino. Bridget nodded.

"I was saying how this cider would taste good with mead," she said. Celestino raised an eyebrow.

"I don't think I've ever had mead," Celestino said, sitting next to Bridget. Her eyes widened comically.

"You've never had mead?!" she asked. Sailor patted his back.

"Bestie you are missing out!" Sailor said. Bridget went on to explain mead animatedly to Celestino while Sailor backed her up. My shoulders relaxed and I couldn't help but grin. My little sister was sitting across from me with a smile. She was hanging out with my friends. It almost felt normal.

"How do you know so much about mead?" Celestino asked.

"I tried it at a renaissance festival during college. They gave me mead mixed with cider. It was awesome," she said. Her eyes sparkled at the memory.

"There's a traveling renaissance festival and they stop in Coralia Coast every year during the late spring. We used to have a local meadery that would set up a booth but it closed down," Sailor said.

"A meadery? That is so cool," Bridget commented. My heart swelled. She had the same look in her eyes Flynn had when he realized he could do something for our family's whiskey distillery. Maybe hers was mead. I handed my friends their beers.

"It's very cool," I said, clinking my own glass against Bridget's.

ELEANOR

The festival began today. I spent the entire week visiting the Hollow Tree, using my magic to keep things under control as best as I could. I had been trying to figure out what my father was hiding but the Hollow Tree wouldn't tell me anything. It only kept repeating, *what once is lost or gone can be found or reborn.* I had no idea what that meant. What had been lost? What was gone? What needed to be found or reborn?

At least everything was going smoothly with the festival. Competitions and carnival rides were already starting. Winners would be announced later today and tonight would be the official ceremony welcoming the winter solstice. We had to remind the supernatural folk that during the snowball competition no magic was allowed. Lola was with the reindeers at the petting zoo to make sure they were grounded for the day.

My mind wandered to the stoic elf who worked at my favorite pub. I felt myself softening around him and I think I was okay with that. I was seeing that it was okay to let your guard down with someone. But a part of me felt guilty. My father unconsciously taught me to rely on no one. But Caleb has never tried to cage me.

The door to Priscilla's Lotions and Potions dinged as I entered. I was hit by the smell of lemon, cinnamon and sage. Priscilla was running around her shop, throwing things together. She looked tired.

Fuck. She's been working over time preparing tonics for the tree. On top of trying to use what magic she could with the tree messing up the ley lines and flow. My heart continued to break.

"I'm sorry!" I blurted out. Priscilla jumped at my voice. Her eyes softened.

"Don't you dare Eleanor Silva. I'm doing this for us and for the town," she said firmly. My shoulders slumped as I walked over to wrap her in a hug.

"We have been slowly down the rot which is good!" she said, confidently. I nodded although it didn't feel like enough.

"Today's the festival. Who knows what could go wrong," I confessed. She nodded.

"It'll be okay," she assured me. She handed me a few salves. "For

214

you to use on the tree. I added the last bit of sea moss." I placed them into my bag.

"Thanks again. I have to go meet up with Crystal but I'll see you soon," I said, giving her a hug. Priscilla squeezed her arms. The smell of citrus filtered through the air.

"You got this Silva," she said.

I WAS WALKING up to the tavern when I noticed Crystal outside talking to Sailor. I bit the inside of my cheek to keep from smiling. Sailor wore a white hoodie with a light blue flannel that made his skin glow and eyes appear brighter. He had some distance between himself and my sister. His head was bent low. He was sheepishly scratching the back of his head while he talked to her.

"So is your whole body covered in scales?"

I snorted out of a laugh at my sister's deadpanned question. She turned around, face red. She waved her hands back and forth.

"I-I didn't mean to say that out loud! It just slipped," she said. She turned to face Sailor whose cheeks were rosy. "I also didn't mean like everywhere. Like legs or your butt or your pen-oh the stars I'm going to shut up," she said quickly. Sailor chuckled and tapped Crystal's hands which were covering her face. She peeked at him.

"It's not a dumb question. I do have scales everywhere but it's more scattered. Like on my cheekbones, my sides and my spine," he said. My sister's shoulders relaxed.

"That seems pretty," she said quietly. I rolled my eyes.

"Alright stop being cute. We have events to check out," I said, wrapping my arm around her and pulling her to walk down the street.

"Bye ladies!" Sailor said as he opened the door to The Drunken Fairy Tale Tavern. I paused my walking and made my way back to the door pushing Sailor inside. "Hey," he protested. Caleb looked up from the bar in surprise. The pub was already getting packed with tourists.

"Hey! The hottie with white blonde hair behind the bar is mine!" I shouted. Caleb's ears burned red and I smiled as the people who were from our town cheered.

"Go do some work or I'm not allowing you inside!" Caleb shouted.

"As you wish!" I said walking out.

CRYSTAL and I checked out the pie bake off and the food truck situation. Afterwards we decided it was best to split up and make sure everyone was okay. I saw Lilianna dipping in and out gathering footage.

Even though there was a dreadful feeling in the pit of my stomach I was happy. So many people were laughing and having fun. Despite the fact that a yeti made its way into our snowball competition or how in the ice sculpture competition one of the statues began coming to life, it was okay.

Thankfully the humans thought the yeti was a mascot and the ice sculpture mysteriously fell over, cracking into shards. Mysteriously of course.

Walking towards the Gasping Greenwood Forest for the ceremony, I tugged my scarf tighter around my throat. I silently prayed to the stars that everything would go smoothly.

Fairy lights wrapped around the trees that circled the clearing. In the center was a giant bonfire and a few fire fairies scattered around to make sure it stayed under control. They were sweating though. We all were anxious about using magic. Everyone spent the day being as limited as they could.

There were stations of caramel apples, apple cider and hot chocolate. Some chairs and tables scattered for people to sit, relax and talk. There were even inflatable slides for the kids and a ball pit where the balls looked like snowballs. I smiled. It was beautiful. Everyone looked content.

Winter brought on the cold and longer nights. People had a tendency to be more sad, lost and lonely. But I always felt alive in the winter. It was a good time to reflect and appreciate what you had. From the corner of my eye I noticed my father talking to Lily's mom. I walked up to Crystal who was standing near the fire.

"Sound check is done. We're ready to begin," Crystal said. Her cheeks were rosy and she looked a bit relaxed. My father made his way towards us along with Mayor Kiana who was bundled up in a red parka. She smiled at us.

"Let's start this!" I said in the most cheerful tone I could muster. Emily came up and handed Mayor Kiana the mic. I took my stance next to her and tugged Emily beside me. The crowd turned to face us. My fake smile began to turn genuine as I stared at the people before me. Fairies, pixies, vampires, werewolves and more. We were all different and yet connected.

This town, the Hollow Tree all connected us. I felt a swell of pride knowing I came from this town. But it was sad my father didn't feel the same way anymore.

"How are we feeling, Lavender Falls?!" Mayor Kiana shouted. Everyone began cheering. Lily and Celestino waved from the side. Lily along with an intern had cameras set up to capture the speech. I waved back. My eyes scanned the crowd for Caleb but he wasn't around. He was probably at the tavern. The pubs were always busy during the festival. Sailor wasn't around either. I couldn't remember if he had a shift at the Siren's Saloon or not.

"We are so excited for this year's Whimsical Winter Wonderland Festival. A mouthful am I right? The day has been filled with so many events. From snowball fights to ice sculptures, sled rides, food and more!" Everyone cheered as she continued.

"We love having these festivals because the community comes together to create the most amazing memories. For those of you from out of town we hope you continue to come to all the fun events we have planned all year long." Claps continued. I felt myself getting restless. I didn't know why.

Something in the back of my head kept telling me to go back to the tree. I snuck a glance at my father. He was drumming his fingers on his pants. He seemed anxious.

"Before we begin I would like to thank all the sponsors for the festival, especially Hale's Lumber Industry! You guys have been a big help with this year's festival." Mayor Kiana handed my father the mic. I tensed up.

"For those of you who don't know, the Hale's have always been a part of this town. While the past few years we've been estranged we plan on joining the community once again," my father paused. "My wife loved this town and for a while I forgot why. But this festival and the people around us are a sign, a remembrance of why. Everyone is a valued, caring and kind member of this community. We are honored to be a part of this event. We hope you all enjoy," he said.

My heart rattled in my chest. I looked at Crystal whose eyes held back tears. We hadn't heard my father talk about my mom in years. It was one small sentence but it was enough to bring tears to my eyes. Looking at him again all I could see was a broken man. He wanted to be a part of the town he looked down on. I wondered what changed. He handed Mayor Kiana the mic again.

"Alright I think that's enough talking. Happy winter solstice everyone!" Mayor Kiana called out. The fire fairies ignited the bonfire, having the colors shift from blue to pink to red. Instead of using magic they used powders to change the flames colors. We needed to be on the safe side and I let out a sigh of relief when it went well. Everyone cheered. Mayor Kiana turned to give me a big hug.

"You've done an amazing job Eleanor. You should be proud," she whispered. I beamed.

"I...I actually loved focusing on the events," I confessed. Her eyes sparkled.

"Oh I know. We'll talk once everything settles," she said with a wink. With one last squeezed she walked over to her family and headed toward the slides. I turned to see Crystal talking to my father. She seemed worried. I took a deep breath.

"Mr. and Ms. Hale. Thank you so much for the sponsorship. The festival is a hit," I said. My father looked at me and nodded.

"You did a wonderful job together. I hope Hale's Lumber Industry can continue to sponsor future events," he said, reaching out his hand. My heart thumped. I wasn't expecting that kind of response from my father. I can't remember the last time he praised me. An emotion passed in his eyes, one I hadn't seen in a long time.

"I hope so too," I said, taking his hand. He shook my hand in a firm grip.

"I have something to take care of. I hope you both enjoy the festival together," he said, walking away. *Together*. He wanted us to spend time with each other. There was a tug on my jacket sleeve. I looked at Crystal's worried expression.

"What's wrong?" I asked. There were tears in her eyes. "Crystal what's wrong?" I pleaded. She gripped my hand.

"Can't you feel it?" she whispered. I looked at her confused. I glanced around the smiling faces. "Focus," she said. I closed my eyes focusing on my magic, on any magic. I could sense everyone around me. I could feel how we were all connected but…wait what was that?

I looked at the path that led to the Hollow Tree and watched the remnants of the father I used to know slink into the shadows. My stomach dropped. The Hollow Tree. It was fading fast. Way too fast.

"Oh no," I whispered as the cold breeze picked up. Crystal nodded. Without another word I ran after my father. The Hollow Tree was on its last breath.

I could feel it.

CHAPTER 26
THE TRUTH IS OUT

CALEB

I dragged my brothers, my mom and my dad into a family meeting while Bridget was opening the tavern with Tatiana.

"What is this about?" My dad asked, via FaceTime. Everyone looked at me.

"Well mom, dad the thing is Flynn, Lola, Eleanor, Celestino, Lilianna, Sailor and Priscilla have all been working hard to figure out how to break my curse." I said. Wow, that was a mouthful. I had a lot of friends now. Saying all of their names was exhausting. My dad stayed stoic. My mom on the other hand began tearing up.

"Why now?" my dad asked, curiously. I rubbed the back of my neck. I hated sharing my feelings, especially with my family. It always made me feel awkward. But I needed them to know the gravity of this situation.

"Eleanor," I stated. My brothers smiled at me.

"The Silva pixie?" my dad asked. His memory of the town and its people faded slightly from spending so many years away. I nodded. My mom clapped excitedly.

"I've always loved her. Strong willed, smart, beautiful," she said. A smile tugged on my lips. Eleanor was all those things and more. My dad's eyes narrowed at me before softening.

"Alright then so your curse?" he said. I took a deep breath and launched into a quick explanation about Lola finding the spell, going to Coralia Coast and how the spell failed.

"I still don't see the reason for the meeting," my mom said. My dad sighed.

"I think I have a feeling," he said looking broken. He figured it out quickly. Greg began shaking his head. My mom gasped when she realized.

"We can't," she said. I looked at my mom, my heart in my throat.

"Trust me guys. I know. Out of all of you I *know*. Okay? I've had to live with keeping her at a distance. Even if it doesn't work she deserves to know why she isn't close to me. She should know why we don't have a normal relationship. I can't take being like this to her. I'm tired of it," I said, squeezing my hands together.

"I agree. She needs to know. I know I was young and therefore don't remember much but Bridget has always asked me why Caleb is so grumpy with her. She hates it," Flynn pleaded. I stared at him. She's talked to him about me? Stars, of course she has. She even spoke to Eleanor. Flynn glanced at me and nodded, sadness in his eyes. Greg sighed.

"I'm hesitant because I remember it all too well, but I agree. She should know the truth. We honestly should have never done the spell in the first place. It's time for us siblings to feel like a family again," Greg said, offering a smile. My mom wiped her tears. It broke her to see her daughter break as a child. I can't begin to imagine how my parents felt during that time.

"*Mo chroí,*" my dad said, softly. We all froze. We hadn't heard our dad call our mom that in years. She looked at the phone, wiping her eyes. They stared at each other, as if speaking in their minds. They were together for years before the divorce. They ended their marriage amicably. Sometimes people grow apart. But no matter the years they spent away from each other they had their own silent language. After a moment my mother sighed and nodded.

"Okay Caleb. We support this," my dad said. My hands began shaking. This was happening. I was going to tell her.

THE CEREMONY WAS BEGINNING and with a quick explanation to Tatiana she tossed Flynn, Bridget and I out the door later that evening.

"Do it and then send them back to me for work," she said, before closing the door in my face. I couldn't help but chuckle at Tatiana. Bridget was confused on why we needed her at Priscilla's but came along anyway.

Her white blonde hair was braided back and her cheeks were pink from the cold. Her brown eyes assessed us all. Flynn and Greg stood off to the side with Sailor. Priscilla was mixing the potion in a bowl. I sat on a stool in front of the table, remembering how I nearly passed out when Lilianna casted the spell.

"What's going on?" Bridget asked, eyes narrowing. Everyone looked at me.

"We have something to tell you," I said tentatively. I motioned for her to sit next to me. She eyed me suspiciously.

"Okay?" she said, perplexed. I sighed and glanced at my brothers who nodded.

"I know we don't have the best relationship," I confessed. She snorted with an eye roll that reminded me of Flynn. "There's a reason for that," I stated. Her eyes sharpened. Fuck, she had that same look our dad would give when we broke a piece of furniture or used our magic to give Flynn a wedgie.

"We, our family, have been keeping a secret from you," I said, nerves slipping into my voice. She crossed her arms, preparing herself.

"Do you remember the divorce?" Flynn asked. She shrugged her shoulders.

"Everything during that time is a haze. I was little," she said, honestly. I could hear Greg sigh.

222

"You were distraught when you found out," Greg said. Bridget looked between us all.

"I did something?" she whispered, her voice already breaking. Fuck. I couldn't do this. I felt a cold hand squeeze mine. It was Bridget's. Her brown eyes watered. "I did something." It wasn't a question. I nodded. Her hand on mine tightened. Priscilla came around.

"If you drink this…you'll remember," she said, offering a bottle with pink liquid. She gripped it in her hand, staring at it. When she finally looked up it was at me. She took a deep breath and placed the bottle on the table.

"Just tell me," she said, reaching for my hands again. I took a deep breath.

"You tried to cast a love potion. You were sad our parents were getting a divorce. But your reading wasn't quite there yet. You accidentally cursed me that if I were to kiss anyone I would turn to stone," I said and I felt the weight on my shoulders fall off. She stayed silent, processing. Then her eyes sparkled.

"The reason I grew up away was because dad wanted to find a way to break the curse. We tried a bunch of ways and met everyone we could. Nothing worked because we weren't sure exactly what you said," I finished. When I looked up she was trying not to cry.

"You guys erased my memory?" she asked tentatively. She shut her eyes, rocking her head back and forth. I nodded.

"You wouldn't go no near him no matter how much we told you he was okay. You would cry all the time," Flynn jumped in. She nodded, squeezing her eyes to keep her emotions at bay..

"I'm-" she began but I shook my head.

"It was a complete accident. Don't you dare apologize," I said firmly. She nodded, eyes on the floor. Her eyebrows furrowed in concentration.

"I-I remember. I was watching Hercules. I was so upset," she said. She paused and cocked her head. "Damn I used some serious magic though." She offered a smile, trying to break the tension. I shook my head, chuckling. Greg slapped Flynn's back laughing.

"You sure did," Greg said.

"Lola found a spell. We had Lilianna cast it but it needs the original caster to cast the spell," Greg said. She eyed the book by Priscilla. Taking a deep breath she stood up.

"I'm breaking this curse and you're going to be with Eleanor and we're all going to have sibling game nights from now on so I can kick everyone's ass," she said, wiping her face. Flynn let out a chuckle. "Oh and memory wiping spells are probably *not* the healthiest route to go. We could have done therapy."

"What?" I asked in shock. She offered a smile and wrapped me in a tight hug.

"The whole town knows about you and Eleanor and we have years to make up for," she said, kissing my cheek. Letting go of me she walked over to the spell book and nodded at Priscilla. Bridget was a lot stronger than I gave her credit for. And I couldn't wait to learn more about her. Priscilla handed me a bottle with blue liquid. Our eyes met.

"By the way we're having a serious family meeting about the whole memory wipe thing," she said, looking at me, Greg and Flynn. We each nodded. I forgot how deadly Bridget's looks could be. Taking a deep breath I began drinking as she called out the spell with a hand outstretched.

"A mistake was made so let the past fade. Fix what has been broken. Through love, let light be awoken," she said firmly. Once again, I fell forward as my whole body heated up. But unlike Lilianna this was hotter, more intense. I grunted. I faintly heard Flynn and Greg asking me something. And then I felt a snap within. I gasped for air.

"Holy shit," Sailor hissed.

"What happened?" Bridget's voice broke. I stared at her with wide eyes. My body felt lighter, looser. The tension I always had, the heaviness on my heart, melted away.

"It's gone. The black stain is gone," Sailor said, clapping the back of Flynn's shoulder. I stared at Bridget. She had the biggest smile on her face. She ran into my arms and barreled me into a hug.

"I have my brother back?" she asked. I squeezed her.

"And I'm never leaving," I said.

One second everything was peaceful but then a deep rumble shook the ground.

"A fucking earthquake?" Flynn shouted, gripping Greg and Sailor. I held Bridget and Priscilla gripped the table. The bottles rattled against each other. My phone buzzed in my pocket. It was an unknown number.

"Hello?" I said.

"Caleb! It's Eleanor. Come to the tree!" Crystal's voice cried out. My heart stopped.

"Sailor, tell Lilianna, Lola and Celestino to go to the tree," I shouted as I ran out of the shop and made my way to the Hollow Tree.

CHAPTER 27
THE TRUTH IS OUT
PART 2

ELEANOR

My father was staring at the tree. I stood off watching on the side. "Please," he pleaded. He sounded broken. I had never heard him sound so broken, not since mom passed. The tree rustled, tiny twigs falling down.

"Let me help you," he pleaded again. The tree shook again. I knelt down, pressing my hand to the ground to connect to the tree. They had to be having a conversation. A part of me felt guilty for eavesdropping but I needed to know.

You can't stop this my child

"Please," he said, getting down on his knees. My eyes widened.

What once is lost or gone can be found or reborn.

"There has to be a way. The town is at stake," he said. I sat in shock. His voice was twisted with regret and helplessness. I had no idea my father cared this much.

My time has come. Cut short it was. You could...

"No," he practically shouted. He could what? Was he keeping a way to save the tree to himself?

"What does the tree mean?" I asked, standing and breaking out from the shadows. My dad stood up quickly.

"Eleanor!" he exclaimed. I began walking forward.

"There's a way to save the tree isn't there?" I confronted him. He shook his head. "There is," I said. How could he keep it from me? "What is it?" I asked.

"No," he said, taking a step forward, blocking me from the tree. I looked at him in shock

"There's a way to save the Hollow Tree. Now tell me!" I demanded. The tree shook. He glanced at the tree.

"No," he said, firmly. I felt anger rise inside of me. I took a deep breath and connected to the tree again. There was a deep rumble.

"Tell me," I demanded. For a second I thought the tree wouldn't answer.

You and I are connected child

"Connected how?" I asked, heart racing.

"Stop," my father hissed.

When you were a baby you got really sick. Your parents did whatever it took but nothing worked so they came to me

I glanced at my father. His hands were fisted at his side, his eyes were sorrowful.

I gave you a blessing. This blessing was a piece of me.

I stared up at my father, stunned. I had a piece of the tree inside of me?

"Is this why I've always felt a connection?" I asked, my hands trembling.

Yes child.

"You were sick," my father said, interrupting. "You're mother and I tried everything, saw everyone we could. But nothing worked. Instead you got worse. You kept growing weak. Your mother suggested we see the Hollow Tree." He choked up at the mention of my mom. His eyes shone brightly at the tree with tears.

"We asked for help to save our little girl. And we were blessed. Your mother...she was so happy and you got better." He wiped a hand over his face. I took a shaky breath, turning to the tree.

227

"What happens if I return your magic?" I asked.

"No," my father said through gritted teeth.

You could save me by giving me back what is mine. But that would mean...

Oh no. My whole body trembled at the realization. I could save the town if I gave back what wasn't mine.

"Eleanor you can't," my father said, breaking in. I glared at him.

"Why do you care?" I asked. He took a step back as if I slapped him.

"You're still my daughter. I already lost your mother. I can't lose you completely. I won't have you give up the life you've carved out for yourself," he confessed. My throat closed. Now? Now he was saying all of this? I cursed at myself for the tears that sprung. I didn't need his acceptance. I didn't need him finally saying I was his daughter again. Taking a deep breath I pulled out the salve Priscilla handed me.

"Please Eleanor," he said, taking a step towards me. I held up my hand and pushed him back with my magic.

"I will always do whatever it takes to protect what I care about. I don't want the town or anyone and anything to suffer because of me," I said. My father shook his head before turning to the tree.

"Take my magic," he said. I stared at him wide-eyed. "Please, just take my magic. Whatever you need. Don't take my daughter. Please," his voice broke. Staring at him I was reminded of how he looked when he heard mom passed. Broken and helpless. He didn't need to sacrifice himself. I'm the one that held a piece of the Hollow Tree. A piece that didn't rightfully belong to me.

Taking a deep breath I dug my knees into the ground. My father took a step but I pushed him back. The wind began picking up and I rubbed the salve at the base of the tree. The ground trembled as I dug my hands into the ground.

Closing my eyes I poured every ounce of love, warmth, kindness that the Hollow Tree has given me in saving my life. I thought of my town, my family, my friends and Caleb. I let it all pour out of me. I faintly heard the sound of footsteps.

Eleanor, what once is lost or gone can be found or reborn.

The Hollow Tree whispered once more before an explosion of gold blinded me.

CALEB

"Eleanor!" I yelled running towards her. There was a flash of gold light and I felt an invisible force try to shut me out. "What the fuck is happening?" I yelled at her father. The man had tears in his eyes.

"Eleanor has a piece of the tree inside of her. She's giving it back," he yelled. The wind roared around us. The rest of our friends gathered.

"There's like a force field around them," Lola shouted with glowing eyes.

"This magic is strong," Lilianna said, her hands glowing. No, this couldn't be happening. I barely had her. I needed her with me. I had plans for us. Dates, vacations, a proposal at some point. She was the reason I found myself opening up to the world and I wouldn't live in one without her.

"No," I hissed as I forced myself into the shield set by Eleanor and the tree. The force field sizzled against my touch. My magic which usually remained dormant awoke. It burned through my veins and pushed out.

"Please," I pleaded to the tree. There was a crack in the air and my hands slipped past the force field. Eleanor was laying at the base of the tree. One hand on a root. She was glowing. She looked like a celestial being.

"No, no, no, no," I muttered, pulling her in my arms. "Eleanor,

229

lovely. Wake up please. For me. Stay with me Starburst," I said, tapping her face. But she wasn't responding. I stared at the tree.

"Please don't take her from me," I pleaded. My heart was pounding, My cheeks were wet with tears. I clutched her in my arms. Her face was serene, like a painting. I couldn't lose my other half. I wouldn't be able to live with myself. She continually gave herself to everyone in this town. She didn't need to give up her magic or her life.

Taking a quick breath, I kissed her. I kissed her with every magic I had running through my body. I gave myself fully to her, the tree and the town.

What once is lost or gone can be found or reborn, I heard a voice whisper. The air around us exploded with thunder. I felt a tentative hand, shaking to cup my cheek. Opening my eyes, gold dust was floating around us. Eleanor slowly opened her eyes. I stared at her in shock. They were both hazel. She offered me a sleepy smile.

"You said you would kiss me with your dick inside of me," her words sounded strangled. I heard a cough from behind me. I threw my head back in laughter. She was back. My Eleanor was back.

"Eleanor," I whispered.

"You're not stone," she said with a wobbly smile, patting my lips. I shook my head, not caring that I was crying. Before I could say anything her eyes looked off to the side. She sighed, happily. I followed her gaze. The tree was gone. Instead there was a tiny sapling.

"What is that?" Lola asked from behind, sniffling. Flynn had an arm wrapped around her.

"A sapling," Flynn said. Eleanor struggled to sit up. I held her close to my chest. She took a deep breath.

"What once is lost or gone can be found or reborn. I couldn't save the Hollow Tree because it would require sacrificing myself. Instead I used a piece of what was given to me plus Caleb's magic, power from the ley lines and what was left of the tree to give birth to a new Hollow Tree," she said softly.

"Reborn," Lilianna said. Eleanor nodded.

"Kinda of like Groot," Flynn commented. Lola giggled, shaking her head.

"Eleanor," her father said. The man looked worn out. She stared at him silently. "I know no words can replace the things I've said to you. I'm just happy you're okay," he said, wiping his eyes. She stared at him for a few moments.

"Help take care of the tree okay? With Flynn. He's an expert in horticulture although Lola might chime in," Eleanor said. He nodded silently. "Oh and give Crystal a break. She's doing great things, you know. She's meant to take over and I think you know that," she huffed. Her father cracked a small smile.

"Oh I know," he said, standing up. Eleanor tapped my chest.

"Can you take me home?" she asked. I nodded, my words clogged in my throat. There was so much I wanted to say but she was tired and we had an audience. Once she was well rested we had much to discuss. "And by home I hope you know I mean the tavern."

CHAPTER 28
ROAD TO RECOVERY

ELEANOR

When I finally woke up I was wrapped in Caleb's arms. With him I felt safe and secured. I could rest without my brain running rampant. I cuddled closer to him.

"Are you finally awake?" His voice rumbled. I nodded against his chest. He kissed the top of my head.

"How long have I been asleep?" I asked.

"Two days," he said calmly. My eyes shot open and I sat up quickly.

"What?!" I exclaimed. I winced slightly, feeling a sharp pain in the back of my head. He chuckled as I stared at his naked chest.

"You used a lot of magic Starburst. You needed to recover," he stated. I placed a hand on his beating heart as the memories flooded back.

"The tree..." I started.

"Healthy and growing," he said.

"Your curse?" I asked. His eyes softened and he cupped my cheek.

"I told Bridget and she broke it," he said. I smiled freely for the first time in awhile. We did it. Everything. The curse, the tree, our families.

"How do you feel?" I asked. He rolled his eyes.

"Shouldn't I be asking you that, Miss Badass Sexy Pixie?" he said, raising an eyebrow. This time I rolled my eyes.

"One I could get used to that title and two I'm serious," I said. He tugged me back against his chest. I stretched my aching body and nestled myself into his arms.

"Well Bridget has demanded we have sibling game nights. So I think we're okay." He played with my hair. I giggled. I couldn't wait to hear about game nights. I knew how competitive Flynn was since I had to witness him and Lola argue about science nearly our entire academic life.

"Now how do *you* feel lovely?" he asked, pressing a kiss against my head again. I sighed happily.

"Better. I feel hurt that I never knew just how deep my connection with the Hollow Tree was. But it explains so much, you know? My father...I don't know," I confessed. "I knew my mom's death broke him. I guess I didn't realize how much since I was so focused on my own grief and Crystal's." I ran my hand up and down his chest.

My father and I would most likely never have a normal relationship which I was okay with. But Crystal had a relationship of some sorts with him and if keeping her in my life meant being cordial with him then I absolutely would do that.

"Wait! How was the rest of the festival?" I asked. He smiled down at me.

"One of the best. Everyone loved it. I heard some tourists talking in the tavern about how they want to come back for the spring festival," he said. My heart warmed. Was putting on the festival on top of everything stressful? Yes. But it felt so fulfilling seeing everyone's smiling faces.

"I was thinking that for the spring festival we might do a theme," I said absentmindedly. "Well that's hoping that Mayor Kiana lets me help again." Caleb's fingers rubbed the side of my hip.

"Really? Like what?" he asked. I did have an idea but I would have to run it by Mayor Kiana first. I was going to have to ask if I could work on the festival with Ben and Celestino. The only reason I was in charge of the winter one was because I had to work with my father's company.

"A flower festival. I was thinking about hosting a flower parade. All the shops could have their own float. Bring awareness to all the amazing places, activities and businesses we have here," I said, smiling.

Caleb pressed a kiss against my temple again. "That sounds wonderful, Starburst." He squeezed me.

I loved this. A whole fucking lot. I loved that I could be myself with him. I loved that he didn't temper me down. I...*loved him.* My eyes watered. Fuck this felt wonderful. I coughed and he held me tighter.

My fingers traced absentmindedly against his chest again as I settled with the feeling of love. Caleb didn't hold me back. He lets me run and dance. With him I could relax into the person I was and wanted to be. For once I didn't hold back the smile that came when my mind was on Caleb.

"So...you can kiss now..." I trailed off. He chuckled.

"Starburst, we're not doing anything until you have fully recovered," he said. I sat back up, too quickly. I tried my best to hide the twitch in my eye.

"But-" He pressed a finger against my lips and I nipped it. He narrowed his blue eyes at me.

"You know damn well if we kiss right now we're not stopping. So once you're *fully* recovered those lips are mine," he said. I raised an eyebrow and he lightly slapped my side. "Those lips too," he said with a smirk.

"Fine. I accept this proposition on one condition," I said, crossing my arms.

"Yes dearest Starburst," he said. I smiled and held my arms open.

"Can I be the big spoon?"

IT TOOK about a week for my magic to fully be replenished. The Hollow Tree was growing slowly and we all decided to name it Junior. Flynn was working with Hale's Lumber Industry to keep an eye on it, which I was grateful for.

Tomorrow I had a meeting with Mayor Kiana but this afternoon was all about hanging with my girls. Lilianna brought over a pot of *sopa de marisco* that she had made and Lola brought some chapati. Bread and soup, the most perfect thing for a winter night. Crystal was making caipirinhas the way I taught her in the kitchen. She laughed at something Lilianna said.

All was well in Lavender Falls it seemed. My friends were happy and thriving.

I thought back to a few days ago when I spent the day with Caleb. We took turns being the big spoon. He caught me up on everything that I missed. He massaged my feet and let me take long bubble baths. I smiled. Thinking about the brooding elf excited me and brought me peace at the same time. Accepting him with my heart eased me in a way I never thought it could.

"Can you stop thinking about Caleb for one second. It's ladies night," Lola teased. I rolled my eyes, taking a drink from her outstretched hand. "You're worse than Lily," she said. Lily blushed.

"Hey. I'm not at her level yet. Caleb and I haven't had the talk... technically," I said, wrinkling my nose.

"Yet," Crystal said, sipping her drink. I rolled my eyes at my girls.

"You guys haven't talked about it yet?" Lily asked, moving to sit on the couch. I shook my head, sitting with her.

"He's been helping me recover and tourism in town is still busy so he's been working," I said. Lola nodded and sat next to me. Fabian appeared onto Lily's lap. Crystal took the arm chair across from the couch. "How's father?" I asked Crystal. She lifted her legs to wrap her arm around them.

"He's been less controlling. He's given me more space to do my actual job," she said. I sighed. That was good. I snuck a glance at Lola. She raised an eyebrow.

"Yes, Ellie," Lola asked. I pursed my lips.

"Oh no. She has that look," Lily said. I rolled my eyes.

"I have a weird feeling about this," Lola said as she sipped her drink.

"You guys are making it seem like I'm going to ask you to stick your hand in a dragon's nest," I said. Lola scoffed.

"You think I couldn't? Dragons are honestly misunderstood giant lizards," Lola said. Lily smiled.

"It may have been a few years but you would give me that look every time you wanted to play: *fashion show*," Crystal said. I gasped.

"You loved it when we played fashion show," I exclaimed. Crystal snorted.

"Ellie. The lipstick you painted on my face made it look like I was smiling and therefore loved it," Crystal said, giggling. I sat staring at my sister in disbelief.

"What about makeover Mondays?" I asked. She made a face.

"I like makeup but not that much," Crystal said. Lola and Lily couldn't stop laughing. I narrowed my eyes on my sister.

"You're secretly a grandma aren't you," I said, teasing her. She waved a hand at me.

"I am learning to crochet so give me until the summer and then I'll be in grandma mode," Crystal said with a smile. Lola patted my shoulder.

"What do you want to tell me that will either upset me or excite me?" Lola asked.

"Or both," Lily chimed in.

"So…on the chance that Mayor Kiana and Ben let me work on the spring festival I may have an idea that requires you," I said. Lola took a sip of her drink.

"I'm usually up for all of your ideas but I don't like your tone or the fact your heart rate kicked up," she said, narrowing her brown eyes on me.

"It involves the community garden and you know who," I said with a smile. Despite the frown her eyes held a twinkle.

"Sexual frustrations," Fabian snickered. Crystal reached over to high five Fabian's paw.

"Oh yeah. Sexual frustrations," my little sister said, nodding.

CALEB

Thursdays had been labeled Kiernan Family Game Night according to Bridget and I couldn't be happier. The tavern was closed for the night and we were all in my apartment surrounding the coffee table. We had magical monopoly spread out along with some snacks and Flynn's latest whiskey concoction. This one held a hint of apple for sweetness. Fuck, did my brother had a knack for whiskey.

"It's my fucking turn," Bridget shouted. We all barked out a laugh. Turns out Bridget might be the most competitive out of us all.

"Then roll the dice so we can keep going. I have to be up at three in the morning to bake croissants," my brother Greg said, smiling as he eyed the game. Greg might be the oldest and chillest out of us but he was the sneakiest. Flynn shook his head.

"Just hurry up so I can win," Flynn said, taking a sip of whiskey. I looked at my siblings, a smile tugging on my lips. I didn't realize how much I was missing out on by not telling Bridget the truth. In the short time since breaking the curse we've all become really close. The hole in my heart was beginning to close. The ice between Bridget and I was melting.

237

"Stop fucking smiling it's weird," Flynn, said pouring me another glass.

"Get fucking used to it *Rider*," I teased. His brown eyes narrowed into slits.

"Only one person can call me that and it's not fucking you," Flynn growled. I threw my head back in laughter.

"So you don't mind that she calls you Rider?" Greg teased. Flynn's cheeks turned pink.

"Drink the whiskey. I need to know how it tastes," Flynn said, using the glass to cover his face. Bridget tossed the dice.

"Fuck. I'm in celestial jail again," she huffed. Greg threw her arm around her and pulled her close.

"Don't worry Bridge, you'll make it out in like five more reverse turns," Greg snickered. She shoved him away and glanced at me. I offered her a small smile. She handed me the dice.

"Caleb it's your turn," she said shyly. She still became awkward around me now and then. We both needed time to get used to each other. But we'll work on it. I was her big brother and I refused to be anything less. I threw the dice and smirked.

"Seven spaces which means I'm close to winning," I said, leaning against the couch. My token which was in the shape of a bow and arrow lifted off the board game and moved seven paces. Flynn coughed into his drink.

"When the fuck did that happen?" Flynn asked. I shrugged my shoulders. Bridget leaned towards Flynn.

"It's always the quiet ones," she said, staring at me up and down. I tossed some popcorn from the bowl we had at her.

"Hey! Don't waste the food that way," she said, picking up the pieces from the rug. Greg stretched his arms.

"I love you guys but I have to be up early," he said, getting up.

"Can I sleepover? I've had a lot of whiskey," Flynn said, giving me puppy eyes.

"Me too! Please," Bridget pleaded. I looked between the two of them and sighed.

"Fine but you better not keep me up half of the night," I said as Flynn began pouring us more drinks. Greg waved from the door.

"Shush. We're celebrating the fact you can get lock lips now and that I'm beating your asses," Flynn said, smiling. His brows furrowed. "I think," he said.

It was going to be a long night.

CHAPTER 29
HEALING HEARTS

ELEANOR

Today I was finally meeting with Mayor Kiana after taking a week to recover. While everyone assured me the festival was amazing I was anxious about this meeting. How could I bring up the spring festival? Mayor Kiana was the reason I was able to get on my feet after college. I didn't want her to think I was ungrateful for the opportunity she gave me.

I strolled inside the office and sat in the chair across from her.

"You did amazing Eleanor," she said. I sighed in relief. She reached for my hand.

"The town is incredibly grateful for you. Not because of the festival. But because of what you did for the Hollow Tree. What you did was a great sacrifice," she said. According to Crystal my father had a meeting with Mayor Kiana telling her everything about what happened with the Hollow Tree. Maybe he was really changing. I nodded along.

"Lavender Falls means the world to me," I said. She smiled wide. There was a soft knock at the door. Celestino came in.

"Celestino?" I questioned. He settled next to me grinning. I looked between him and Mayor Kiana. I narrowed my eyes at her and she continued to smile.

"Don't give me that look. I'm going to tell you," she said, waving her hand at me. I sank further into my seat.

"Celestino is stepping down from assisting Ben in the Cultural Affairs and Special Events Department," she said. My eyes widened and I turned to Celestino who shrugged.

"What the stars? Why? You just got the job literally like two months ago," I exclaimed. Celestino chuckled.

"True and I do love it but working on the fall festival made me change my mind," he said. I shook my head in disbelief. "Carpentry, Eleanor. I loved working on the sets for the town. You know wood shop was my favorite class. I like working with my hands. So I want to open a shop." His green eyes brightened with excitement. I sat back in shock. Celestino was a master carpenter. He was always amazing. The bookcase he made Lily was gorgeous. I needed him to make me one actually.

"Wait what does this have to do with me?" I asked, glancing back at Mayor Kiana.

"Eleanor, I've been grateful to have had you by my side these past years. You've grown into an incredible pixie." I tensed, sensing a but. She smiled, knowing. "But the festivals were always your favorite part. I put you in charge of the winter festival to test you," she said. My heart began beating against my chest. Was this what I thought?

"You thrive putting on events. You're great at managing people and bringing ideas to life. I want you to work under Ben as his partner. You would be amazing for the job. It would be…more fulfilling for you," she said. I stared at her in shock.

"And Ben-"

"Is very excited to have you on board," Celestino said, cutting me off. I've always loved events and parties. By the stars I was the party queen through high school and college. Despite having to deal with the tree and the curse I *loved* working on the winter festival. I already had a mega brilliant idea for the spring festival. That is if Flynn and Lola said yes. Well mainly Flynn. Lola was already on board.

"You've already been thinking about the spring festival haven't you?" Celestino teased. I shot him a look.

"Of course," I said, smirking.

"Then it's settled. In the new year you'll begin working with Ben," Mayor Kiana tapped her desk.

"Wait, what about you? Who is going to be-"

"Why do you think I have Emily?" she said with a smirk. I giggled. Of course.

"You had this planned," I pointed out. She shrugged her shoulders. Everything felt like it was falling into place. There were two things left. Talk to my father and make out with Caleb.

I was sitting in The Drunken Fairy Tale Tavern with everyone once the day was nearly over. They were celebrating me being the town's savior and my new job.

"This is literally perfect for you!" Lola squealed. Lily squeezed my hand.

"I'm so happy for you!" Lily said. I couldn't keep the smile off my face even if I tried.

"I already have plans for the spring festival," I said excitedly. Flynn groaned as he handed us our drinks.

"Please can we wait before discussing the next festival?" he asked. I laughed. I had already let it slip to Lola my idea and she proudly told Flynn. With Flynn being in charge of the community garden he would be in charge of the flowers. I was going to need a lot of flowers to pull off the parade. Getting Ben to agree was easy seeing how we've already worked together for the past two festivals. Lola patted his hip from her seat and he froze.

"Don't worry Rider this time you have me helping you," she smirked. He rolled my eyes.

"Don't remind me, *Sunflower*."

LUST, LOVE & PIXIE DUST

Flynn glared at her, but his lips quivered slightly. Caleb walked over and placed a kiss on the top of my head as he personally handed me my drink.

"Thank you," I said. His blue eyes softened.

"Of course, Starburst," Caleb said, giving me a small smile.

"Ew, can we stop with all these heart eyes?" Sailor said, taking a sip of his beer.

"Hey guys!" Crystal strolled in beaming. She seemed lighter. The bags under her eyes were nearly gone. She looked at Sailor, still smiling. Celestino tugged on Sailor to scoot who magically unfroze from staring at my sister.

She glanced at Celestino and mouthed thank you. She turned her hazel eyes to me that finally matched mine. My left eye was a sign of my connection with the Hollow Tree and sometimes depending on my mood and my magic it still would appear.

"So..." Crystal trailed off. I glanced at my sister. I raised an eyebrow. "I need a place to stay," she stated.

"What?!" I nearly shouted. She gave me an awkward smile and started tugging on her black hair. Sailor reached and pulled her hand away.

"Don't do that," he said softly. She flushed and shook her head.

"I'm moving back to Lavender Falls. I wanted to know if you had any space," Crystal said. My sister was moving back?

"I have a one bedroom but I'm sure-" I started but then Caleb tapped my shoulder. I looked over at him. He crossed his arms and looked at me. His eyes were a startling blue. Around his pupils the blue was so pale it almost looked gray. I cocked my head to the side and he did the same but slightly motioned towards the stairs that led to his apartment.

"Are you serious?" I asked, my eyes widening.

"He didn't even say anything," Flynn said.

"They don't even need to speak to communicate," Lola said, sighing dreamily.

"You can take my apartment," I told Crystal, finally breaking away from Caleb's gaze. She gasped.

243

"What-what no I can't do that! What about you?" she asked, leaning over the table. I smiled at her.

"I'm going to be with this brooding elf for a while so it's okay," I said, jabbing my finger in Caleb's side. He grabbed my hand and placed a tender kiss on the back of my hand.

"A long while," Caleb confirmed. Flynn rolled his eyes.

"It's going to take forever to get used to having him be lovesick," Flynn said. Caleb playfully slapped the back of his head. We all bursted into a fit of laughter. Bridget strolled by and slapped Flynn's shoulder.

"What the fuck was that for?" Flynn asked. Bridget smiled and shrugged her shoulders.

"Saw Caleb do it and figured there was a good reason," Bridget teased. Flynn rolled his eyes with a smile.

Looking around I felt a swell of happiness. My life was filled with ups and downs. But I worked hard to get to this point in my life. To be surrounded by people who cared for me, to do what I loved. I glanced at Caleb. *To be with someone I loved.* There was a loud sigh.

"We should probably go guys," Sailor said, breaking the silence.

"Why?" Crystal asked. Sailor looked at her and smirked.

"They're vibes are screaming to have sex," Sailor said casually. Crystal's face burned.

"You...you can see that?" she stammered. His eyes were glowing at her and he tilted his head back and forth. I clapped my hands, getting everyone's attention.

"How about a toast?" I offered. Everyone smiled.

"To friendship!" Lilianna said.

"To family!" I said, glancing at Crystal.

"To Lavender Falls!" Crystal responded.

"To us!" Caleb said.

"And caramel apples!" Fabian said as he appeared out of nowhere.

"No fur on my floor Fabian," Caleb grunted. We cheered and spent the rest of the day laughing until Caleb kicked everyone out. Everyone out but me of course.

LATER THAT NIGHT I was beginning to pack to start moving in with Caleb. I just wanted to bring a few things over tonight. Skincare, hair care, pajamas, jewelry, shoes, my favorite mug, a bottle of wine, my favorite blanket.

I stared at my bed that was covered in things. I told Caleb I wouldn't be gone long. That I just needed a few things but this was way more than a few things. I jumped when I heard my phone ring.

It was *him*. My father. Taking a deep breath I picked up. I took a deep breath. This was the last thing to check off my list.

"Hello," I said. For a few moments there was silence. I bit the inside of my cheek to keep my patience.

"How are you feeling?" he asked. I furrowed my brows. A part of me wanted to yell at him. My inner child wanted to shout at him and beg why do you care now? But the grown up side of me decided to rein in on that anger.

"I'm doing much better," I said, plainly. He sighed.

"Thank the stars," he exhaled. My nose twitched.

"May I ask a question?" I hesitated. He cleared his throat.

"Go on," he stated. I sat on the edge of my bed and stared at the ceiling. What the fuck did I even wanted to ask? About him? My mom?

"Why?" I asked. I heard him begin to pace.

"According to Crystal I have control issues that stem from…your mother's death. I wanted to keep you by me, working for me where you could be safe so I wouldn't lose you like I lost her. We're both stubborn so we kept butting heads as well. I'm also a rich snob," he admitted. I started laughing.

"Wow. She said all of that? To your face?" I asked in surprise. I loved my sister but confrontation was not her strong suit. I wondered how that conversation happened. My father grunted.

"It was implied. She's very much like your mother in the whole feelings department," he grumbled.

"That she is." I agreed.

"Eleanor…" he trailed off. I swallowed the lump in my throat, afraid of his next words. "You never deserved the way I treated you. Not as a child or as an adult. You don't have to forgive me. I understand that. Just take care of your sister while she's there okay? She's sensitive like your mom was. She has a big heart like you." Tears pricked my heart. The hole I've always had in my heart because of him began closing.

"Of course," I said. He sighed in relief. I took a deep breath.

"And if you don't mind I would like to sponsor the spring festival," he said, quietly.

"I think the town would appreciate that," I said, truthfully. "Father?" I asked.

"Yes?" he responded. My father was a broken man attempting to pick up his pieces. I was one of those pieces and in a way I was doing the same.

"I do forgive you."

CHAPTER 30
HAPPY ENDING

CALEB

I was closing up the tavern when I felt a pair of arms wrap around my waist. I turned to see Eleanor with a giant grin and two suitcases. I raised an eyebrow.

"You said a few things," I said. She pouted.

"These are just the essentials," she said, crossing her arms. I reached for the bag that was on her shoulder.

"We're going to have to move a lot of stuff around aren't we," I said. She smiled wide, her freckles spreading.

"It's cute how you said we. Now, are you done yet?" she asked, tapping my lips with her fingers. I nipped them slightly and she giggled.

The first time I kissed her she was technically knocked out. Then I gave her some time to recover. It's been over a week with us making eyes at each other, waiting for the right time. But I knew what was going to happen tonight the second she came to the tavern. Sailor was definitely right.

"Meet me upstairs," I said. She squealed and ran off. I let out a chuckle. She was fucking adorable. My sexy pixie vixen. *Mine.*

It didn't take long to finish locking up. As I made my way up the stairs I could feel my cock straining against my jeans. It was finally fucking happening. The door was slightly open and when I walked in I smelled cinnamon.

"Fuck," I whispered. I locked the door behind me. Eleanor's clothes were all over the floor, leading to my bedroom. I decided to do the same. I stood outside the bedroom door. My dream woman was laying in my bed, naked, waiting for me.

If you had asked me four years ago if I would be in this position I would have rolled my eyes. But Eleanor pushed me. She made me realize I was living half of life by letting the curse rule over me.

"Don't hesitate now Caleb," Eleanor called out. I groaned, pressing my head against the door. So fucking demanding but I loved it. I opened the door and froze. She stood in front of the bed covered in baby blue lace. Her eyes wandered down to my cock.

"Mhmm. I knew you would like this," she said as her hand dragged down her chest. "I saw it and had to get it. It matches your eyes," she continued. I nodded tightly. "I figure every time I wear it..." My eyes continued to follow her hand that was teasing the waistband of her panties. The material stretched across her curves. My hands clenched into fists.

"I could think of you," she finished. My breathing grew ragged. With a few steps I had her in my hands, gripping her hips. She gasped at the sudden strength. I pressed my cock between her legs and she arched, mouth hanging open in a moan. I cradled the back of her head.

"I'm going to kiss you and fuck you," I said through gritted teeth. I gently pushed her flushed against me with my magic. Her smile was carefree and it made my heart sing. She filled me with wonderment.

"Then fucking get to it," she said, softly, stroking one of my ears. I crushed her lips to mine. They were soft and full. My body roared to life as if she lit a match within me. She bit my bottom lip, harshly. I hissed at the pain.

I gripped her head and pulled her hair as my tongue entered her mouth. She moaned as I began grinding against her. I drowned in her taste, in her scent, in *her*.

We've spent years building up to this moment and now I knew in the depths of my soul I would never let her go. She whimpered slightly when I pulled back to catch my breath.

My thumb traced her bottom lip that was beginning to swell. Her tongue poked out in a tease. I smirked.

"My beautiful pixie," I whispered. Her eyes fluttered closed as if savoring my words. This time she gripped my neck, bringing me back for another taste. This time we moved slower. We had all the time in the world to explore each other. There was nothing keeping us apart.

Her hand scraped through my hair, tugging at my braid. She moaned as my tongue slipped along hers. My hands slipped to grip her ass and I placed her gently on the bed, never breaking away. I couldn't. The taste of cinnamon was addictive. I wonder if I could make a cocktail that tasted like her lips.

She wrapped her legs around my waist, pushing her cunt into my hard cock. I rocked into her as I gave her a bruising kiss. My magic caressed her body and Eleanor gasped, eyes wide. My magic pushed and pulled at the parts of her body that my hands weren't touching. I wanted to seduce my pixie into an orgasm with everything I had.

She nipped at my bottom lip and her tongue slipped in to tangle with mine again. We laid like that, wrapped in each other's bodies. Figuring out our dance as our mouths learned each other. My hand, gingerly pressed into her collarbone and Eleanor sucked in a sharp breath. Her hands wandered down my body until she gave my ass a sharp slap. I groaned.

"Dick. Now," she choked out. I bit into her neck and she arched her back. I soothed the pain with a gentle suck. "Now," she demanded again. I chuckled and cupped her breasts through the lace, watching her nipples poke through.

I licked my lips before flicking one roughly against the lace. Eleanor cried out. I enjoyed sucking on her nipple through the thin fabric as my other hand dipped to find her panties drenched. She was thrashing under me, panting.

"Please Caleb," she begged. *Fuck* I loved the sound of her begging.

"Strip," I demanded as I reached over the nightstand for a condom.

Eleanor took off her underwear and bra with shaking hands. I tore open the package and stroked my dick.

"Starburst?' I panted out. Her eyes were focused on my cock as she licked her lips. If she didn't stop eyeing my dick like that I was going to blow.

"Yes?" she asked while rubbing her nipples. I groaned at the sight.

"I'm giving you a choice," I said. She raised an eyebrow before a soft whimper escaped her. She pinched her nipple. I was definitely going to blow soon.

"On top or bottom?" I asked, my eyes focused on the perfect pussy that was making a mess on my sheets.

"Both," she said quickly. I chuckled as I sheathed myself. I sat against the headboard and tapped my thigh.

"Then, how about you take a seat first," I said. She placed her hands on my shoulder and moved to hover over my lap. My hands gripped her hips. This was finally fucking happening. We were doing this.

We stared at each other. Her eyes were like warm honey with flecks of green. Worry flashed in her eyes as she took in a deep breath. I cupped her face and offered her a small grin. Eleanor leaned her forehead against mine and she took my cock in one of her hands. My body tightened with anticipation.

"Please don't look away," she whispered. She rubbed the head of my cock through her folds, getting it wet. I gripped the back of her head with one hand and nodded. She sucked in a breath as she began to lower herself. Her walls squeezed me like a vice. Her eyes held me in a trance.

They were wide, filled with trust and awe. It hurt to look at how beautiful she was opening up to me. She nodded in silence as if understanding what I was thinking.

"Tight…Caleb," she panted out.

"I'm going to fucking blow," I said as I tried breathing through my nose. She felt so fucking good. So fucking tight. She shook her head, rocking slowly to lower herself until she was fully seated. I pulled her in for another harsh kiss. Her body twitched, needing to move.

"Have…move…Caleb," she said as she began to slowly rock.

"This is paradise," I grunted. "I never want to leave," I said as my fingers dug into her hips and her pace picked up at my words. I opened my eyes to her tits bouncing up and down. *A fucking sight.* I leaned forward and wrapped my mouth around one of her nipples, sucking. Eleanor mewled loudly. I slapped her ass and she yelped.

"Yes," she cried out as her hips began moving unsteadily. She was getting close, her walls twitching.

"Fucking stars," I grunted out. I lifted her up and pulled out quickly. She whined, slapping me in the chest. I flipped her over taking control again. There was no fucking way we weren't coming together and with her on top I was close to blowing it all. I slid a pillow under her hips, readjusting our position. Her hands gripped my shoulders and she nodded.

I thrusted in roughly and Eleanor opened her mouth in a silent cry, her nails digging into me. I set a rough pace, wanting to meet her. I drove in and out of her. Her cries and my grunts filled the room. Our magic pulsed through the air, mixing, pulling and pushing.

"Harder!" She planted her feet on the bed and pushed her hips higher. She was choking my dick. Her body began trembling as the angle helped to rub her clit. With a shaky hand she stroked my ear and I nearly collapsed on top of her.

"Kiss me," I growled, feeling the last bit of my restraint snap.

"As you wish," she said, her voice laced with what I hoped was love. She gave me a harsh kiss, the pain mixing in with the pleasure as I pounded into her.

I faintly heard the furniture around me shaking. I snaked my hand down to play with her clit and Eleanor shoved my face away crying out my name in release. With her walls clenching me, her body shaking, I met her at the finish line.

I was definitely going to need to make this room soundproof and probably figure out a way to keep the furniture nailed down.

My body continued to convulse as Caleb rubbed circles around my clit. He panted into my neck and I waited for my eyes to go back to normal. Stars still hung in the corners and my magic buzzed under my skin. I could hardly catch my breath. Caleb made me feel possessed, consumed and craved in the most beautifully chaotic way. I smiled.

"Fucking stars," I whispered. Caleb took a deep breath.

"We can fuck under the stars if you wish," he said, breathlessly. I let out a laugh and slapped his delicious butt. He slowly pulled out of me and I hissed at the emptiness. While he went to handle his business I continued to stare at the ceiling. The door creaked and Caleb came back with a warm wet towel. I smiled at him.

Instead of fighting him I let him take care of me. Something he was teaching me was that I didn't need to do everything on my own. There was nothing wrong in allowing someone to take care of you. It didn't make you weak but showed your strength to trust someone else. He kissed my cheek and quickly left again. I sighed happily.

That was the best fucking sex I ever had. Mind blowing honestly. He made me feel warm and safe. My heart began pounding as the door creaked back open. The bed dipped with Caleb's weight. He pulled me on top of his chest. I hadn't realized I started crying when I felt his hand wipe away my tears.

"Happy tears?" he asked softly. I bit my lip. He tugged it free. "Don't close up on me now," he said. I looked up into his blue eyes. He was everything and more to me.

"I love you," I said quickly. He broke out into a breathtaking smile. His eyes softened with crinkles, his lips a deep pink from kissing and his cheeks flushed. He looked happily relaxed. He brushed hair away from my face.

"I was wondering when you were going to admit that," he said. I slapped his chest. He pressed a sweet kiss against my lips. "Eleanor Silva, I have been in love with you for four years. You're a tornado of color. I love your honesty, your loyalty and compassion. You've brought color to my dull world," he said with sincerity. Tears flowed freely with love down my face. This was frighteningly beautiful.

"I would never tie down a pixie that is meant to fly," he said, wiping my tears. "Instead I'll be here for you when you need rest, a shoulder to lean on, someone to share your fears and happiness with. I'll even throw a punch so you don't ruin your manicure," he continued. I shook my head.

"You know I would hate to ruin a good manicure," I said with a giggle. He tugged my chin, forcing me to look at him again.

"*Sempre minha estrela.*" His voice caressed my heart as his tongue tumbled around the foreign words. This was almost more than I could take.

"How fucking dare you say that in Portuguese," I exclaimed. He laughed, wrapping his arms around me. He rolled us so that he was back on top of me. In his arms I was safe. Safe to fly as I please. I leaned up to kiss him.

"*Mo anam cara.*" My Gaeilge was rough but the look on Caleb's face was worth it. My soulmate.

"*Alma gêmea,*" he responded back in my language. My cheeks hurt from smiling but the pain was worth it.

"Let's learn the dirty words," I teased. Caleb broke out into another laughter. He's been laughing a lot easier lately and I loved being the one reciprocating it.

"Whatever my pixie wants she gets," he said as he began kissing me. Oh it was going to be a long fucking fantastic night.

"I like the sound of that Elfie," I said.

EPILOGUE

ELEANOR

I t took awhile to have Crystal fully moved into my apartment because I was slowly transferring my stuff to Caleb's place. I had a ton of shit and I could tell Caleb was struggling to fit everything, everywhere. It was almost new year's and I couldn't wait to start my job in the upcoming year.

Ben was very excited to have me join his team and Celestino had found a building to have his carpentry store. Crystal said that Hale's Lumber Industry would help supply the wood as a way to integrate back into the town. She had a lot of ideas for expanding the company into other supernatural towns.

I requested to keep my same office desk due to the fact that I needed to be around my best friend Lily for our daily passing note sessions. Caleb and Bridget had been hanging out so much you can finally see just how similar they were as siblings. Everything was finally settling in place.

"I told you not to over water it!" Lola's voice cut through The Drunken Fairy Tale Tavern. Flynn scoffed from behind the bar. Okay well almost everything.

With the spring festival in a few months those two have been at each other's throats. The problem was I couldn't tell if they were doing it on purpose or not. Either way I needed them both to get along just enough to make sure we had enough flowers for the festival.

"I did not over water the peonies," he exclaimed. I let out a giggle. Lola rolled her eyes. Lola was rarely riled up by anything and anyone. But then again they've been in competition with each other since forever.

"Sure, *Rider*." She stressed her nickname for him. He huffed and leaned over the bar.

"I told you I'm not some Disney prince," he said through clenched teeth. She leaned closer and I swore his cheeks flushed.

"You're right. At least he's good looking," she said, eyes narrowing. His nose scrunched. I shook my head laughing and turned to watch my hunk of an elf pour my drink. He glanced over at me and smiled.

"What should we do for dinner besides each other?" I asked. Caleb closed his eyes briefly, fighting back a smile.

"Depends. What are you in the mood for?" he asked, not phased with my blatant teasing. I glanced out the window where the streets were piled up with snow.

"Maybe chili? Oh! With fries," I said, excitedly. Caleb offered me a small smile and leaned against the bar.

"And for dessert, how about some brownies," he said.

"With whipped cream but make sure it's the can stuff so we can use it later," I said, tapping his nose with my finger. Caleb chuckled and it made my heart swell. He was a beautiful man. He was also *my* beautiful man. He was mine and I was his and we were disgustingly happy with each other. It was hot. Like a fire breathing dragon hot.

"I love you," I said with a stupid smile.

"You've said that five times since being here," he pointed out. I rolled my eyes.

"Screw me for being happy," I said. Caleb handed me my drink and leaned close.

"I will. We have to break in the new place." His voice was low and it sent shivers.

"But your apartment isn't new," I pointed out. His eyes darkened as he leaned to whisper in my ear.

"It is because now it's ours and I will fuck you in every inch of the place that you've made *ours*." He nipped my ear and I felt a jolt deep in my belly. We went from lust to love. Caleb made me so frustratingly happy that I could explode like pixie dust. Mhmm, that gave me a few ideas actually.

"Don't make me wait long," I said, kissing his lips. I slapped his ass and headed up the stairs with my drink.

The end

Sneak Peek Book 3

LOLA

"I KNOW WHAT I'M DOING," Flynn barked at me like a hellhound. I scoffed, irritation grating my skin. I was so excited to be back in Lavender Falls after graduation. I finally finished vet school and couldn't wait to be working with the animals and creatures of the town. When Lily said I would be Ms. Heinstein's assistant I was ready to explode.

Although if I'm being honest Ms. Heinstein has been making more of a partner than an assistant which I was totally grateful for.

What was even more exciting was she loved my idea of implementing more natural remedies for our patients. I'd been partnering with Priscilla, the owner of Priscilla's Potions and Lotions, to come up with different medicines. My best friend Lily had been helping with logo designs.

Everything was falling into place until I had to face Flynn Kiernan. Flynn was one of the bartenders of The Drunken Fairy Tale Tavern in our small town and also part owner of Kiernan's Whiskey Distillery. He was also my science rival from elementary through high school. I figured that now that we were adults he would have grown up a bit.

But he was still acting like a teenager. Well in one area he definitely grew up. I felt my cheeks heat up as I stared into his honey brown eyes. His messy dirty blonde hair was being held back by a headband. He was giving total 90s heartthrob vibes. I hated the fact that he set my blood pumping in more ways than one.

I was Lola Luna, the wickedly smart sunshine vampire. And this elf of a man liked raining on my parade. Something about Flynn just made me want to fight him. I loved getting under his skin. He was so easy to rile up.

Flynn was also the man in charge of the community garden. Despite the fact he got on my nerves that man had a green thumb. I shook my head, not wanting my brain to start thinking about his fingers and what they could do. I mean the man made pouring mulch sexy. Mulch! Even surrounded by the smell of pegasus manure I couldn't help but gawk at him.

Ever since my idea for natural remedies became approved and he needed to open a bigger section of the garden to me he's been in a sour mood. I could only blame growing up with Greg and Bridget for his possessiveness of things he considered his.

What made matters worse was that Eleanor, my other best friend who is in charge of the Spring Floral Festival, wanted us to work together. She had the brilliant idea to have a flower parade. It was a good thing we were a magical town because I had no idea how we were gonna manage creating that many flowers.

The Hollow Tree which helped nurture the magic of pixies was recently tied to our town's ley lines. The tree was dying and the connection was wreaking havoc on our town's magic. Eleanor managed to save the day. But Flynn, the fairies, pixies and I have been working overtime to heal all of the vegetation that suffered.

Today I noticed he overwatered the peonies and decided to bring it up to him. *Nicely.* Sort of. He was wiping down the bar when I popped onto the bar stool.

"I did not over water the peonies," he exclaimed. I rolled my eyes.

"Sure, *Rider*," I stressed my nickname for him. He huffed. He hated it when I called him the male love interest from the Disney movie Rapunzel. But it was because I really thought he looked like him aka my favorite Disney lead. He just didn't know the Rider was my favorite.

"I told you I'm not some Disney prince," he said through clenched teeth. I leaned closer, enjoying watching his nerve break. There was a delicious flush on his cheeks.

"You're right. At least he's good looking," I said, eyes narrowing. His nose scrunched. He leaned over to me and I sucked in a breath. He smelled like sunscreen and rainwater. I stifled a moan as I felt his breath sear across my neck. His lips brushed my ear lightly. For some reason everything he did made my senses heighten and I was a vampire.

"If you think I'm some PG prince you're sorely mistaken, *Sunflower.*" His voice was low and gravely.

"Are you more of the big bad wolf?" I teased, my heart pounding in my ears. The scent of arousal hung heavy in the air and I was ready to choke on it. This is why I pushed Flynn. I knew he was attracted to me. My vampire senses saw it all.

I could see the pupils of his honey eyes dilate, hear his heart race every time I got close and I could fucking *smell* he wanted me. It's been absolutely intoxicating ever since I've moved back. He leaned away.

"Bite me," he said. I tightened my jaw, forcing my fangs to retract.

"Don't tempt me Flynn," I said, pushing away from the stool.

"Lola," he said firmly. I fought back a shiver. I melted every time he used that tone.

"You know for the festival we're going to have to get along. It won't be a competition," I pointed out. He crossed his arms.

"Not everything is a competition between us," he said. I threw my head back in laughter.

"Should I remind you that after I planted cilantro in the greenhouse you decided to grow some and then used magic to increase the growth rate," I said crossing her arms.

"Greg needed cilantro for the flatbreads he was making," he said. Fuck. Greg had been making more flatbread.

"And the reason you keep trying to get to the garden before me in the morning?" I asked.

"I have to make sure the flowers are growing," he said. I raised an eyebrow.

"I understand that but I see you double checking my section. Do you not have confidence in my skills?" I asked.

"Well I did study horticulture and you studied creatures," he pointed. I shook my head.

"And yet I was the one helping you move plants into the greenhouse when the Hollow Tree was affecting the garden," I pointed out. He rolled his eyes.

"We're having a floral festival. It requires a shit ton of flowers," he said.

"I can grow a damn daisy, Rider," I said. His lips stretched into a smirk.

"Shall we make a bet?" he asked.

"A bet about who can grow the most flowers?" I asked. He nodded, leaning against the bar. "What do I get when I win?" I asked. He barked out a laugh that had my stomach twisting.

"*If* you win," he emphasized. "Winner get's anything they want."

"Anything can be dangerous," I said, smirking. I offered my hand. He took it and shook it with a firm grip. My heart skipped faster.

Flynn Kiernan was going down.

FLYNN

Fucking hellhound's lair. She was sitting in my family's tavern accusing me of over watering the peonies as if I didn't have a degree in horticulture. She stared at me with her big dark eyes and I looked away. Her eyes sparkled like the night sky, enchanting me.

Every time I stared for too long I felt myself get lost in them. She had her natural hair out creating a dark halo around her soft round face. She always kept her hair out during the colder season.

Regardless she was beautiful with whatever look she decided on.

She leaned on the bar with a wicked smile. My eyes flickered to her full lips and I was once again tempted to kiss the senses out of her.

I've known Lola Luna my whole entire life. She was my academic rival. It all started in potion making class in the second grade when she corrected my ratio for a plant spell.

Growing up as sort of the middle child I had a thing for wanting to prove myself. Greg was the oldest and figured out quickly what he wanted to do with life. Caleb lived away with our father but that didn't stop our mom from constantly worrying about him and then there was my baby sister Bridget who was the only girl.

Sometimes I felt lost within my own family. The only time I was sure about anything was when I was competing with Lola and making whiskey.

I thought I was saved from my feuding days with her but then she waltzed back into my life and into *my* garden. The community garden was my safe space away from everyone and now she was filling my safe space with sunflowers and sage.

I hated it. I hated how she made me feel. The day she moved back she walked into the bar with her megawatt smile, curves for days, an ass meant to fill my hands and a mischievous gleam in her eyes. That said ass was now walking out the door and I couldn't stop staring at it after making that stupid bet.

"You're so fucking screwed," my brother Caleb said to me, breaking my perverted thoughts.

"I don't know what you're talking about," I grumbled. He rolled his eyes at me before flickering them back to his girlfriend who was walking up to their apartment. I smiled. I was happy those saps were finally together. My brother finally lost the icicle that he had stuck up his ass since getting with Eleanor. His blue eyes landed on me again.

"You've been wiping the exact same spot since Lola came in and left," he said pointing to the bar. My eyes widened as I stared at the rag. *Fuck.*

"Whatever man, she has gotten on my nerves ever since we were kids," I said, tossing the rag into the bar sink.

"You're not kids anymore," he pointed out.

261

"She's in my garden," I pointed out.

A customer waved for a beer and I watched Caleb pour him a pint. I sighed, feeling exhaustion hit. I had woken up at the crack of dawn to tend to the garden.

Ever since the winter festival and the Hollow Tree dying the garden has been needing extra attention. When the tree died, Eleanor ended up doing some magic and the Hollow Tree was reborn as a sapling. It's been slow progress for the vegetation to regrow even with magic and I've been having to keep an eye on the sapling.

"You could let her into *your* garden," Caleb said with a smirk. "Oh wait you did…sorta." I reached for the towel and whacked him.

"Caleb!" I hissed. He let out a laugh. Ever since being with Eleanor he's been laughing and smiling a lot more. At first I thought it was fucking weird but after a few family game nights per our little sister, Bridget's request I've been getting used to it. He arched an eyebrow.

"You know you want to," he pointed out. I shook my head.

"All I need is to win this bet and for the Spring Floral Festival to be a success without Lola and I biting each other's heads off," I said, crossing my arms. My brother patted my shoulder.

"I've heard vampires like to bite," he said, walking away. I sighed and looked at the door the sunshine vampire strutted out of. Sometimes I wished I could just give into my wants and needs. But-

My phone blared, breaking my thoughts. It was Priscilla.

"Hey what's up?" I asked her. Her next few words had me running out the tavern after Lola. "Lola!" I yelled. She was only up the street.

"What's wrong?" she asked, reaching for my shoulder, but pulled her hand away before making contact.

"Priscilla called. We need to head to the garden. Now." I grabbed her wrist and we ran.

Once we reached Boogeyman's swamp we took a turn away from it and towards the community garden. Priscilla was at the gate crying. Lola reached to hug her.

"Q-quick, please," she said in between sobs. We made our way towards the back of the garden that bordered near the Gasping Greenwood Forest. My eyes widened in shock.

"Oh no," Lola whispered. A trail of rot that started from the forest, slithered its way towards the peonies and nearby flowers. Just this morning they were a vibrant pink and now they were wilting and turning yellow.

The sound of a broken branch caught my attention. I took a step in front of the ladies. Tumbling out of the forest a gentle animal with pure white fur stumbled out. My eyes widened.

This was fucking bad. The creature collapsed once it made its way from behind the trees. Lola pushed me out of the way and ran towards it. The creature eyed her. It was clearly too tired to move away from her. Lola's hands were gently brushing its belly. The creature continued to stare at Lola. Lola's eyes glowed slightly.

"It's pregnant and it's dying," Lola said.

"I can't believe they exist," Priscilla whispered. Lola eyed the forest.

"Something is wrong for it to come to town, to be around us," Lola said, getting up. "It says death is coming," Lola said, facing me.

"How do you know that?" I asked her.

"What do we do?" Priscilla asked. I looked back at the peonies and dug my hands into the earth, closing my eyes. I let my magic seep out and connect with the dirt. I felt a sharp sting race up my arm. Something was off. I yanked my hand back.

"A rot is spreading and if we don't act fast the creatures, the vegetation could all be at risk," I said. Lola nodded and began walking. "Where are you going?" I asked, grabbing her wrist. She pointed towards the creature.

"Go do what you're trained to do and take care of the garden and I'm going to do what I'm trained to do and save this unicorn's life." There was a silver glow around her pupils. My eyes widened.

I had never seen that happen to her. Why did I have the feeling that there was more about this vampire I grew up with then I thought.

"Go Flynn," she pushed my shoulder, heading out.

"Can't we have one normal festival," I said, rolling up my sleeves as Pricilla went to get the garden tools.

ACKNOWLEDGMENTS

Wow a second book is done! Isn't that cool? This book was a wild ride. Eleanor and Caleb were so much fun to write. While both of them are headstrong they have a big heart. Some of my favorite moments were how they were able to communicate without saying much. Their connection runs so deeply for each other.

This book wouldn't have happened without so many people. Thank you to Mel and the Steamy Lit family for always supporting me. Thank you to Jennette for designing my cover once again and listening to my rants. Thank you to Miguel for the endless supply of memes that related to Eleanor and Caleb.

A big thank you to Bear for always inspiring the heartfelt moments in my books. Thank you for showing me what love is meant to be like.

Thank you to AJ and Bridget for their absolute love for the small town that I created. You two have been in my constant corner and I hope you're excited for book 3.

Thank you to my mom. Thank you for helping me fall in love with books. I promise one day it'll be worth it and you'll rest easier.

And lastly to me. You wrote TWO BOOKS! Isabel you did that. I know you get depressed and lonely sometimes but you've made it this far and you have so many more worlds to write so keep going. Listen I kept the acknowledgments short this time. Also who even reads these? If you read this, remember to drink water.

ABOUT THE AUTHOR

Isabel Barreiro is an anxious bookworm who loves being a dork and knowing random facts. Did you know a bumblebee bat is the world's smallest mammal?

During the day she's a freelance social media manager and at night she's binging anime shows or sewing clothes. Her brain has five hamsters running around on fire which makes the day to day interesting.

Despite being born and raised in Miami she prefers mountains and the fall/winter season. Maybe one day she'll have her small town life that she loves writing about. She loves cooking and crafting and being an extroverted introvert.

You can follow her on Instagram/TikTok:
@authorisabelbarreiro
You can receive my newsletter on substack:
A Bookworm's Diary by Isabel Barreiro

You can also check out the first book in the Lavender Falls series, Falling For Fairy Tales on Amazon! A workplace romance between two childhood best friends who reunite to put on a magical pub crawl.

Made in the USA
Columbia, SC
10 June 2025